Fall 1999   Vol. XIX, no. 3
ISSN: 0276-0045   ISBN: 1-56478-222-0

THE REVIEW OF CONTEMPORARY FICTION

Editor

JOHN O'BRIEN
Illinois State University

Senior Editor

ROBERT L. McLAUGHLIN
Illinois State University

Associate Editors

BROOKE HORVATH, IRVING MALIN, DAVID FOSTER WALLACE

Book Review Editor

AMY HAVEL

Production & Design

TODD MICHAEL BUSHMAN

Editorial Assistants

ELIZABETH HRITSUK, LORI LITTLE,
SARAH McHONE, KRISTA VEZAIN

Cover Collage

TODD MICHAEL BUSHMAN

visit our website: www.dalkeyarchive.com

The Review of Contemporary Fiction is published three times a year (January, June, September) by The Review of Contemporary Fiction, Inc., a nonprofit organization located at ISU Campus Box 4241, Normal, IL 61790-4241. ISSN 0276-0045. Subscription prices are as follows:

    Single volume (three issues):
        Individuals: $17.00; foreign, add $3.50;
        Institutions: $26.00; foreign, add $3.50.

DISTRIBUTION. Bookstores should send orders to:

Dalkey Archive Press, ISU Campus Box 4241, Normal, IL 61790-4241. Phone 309-438-7555; fax 309-438-7422.

This issue is partially supported by a grant from the Illinois Arts Council, a state agency.

Indexed in *American Humanities Index, International Bibliography of Periodical Literature, International Bibliography of Book Reviews, MLA Bibliography,* and *Book Review Index.* Abstracted in *Abstracts of English Studies.*

The Review of Contemporary Fiction is also available in 16mm microfilm, 35mm microfilm, and 105mm microfiche from University Microfilms International, 300 North Zeeb Road, Ann Arbor, MI 48106-1346.

visit our website: www.dalkeyarchive.com

THE REVIEW OF CONTEMPORARY FICTION

BACK ISSUES AVAILABLE

Back issues are still available for the following numbers of the *Review of Contemporary Fiction* ($8 each unless otherwise noted):

NOVELIST AS CRITIC: Essays by Garrett, Barth, Sorrentino, Wallace, Ollier, Brooke-Rose, Creeley, Mathews, Kelly, Abbott, West, McCourt, McGonigle, and McCarthy

NEW FINNISH FICTION: Fiction by Eskelinen, Jäntti, Kontio, Krohn, Paltto, Sairanen, Selo, Siekkinen, Sund, Valkeapää

NEW ITALIAN FICTION: Interviews and fiction by Malerba, Tabucchi, Zanotto, Ferrucci, Busi, Corti, Rasy, Cherchi, Balduino, Ceresa, Capriolo, Carrera, Valesio, and Gramigna

GROVE PRESS NUMBER: Contributions by Allen, Beckett, Corso, Ferlinghetti, Jordan, McClure, Rechy, Rosset, Selby, Sorrentino, and others

NEW DANISH FICTION: Fiction by Brøgger, Høeg, Andersen, Grøndahl, Holst, Jensen, Thorup, Michael, Sibast, Ryum, Lynggaard, Grønfeldt, Willumsen, and Holm

THE FUTURE OF FICTION: Essays by Birkerts, Caponegro, Franzen, Galloway, Maso, Morrow, Vollmann, White, and others

Individuals receive a 10% discount on orders of one issue and a 20% discount on orders of two or more issues. To place an order, use the form on the last page of this issue.

Introduction

The *Review of Contemporary Fiction* has become swept up in the ubiquitous fever of retrospection connected with the end of the decade, the century, and the millennium. Thus we've decided to devote our last issue of the 1990s to looking back over the past nineteen years and choosing some of our favorite essays by some of our favorite authors. The unifying theme here is "Writers on Writing." In each of these essays one of the innovative authors of our time addresses the aesthetic, cultural, social, political, or technological aspects of fiction and fiction writing. The result, we think, is a remarkable dialogue on the state and practice of contemporary fiction as we prepare to enter a new century.

Contents

The Act of Creation and Its Artifact

Gilbert Sorrentino

> No poem is intended for the reader, no picture for the beholder, no symphony for the listener.
>
> —Walter Benjamin

I don't think that it has been fully acknowledged, or even admitted, that the writer's finished product, the artifact, is not as important to its maker as it has been made out to be by critics and scholars; or, to be more precise, that its importance to critics and scholars is infinitely greater than it is to the writer. This is a state of affairs that is totally at odds with the idea of "the job well done" as that idea exists in professions or vocations other than the artistic. This latter concept is often almost the entire rationale for a given job's being done at all, and, indeed, the so-called empty job is usually described as that one which has no end product that can be identified with the labor that went into making it, or the job that has no tangible end product at all. I set aside the profit motive, since what a man is paid for his work most often only accidentally reflects that work's value. But, curiously enough, for the writer, the end product, the artifact, but testifies to the fact that he is once more unemployed. It is a truism that the successful completion of a poem or a work of fiction leaves the writer with a feeling of relief mixed with a sense of loss and anxiety, but I would go further and say that this completion also leaves him abashed, disgruntled, even in a state of what might be called intellectual despair. A writer discovers what he knows as he knows it, i.e., as he makes it. No artist writes in order to objectify an "idea" already formed. It is the poem or novel or story that quite precisely tells him what he didn't know he knew: he *knows,* that is, only in terms of his writing. This is, of course, simply another way of saying that literary composition is not the placing of a held idea into a waiting form. The writer wants to be told; the telling occurs in the act itself. And when the act is completed its product is, in truth, but a by-product. The bringing to conclusion of a work guarantees the writer nothing, that is, he cannot, because of the artifact's presence, know if he will ever produce anything as good as that which he has just produced. Nor does the artifact preclude the question: Is this as good a job as one can do? These things are answerable only in the act of writing. By some subtle contradiction, the finished work attests to the writer's reality only in the eyes of its audience. It is, for them, since they had no hand in its making, almost the writer himself, or at least a legitimate surrogate for him. The writer's reality is, however, proved to him only in the act of composition. His finished work is before him as it is before anyone else; he, indeed, is usually as much in the dark about it as the reader who comes upon it for the first time, with the burden that it often proves far inferior to his intention. Eliot, in "The Use of Poetry and The Use of Criticism," writes: ". . . what a poem means is as much what it means to others as what it means to the author; and indeed, in the course of time a poet may become merely a reader in respect to his own works, forgetting his original meaning—or without forgetting, merely changing." There is a story told of the late Jack Spicer, reading proofs of one of his books with friends, who pointed out to him that one of the poems in the book was exactly—word for word and line for line—the same as another poem in the book. To which Spicer replied that the poem had to stay because it was written at a different time and was, therefore, a different poem. This is only truly understandable in light of Jack Spicer's practice of writing poems by the process of what he called "dictation," which I will return to later. We may go back to the middle of the twelfth century, and discover Marcabru, the Provençal troubador, writing:

> I'll take him on as critic,
> who'll call the meaning in my song,
> of each word,
> who's analytic, who
> can see the structure of the vers unfold.
> I know it'll sound absurd, but
> I'm often doubtful and go wrong myself
> in the explication of an obscure word,
> for I myself have trouble
> clearing up obscure passages.

I think these comments on completed work, by three totally different poets, writing out of three totally different traditions, help point to the fact that the act of writing has, for the writer, little to do with the product that issues forth from it: for him, the act itself is the product. When the writer reads his own work he sees, as it were, *through* it, not to anything so shifting or profound as its meaning, but to the fact of his existence as *the one who wrote*. The work does not testify to his existence, but to the recollection of himself in the act of writing: for the writer to be alive as a writer he must re-create himself or discover his reality again and again. Pound's disavowal of his early poems as "stale creampuffs," Dahlberg's refusal to acknowledge the worth of the remarkable social-protest novels he wrote during the thirties, Joyce's impatience with people who wanted to talk about *Ulysses* after he had begun work on *Finnegans Wake:* these are not examples of eccentricity or perversity, but instances of candor. The finished work is, for its maker, a kind of intrusion into his life, almost an affront to it. It marks a full stop and guarantees nothing but that which is self-evident: that his work is over. What is most disturbing to him, as I have suggested, is that this completion does not presage anything in the way of future work. The well-known state called "writer's block," and the equally frustrating state in which the writer writes, but writes badly, are bitter and destructive not because they obtrude between the writer and the finished product, but because they cut him off from the process of creation itself, that process which tells him that he is alive. Perhaps most unsettling of all is the situation that obtains when one has written with excellence, for excellence does not foreshadow as great or greater excellence to come. The idea that an artist's work becomes increasingly more sublime as he grows older and, if you will, wiser, is a critic's idea, a neat method whereby one may judge what critics like to call "growth" or "development." Writers know better, and it is not at all uncommon that a work of great power and beauty is succeeded by a lesser work. Literary style is not sharpened or refined by diligence. Rémy de Gourmont writes, with his usual unsentimental clarity: "So little can be learned in the way of style that, in the course of a lifetime, one is often prone to unlearn: when the vital energies are diminished, one writes less well, and practice, which improves other gifts, often spoils this one." To retreat into a cliché, for the writer each work, each phrase and sentence, is new, and he is as much working by feel when engaged with new work as he ever was in the past. It is quite literally the fact that the writer's controlling motto is "Scribo ergo sum": and the verbs of that sentence are always in the present tense.

In Baudelaire's great and harrowing prose poem, "À Une Heure du Matin," he writes: "Dear God! Grant me the grace to produce some beautiful lines that will prove to me that I am not the basest of men. . . ." The grace that he asks for is the grace that will enable him simply to work, to prove to himself that he is real, that he is what he is—a poet.

If what I have said has any value, then there must be something particularly ecstatic, mysterious, and sublime in this act of creation, something so infinitely finespun and elusive that no one, including the artist, has ever been able satisfactorily to describe it, much less describe the reasons for its power over the artist. No one has ever been able to isolate and analyze the link between this act and the artifact that it produces. Why this word and not that one? Why this startling and defining image? Why this metaphor, so blinding in its clarity that it remains unforgettable, and, indeed, often colors the way we see and think of whole areas of experience forever after? When Yeats writes:

> But Love has pitched his mansion in
> The place of excrement

he has, in eleven words, isolated a bitter, unidealized, and absolute fact about sexual love, the kind of carnal love that the Greeks called ἡ ἄτη, delusion and madness, what love was understood to be by the Greeks, and Romans as well, before its idealization as courtly love and its further transmutation into romantic love, which concept still possesses our modern spirit. Yeats, in two lines, recovers 2500 years of pre-medieval Western thought and, more importantly, allows us to see ourselves in its mirror. And when Yeats writes:

> Locke sank into a swoon;
> The garden died;
> God took the spinning jenny
> Out of his side.

he encapsulates epigrammatically the cultural, ethical, moral, economic, and sexual changes wrought by the industrial revolution on a society that had no idea of how to cope with it. These poetic truths are carried to us by metaphors, those sudden flashings into the light of what has hitherto been hidden from our understanding. Poets know that metaphors are not literary ornaments that give the poem a pleasing surface polish; they are the very bones of the poem, ways of translating what is unknown or inchoate in the poet's mind as it has absorbed the data of the world. St. Thomas says:

Now these two—namely eternal and temporal—are related to our knowledge in this way, that one of them is the means of knowing the other. For in the order of discovery, we come through temporal things to the knowledge of things eternal, according to the words of the Apostle (*Rom.* 1.20): *The invisible things of God are clearly seen, being understood by the things that are made.*

And it is the metaphor that allows us to understand "the things that are made." Our word comes from the Greek μεταφέρω, to carry from one place to another, to transfer. And metaphors come, by and large, unbidden, they are part and parcel of this mysterious creative act, they are, indeed, sometimes the entire creative act, for some sublime works of art are, in their entirety, metaphors.

Shelley has said that "the mind in creation is as a fading coal, which some invisible influence, like an inconstant wind, awakens to transitory brightness." "Some invisible influence." Lest that be considered the purple effusion of an arch-Romantic, here is Wyndham Lewis, a writer whose devotion to classical principles of composition has perhaps no equal in this century: "If you say that creative art is a spell, a talisman, an incantation—that it is *magic,* in short, there, too, I believe you would be correctly describing it. That the artist uses and manipulates a supernatural power seems very likely." Despite the fact that Shelley says that the artist is used by, and that Lewis says that the artist uses, some outside power, both concur that the power is not, in fact, "theirs." All right: "Some invisible influence"; "a supernatural power." We may recall Baudelaire's "grant me the grace," in which we hear him asking for the power to create. There are dozens of other comments by dozens of writers on the creative process—from Lorca's belief that the artist at the peak of his powers is possessed by a *duende,* a spirit, that permits him to make his art, to Eliot, at the opposite pole, who denies the existence of a friendly demon who presents the writer with the "gift" of a poem, but concedes that the creative act is the lifting of "an intolerable burden" and that it is *effortless.* His figure is that of a bird who hatches an egg after a long period of incubation, but doesn't know what kind of an egg it has been sitting on until the shell breaks. And in Kafka's *Diaries* we read, on his writing "The Judgment," "The fearful strain and joy, how the story developed before me, as if I were advancing over water." Andrew Marvell, in "The Garden," writes:

> The Mind, that Ocean where each kind
> Does streight its own resemblance find;
> Yet it creates, transcending these,
> Far other Worlds, and other Seas;
> Annihilating all that's made
> To a green Thought in a green Shade.

Yeats's "automatic writing" may also be adduced here, as well as Jack Spicer's reliance on what he called "dictation," that is, that it is the poet's "outside" that is important, not his "inside," and that true poems issue from the former, unclouded by the opinionated ego.

I have gone on at some length about this process of creation in order to make clear my argument: that the process is sublime and that one of the writer's rationales for his vocation, if any rationale is needed, is the recapture, the re-experience of this sublime state. I don't agree with Eliot that creation is the shedding of an intolerable burden, or, I should say, that has not been my own experience. Rather, it has been, for me, a release from a rootless anxiety, the excursion into a state of exhilaration, of freedom, that is explicable neither in physical nor intellectual terms, since it is an uncanny blend of both the physical and the intellectual. It is as if one could think through and into corporeal pleasure, so that the mind might delight in what is rightly the body's province; or, conversely, as if the body could feel the pleasure that the mind takes in thought. It is a curious truth that when everything is going well, nothing is easier than writing. When nothing is going well one cannot write at all. In the first instance, one works, certainly, but one works almost flawlessly; in the second, the work is wearisome and frustrating and fruitless, the language that one thought so familiar and malleable becomes intractable and gluey. At best, one writes, at these times, "decent prose"—grammatically correct, syntactically rigorous, logically cohesive—and absolutely wooden. The work has everything but the one thing that all good writing must have—style. One might almost say that to fight the language is to court failure.

Excellence, stylistic excellence, is somehow achieved by that part of the mind that has nothing to do with thought, as we generally consider thought; nor is it done by that part of the mind that says "good morning," or "pass the butter," or "I love you." It is far removed from linear, or logical thought, and is done in a kind of trance or semi-trance state, in which this dark corner of the mind performs quite independently. Proust has gone so far as to posit the idea of the writer as two distinct beings, when he writes:

Any man who shares his skin with a man of genius has very little in common with the other inmate; yet it is he who is known by the genius's friends, so it is absurd to judge the poet by the man, or by the report of his friends. . . . As for the man himself, he is just a man and may perfectly well be unaware of the intention of the poet who lives in him. And perhaps it is best so.

Proust was speaking here of Saint-Beuve's denial of Baudelaire's genius because of his disapproval of the poet's scattered and wretched life. But the Baudelaire who whined and begged and pitied himself was a Baudelaire who had nothing to do with the poet who wrote *Les Fleurs du Mal.* That is one of the reasons why "À Une Heure du Matin" is such a great poem, for in it we are privy to the first Baudelaire addressing God and asking Him to allow the second Baudelaire the grace to write; or, to put it more precisely, we see the poet recognize the fact that his poems come from some "other" part of him, and are produced with the aid of some power which he does not normally possess.

I have said that the writer works in a kind of trance, or semi-trance. I don't really like these words, because they conjure up the image of the artist as a kind of idiot savant, a comfortable image for many people, since it reinforces their prejudice toward the artist as an overgrown child, still dabbling in fantasies. I think it is instructive that the word "fantasy" has taken on a totally different meaning from its roots, which are Greek. The noun, ἡ φαντασία, means *a making visible,* from φαντάζω, *to become visible, appear,* from the verb φαίνω, *to bring to light, make to appear.* We have, by denying the etymology of this word, tried to make the artist as discoverer or revealer into the artist as daydreamer. So, instead of using the words trance, or semi-trance, let's rather define this state as one in which the writer is possessed by the will to make, to the exclusion, during this act of making, of all other things. In a sense, he *becomes* the act itself. In this state, he does not so much invent as *find* what is already there, find, to return to Proust, the "intention of the poet who lives in him." Our word, "troubadour," is the French version of the Provençal "trobador," which means, precisely, "finder." In this state, this magic state, things that are unknown to the writer in his everyday life are *found,* the clearest example being the discovery of metaphors that will reveal to him what he does not know, that will express to him those things that are there, but there in darkness and obscurity. This state is surely what Shakespeare had in mind when he spoke of "the poet's eye in a fine frenzy rolling," if we understand "frenzy" to mean a state of temporary "insanity," and not, as the vulgar would have it, a description of The Crazy Artist, still one of the philistine's most cherished inventions, an invention that reinforces his belief that art, since it is produced by maniacs, who are also, let us remember, children, is not to be taken seriously, or not to be taken at all. To this point, it is interesting to note here that I've recently read of psychological studies that have found links between the voices heard by paranoid schizophrenics and the "voices" heard by writers in the act of composition. These latter are not necessarily "heard," but may be considered to be the power that effortlessly directs the writer's thought or that he directs. When he is not composing, he does not hear these "voices"; or, to paraphrase Jung on Joyce, the artist is different from the psychotic because he can will his return from the state in which the psychotic is helplessly trapped. We might say that the "everyday" man in whom the poet lives never enters that state, but the interior poet lives in it always, waiting to assert himself in the act of creation. It is to the point to remember that *Finnegans Wake* is in essence a world of voices, all of which continually and unpredictably shift into other voices; it is as if Joyce's interior voice has been consciously splintered in order to evoke and reveal a state divorced from what we think of as temporal reality. His methods, as he once said, in elaboration of criticism that called the *Wake* "trivial," are also "quadrivial," an absolute exploitation of the mind's detritus.

But how does this poet who "lives in" this otherwise very ordinary human being select and order the materials used in the work? How does he go about setting down on paper specific elements in specific ways? Writers' minds are as full of trash as is the mind of anyone else; writers are subject to the same weaknesses and temptations as anyone else; they are, as is everyone else in the industrialized technocracy that the world has become, bombarded daily by the same endless and disconnected data. How then does the writer, *writing,* work? What happens that permits him to select, from all this jumble of garbage, the items that go to make his poem or work of fiction? If he is lucky, information long lost, or partially remembered, or completely forgotten by the "ordinary man" is held gingerly by the "other man," the man inside, and released as it is needed. This release of data is not neat and orderly; the process might be compared to working a jigsaw puzzle which not only does not have an illustrative paradigm as guide, but one in which the pieces themselves are continually changing shape.

While it is presumptuous to speak of how other writers compose, and while it is well-nigh impossible to give a coherent account of how one composes oneself, I hope I may be forgiven if I end these remarks with a brief account, one that is remembered as exactly and honestly as possible, of how I composed part of a chapter of one of my books, *Splendide-Hôtel.* The chapter under discussion is the one titled "R." First of all, it is necessary to know a little about this book. It is 1.) an imaginative and critical foray into the life of Arthur Rimbaud; 2.) Rimbaud wrote a famous poem, "Voyelles," in which he assigned colors to vowels; 3.) my own favorite color is orange. I quote the pertinent passages of the chapter:

> R is a beautiful letter, ultimately deriving from the Phoenician ꟼ a tiny pennant. I will it to be an orange pennant, since orange is my favorite color.
>
> *
>
> R is a letter of enormous beauty. I take it to be orange. In the context of this work it stands for the poet's very name.
>
> *
>
> In 1876, the poet, the monarch of colors, sailed to Java. I imagine his slight smile as he discovered that the ship that would take him there was the *Prince of Orange.*

The tiny pennant, the Phoenician letter that has the exact shape of a pennant, I have made into an orange pennant, since orange is a color, my favorite color, that appears elsewhere in this book. Its assigned color allowed me to partake of Rimbaud's invention of vowel colors by here giving a color to a consonant. The "R," which is the title of the chapter, gave me the occasion for permitting it to stand for Rimbaud's name, thereby weaving his name into his color inventions, and, by extension, into my own, and, by further extension, into my designation of him as "the monarch of colors." If the poet may invent colors for vowels, why may he not invent colors for all letters? And if Rimbaud, my subject, did not invent all the colors, I, as his surrogate, invented at least one of them, this orange "R." At this point I stuck. The chapter needed closing, some paragraph or phrase or even sentence that would snap it shut as well as coherently incorporate the elements I had already composed. At this point the "poet inside," if you will, declared his intentions.

The orange pennant, each time it came to mind, presented itself as the sort of signal pennant flown from ships; I have no idea why. It may have been because of my recollection of the Phoenicians as mariners *par excellence;* it may have been because of my memory of the "Death by Water" section of *The Waste Land,* in which maritime imagery and language are used for effect and whose figure is that of Phlebas the Phoenician. I have no idea. I submit these data in retrospect, as the reader of my own work; at the time, these shards and bits and pieces of information entered my mind willy-nilly, urging me, it now seems plausible, toward something of which I had no knowledge, or let me say toward something of which I had no inkling that I had had knowledge. Buried in the detritus of my mind was the dim recollection of something—but what?—something I had long ago read in a biography of Rimbaud, the celebrated study by Enid Starkie. Its information had settled in my conscious mind as a series of "major facts," but it was not "major facts" that the poet within needed. I was sent from my orange maritime pennant to Professor Starkie's biography to look for something that I was not sure existed; but that "something" was what the "other" Sorrentino knew all about. The poet within knew exactly what he was searching for; I was, as it were, his agent. And then, in Starkie, I read that Rimbaud "made his way to Holland where he enlisted in the Dutch army to go to Java. He signed on for a term of six years and was given a bonus of twelve pounds. He sailed on 10 June 1876, on board the Prince of Orange. . . ." When I saw that sentence, my chapter had what it needed, my orange pennant, which was also an "R," which was also the sign for Rimbaud's name, now flew from this ship, the *Prince of Orange,* on which Rimbaud, the prince of colors, had sailed, taking with him my personal color.

I tell this story to point to the fact that I insisted on my orange pennant being a marine pennant and I went to Professor Starkie's book almost as if I had certain instructions to do so. In this act of composition, what I had forgotten was not forgotten by the writer who knew how to end the chapter. I was, very calmly and aloofly, manipulating, in some way I did not understand, some outside power, one that enabled me to find what I needed. The entire process was exhilarating, an instantaneous release from anxiety. What seemed to be unsayable become possible to say. Kafka writes: "How everything can be said, how for everything, for the strangest fancies, there waits a great fire in which they perish and rise up again." The chapter, as it now stands, written, exists for me as a memory of the act that made it. In a very real sense, a writer's finished work is, for him, a mnemonic device that allows him the recollection of its creation. The finished work is an artifact, and if it gives its maker pleasure to regard it, it is a cold pleasure.

Thomas Middleton writes, in his great tragedy, *The Changeling:*

> A cunning poet, catches a quantity
> Of every knowledge, yet brings all home
> Into one mystery, into one secret
> That he proceeds in.

The "mystery," the "secret that he proceeds in" is the essence of his vocation, made intense precisely because it is as much a mystery and secret to him as it is to anyone else. The artifact that emerges from this procedure attests to the latter's absolute reality but can never explain its workings.

This essay was originally delivered as the Edwin S. Quain Memorial Lecture at the University of Scranton on 25 April 1979.

First published in issue 1.1 (Spring 1981)

Address to the
New York University Conference

Robert Pinget

I have not a great deal to add to the remarks I made at the Cerisy conference on the New Novel a few years ago, for I have always worked along the same lines. (These remarks, incidentally, were reprinted as a postface to the translation of one of my novels published here by Red Dust, *The Libera Me Domine.*) What I can do, though, is go into greater detail about the way I treat the material of my novels, and try to explain how I write them.

In fact, since what is still, I believe, called "The New Criticism"—an offshoot of the science of linguistics, with which it is even sometimes confused—since the New Criticism has seized on our work, it seems that we authors have no option but to take a stand on this discipline, whether it be to reject or to accept it. It has to some extent impugned the author, even going so far as to throw doubt on the importance of his role. These critics no longer talk of creation, they talk of production, which they see as something like the result of all the forces arising out of intertextuality as a generalized phenomenon.

The positive aspect of this way of envisaging literature is the importance the New Critics attach to the study of the text as such: that is to say, as the field of interaction of signifiers.

But the risk it runs, if I understand it aright, is that, if taken to extremes, any text by any writer would qualify as food for thought, as if all texts issued, and could only issue, from the same universal mechanism, and as if the only thing that mattered was to understand its functioning, without bothering any longer to ask ourselves either why, or with what aim, it functions. If that were the case, it would be the end of any scale of values.

Unless this criticism were to decide to confine its attentions to the texts of a few elite writers whose sole preoccupation was precisely to please it, and who refused themselves the flights of fancy arising, for example, from spontaneity—the bête noire of this criticism. In that case, however, it would have become too selective, and no longer have the audience which, after the improvement of its methods and the broadening of its views, it deserves to reach.

It would be logical, as things stand at the moment, for the authors who have wholeheartedly subscribed to the spirit of this discipline, to stop signing their texts, since they admit that they do not have exclusive rights to them. Yet they continue to sign them. This, then, is a phenomenon we should keep in mind.

So far as I personally am concerned, I have taken a great interest in the work of this new school because it has helped me to a better understanding of the movement of my texts, and to become aware of an element of their significance that is not negligible. But it is ideally impossible for me to exclude from my writings the totally subjective side they contain, and the light they throw on my most secret intentions. My work does not solely consist in discovering the functioning of the text on the page, but also in trying to discover where my choice of words comes from, and the relationship to my aspirations that they may signify.

What I call the *tone of voice* is nothing other than the deliberate choice of a certain vocabulary, and it is the sum total of this vocabulary that is alone responsible for breathing life into the text. This choice differs in each of my books, and is the result of a simple preoccupation with change and renewal. In the same way, it implies a different syntax from one book to the next.

This means that I only partially subscribe to the idea that a text is merely a production; in other words, a game deliberately played with the purely material interrelationship of signs. Even though, of course, my writings no longer contain any representation in the classical sense, they do still contain something eminently subjective, which is the search for a personal expression. It is just possible that my books may simply be exercises in the control of my creative faculty, of my sensations, of my memory. Exercises in the mastery of the tone, which may take various forms.

People today still talk a great deal about Mallarmé, and about his dream of the ideal Book—an object independent of any other concept than that of pure beauty. But they forget that, apropos of *Hérodiade,* he wrote in a letter: This poem . . . "into which I put the whole of myself without realizing it . . . and to which I finally found the key."

This is to say that he himself, whose all-embracing consciousness has been so much praised, accepts not only the participation of the unconscious in writing, but also the fact that a poetic text reflects the temperament of the author, and that it can therefore be a way for him to know himself.

Mallarmé also wrote, elsewhere: "On paper, the artist creates himself," and not: "the artist creates." Here he implicitly recognizes the expressive role of the text, and he never, to my knowledge, went so far as to deny the author as a unique individual, or, consequently, the significance of writing insofar as it is concerned with other than purely functional phenomena.

On this same subject, it would be difficult to be more lucid than Baudelaire, who wrote in the preface to one of his translations of Edgar Allan Poe, *Nouvelles histoires extraordinaires:* "But above all, I want to say that, having allotted the proper share to the natural poet, to *innateness,* Poe also allotted a share to science, to work, and to analysis—which will seem exorbitant to those who are arrogant but not erudite."

And again, comparing Poe to those poets who believed solely in disorder and whose aim was to write poem with their eyes closed: ". . . likewise, Edgar Allan Poe—one of the most inspired men I have ever known—made an effort to hide his *spontaneity,* to simulate sang-froid and deliberation."

Innateness, spontaneity, inspiration, which I assimilate with the unconscious, with its most immediate manifestations which will then be controlled: on reflection, this is self-evident.

I have great respect for the present-day critical methods, and I even owe a debt of gratitude to those who employ them, since they have been good enough to turn their attention to my work, but I don't think that, given the still very new state of the science from which they are derived, these methods are the only ones capable of making an exhaustive assessment of the value of a text.

It is not solely in the light of pure deductive reasoning that my books should be approached, for insofar as it is possible I allow them to be activated by the irrational, particularly in their sequences. Why? A question of idiosyncrasy, of temperament. In my eyes, the share allotted to the irrational is one of the ways that may help me to arrive at a personal "truth," which is only to a very limited extent present in my awareness of it. This is a kind of open provocation to the unconscious. This "truth," while it is no more important than that of anyone else, is nevertheless more valuable to me, if only because it helps me to a better informed approach to the truths of other people. We are all, indeed, more or less dependent on the collective unconscious, whose nature we can only glimpse by examining as best we can those manifestations of it which we perceive in ourselves.

I don't know whether this proposition is orthodox: I mean, that the fact of intentionally having recourse to the irrational causes some revelation of the unconscious to emerge, but it seems to me that the magic of primitive peoples did not work otherwise, and that the study of its practices has taught us many things; side by side, of course, with the interpretation of dreams, which doesn't date from today, though the irrational discourse of dreams is not released intentionally.

All this does not mean to say that the "psychological" significance of my work is more important to me than its aesthetic significance; I am merely trying to avert the error people may fall into if they consider that once my book has been closed, nothing should remain but the pleasure—or the boredom—of having read it. Something more, something indefinable, fortunately, is intended to be its distinguishing characteristic. To my mind, this characteristic can only be perceived by a kind of criticism that does not belong to any school but which dips more or less at random into my work.

In short, it is by a very personal method, and in the actual process of writing, that I criticize my manner of understanding literature, and I can only do this in terms that are not in common use. This criticism is an integral part of my work. And it is the reason why I have never felt a need to construct a theory independently of my writings.

If it is de rigueur, in this assembly, to speak of technique, I will very briefly say that the structure of my novels is often built on recurrences. These recurrences, or repetitions, are of four kinds.

1) Complete recurrence, *ab initio,* or repetition of the first part of the book in the second. Bipartite structure, then. Typical examples: *No Answer, Fable, The Apocrypha.* What is important here is the repetition of all the themes, but with perceptible or imperceptible modifications, distortions, variations, transfigurations, which finally destroy, or at least shake, the certainties that the reader may have fastened on in the first part. Hence the impression that the book is being composed, and decomposed, under his very eyes. The formula I have employed to define this procedure and which applies to all my books is: *Nothing is ever said, since it can be said otherwise.*

2) Partial and progressive recurrence, all the way through the book. After a certain number of pages, let's say, recapitulation of themes with variations, and so on with different themes. Typical examples: *Someone, The Libera Me Domine, Passacaglia.* "Unipartite" structure, then.

3) Complete but reversed recurrence, starting from the middle of the book, of the first part in the second, which thus repeats it by going back to the beginning. Bipartite structure, but disguised as "unipartite," as the book is all of a piece. This is what I have called anamnesis, Unique example: *That Voice.* Variations and hypotheses proliferate as in 1) and 2). It is only the stimulus that differs. I would therefore stress the fact that in order to write, I need a positive stimulus to trigger the creative process.

4) A fourth kind of recurrence is the pure and simple repetition of certain key-phrases or leitmotifs throughout the book, which thus

increase its resemblance to a musical composition. These repetitions, or refrains, are additional to the three other kinds of recurrences and are to be found in almost all my novels. I like to use them, because they are more effective than all the others in creating an impression of surface unity. The difficulties in reading caused by the variations on the themes are thus, in my eyes, or rather, in my ears, smoothed out. And the reason why it is these leitmotifs that I am the most attached to is, it seems to me, because they persuade me that in spite of my liking for combinatorial games, the most important thing to me is to convince myself, and to make the reader convince himself, that once a work of art has assimilated all possible complexities of expression, its aim must be to say only one simple thing which, I think, is called poetry.

This part of my technique, which I can describe only very succinctly here, is relatively easy to apply and to analyze. Its effect on the writing itself, on what the reader reads, is another matter. He is hindered by an abundance of assertions and negations, of alterations, second thoughts, parallels, distortions; in short, by an apparent absence of logic.

But the logic, or reasoning, of art is not that of logic. Art is always founded in nature, but reconstitutes it in a different way, makes it into something greater, more beautiful, more true, less immediately apprehensible. Of course, the criterion of this beauty and this truth changes from century to century and from artist to artist. This is a truism.

My own way of exalting nature has been to make people discover, or to try to make them discover, its infinite variety. What I have called its *potentialities,* which are all included in a given reality. The imagination is in fact a constituent part of our being, and is just as necessary as dreams and observation.

Every time I tackle a new book, my temperament incites me not to give it exactly the same form as its predecessor, in other words, the same language or the same tone, which are indissolubly linked to its form. The result of my way of working is that each book is different right from the outset. But very fortunately, whatever I do, my readers say that no matter which of my books they tackle, they recognize the same voice in it. I say very fortunately because, all things considered, the essential for me, in these experiments, is to explore and throw light on what my innermost depths conceal, and this I can only achieve by means of successive trial and error.

My attachment to the technique of the intermingling of themes and their variations is due to the admiration I have always felt for so-called baroque music. When I was very young I was already captivated by it, and for years I tried to exalt its spirit in rather maladroit poems. It was only later that I pursued the idea of taking inspiration from it in the novel. This may seem inconsistent, after what I have just said about the deliberate irrationality of my writings, for the type of music in question goes to great pains to set an example of the most rigorous geometry. In this connection we should remember the accusations made in the nineteenth century against baroque music, and against its grandiose and disconcerting discoveries. Invention, experimentation, and the unexpected are triumphant in this music thanks to an exceptional mastery of means. Is there any need to mention the mirror-image technique employed by the greatest representative of this school? The irrational, controlled and measured in masterly fashion, is the very wellspring of his creative power.

It is piquant to remember that in the last century this form of art was considered to be "chaotic, cultural muck"!

But to pursue this analysis of the relation of my work to that of composers, who include one of the most formidable of past-masters of all time, would be to condemn it to the most inevitable shipwreck.

I would be better advised to say, merely, that for thirty years I have devoted myself to a kind of experimental writing that is intimately linked to oral expression. My exercises in vocabulary, syntax, rhythm, punctuation, have always been aimed at trying to match this writing to the voice that inspires it. My ear catches something that my pen endeavours to transcribe. My books are to be listened to, rather than to be read.

As for the subjects treated in my novels, they are taken from the most banal, apparently derisory, everyday events, *in which there is nothing that can make a novel,* but which I have chosen for my material. This is to say, given the importance I attach to every well-thought-out formulation, that I play on this appearance to the point of exhausting it, in order to make anyone who listens to me admit that, beneath or beyond appearances, a drama is being played out, Now, if this drama is being played out, the game must be to give the listener a premonition of it—one must play fair—or "play the game." A ludic activity, in other words gratuitous, hence necessary. Every work of art is a more or less dangerous game, which may well be mortal. Let us not forget that drama is an essential act of nature which is played out in the innermost depths of the being, and hence moved by passion, moved by pathos. Once again, these are all truisms.

Their horror of passing time, of the everyday, has the paradoxical effect of making my narrators cling to these everyday events in order to reduce them to nothingness. Hence their constant, liberating repetitions, and their open access to the world of the imagination.

The systematic confusion of grammatical tenses and of situations is symptomatic of this need to annihilate the obstacle. This quest to discover something else through the medium of the imagination only retains its character to the extent to which the narrators decide to forget what they are looking for, fascinated as they are by the discovery itself, and fearing more than anything else that they might glimpse the beginning of the end of their spiritual adventure. In other words, they have no option but to despise death, which would be the end of the Word; this they do by flushing it out everywhere, and demystifying it with humour. A task which could not be more vain, as they well know, but they accept it, once again because of their liking for the game. They are therefore perfectly cognizant of their extravagance but it is the rule of this procedure, which might seem absurd to anyone who had no sense of liberty.

Let me repeat that my work belongs to the domain of art, and that I use every artifice of language in it, amongst which contradiction is by no means the least. Thus, to go no farther than this element of contradiction, which is the most obvious and simplistic form of variation, a casual reader may well find that contradiction is the only thing he remembers after his quick reading of my books, but this would be to amputate them of three-quarters of their content, not to say the whole.

If I do not quote any of my other books here, it is because their composition is simpler and more apparent. They are no less typical, each in its own way—I am thinking in particular of *The Inquisitory*—of my constant and primordial concern with tonality, with the exigencies of my ear, and of my declared intention, from my very first book, to extend the limits of the written word by replenishing it with the spoken word. I felt an urgent need to adopt this language deliberately, with its particularities of syntax, its inventions, and its rich vocabulary.

My first novels all reflect this fascination with these potentialities, which then manifested themselves more freely. All the suggestions, refutations, prolongations and metamorphoses of fragments of speech are deliberately expressed in them. A more rigorous disposition or composition of these fragments imposed itself later, but the material has remained the same.

But if I were to try to make this exposé more systematic, I would run the risk of falsifying or restricting the meaning of my writings, and that would be to betray them.

After thirty years of publication with Les Editions de Minuit, I am still affiliated to the New Novel and I still stand by its efforts and discoveries, which are of great diversity and undeniable present-day significance. For my part, by the choice of a method of which I have given you only the barest outline, I have attempted an approach to the dark face of language, in order to make it easier for unconscious values to break through and thus enlarge the field of my conscious activity. This has involved reconciling innateness with calculation, and often putting the accent on paradox which, as Jung said, is one of our supreme spiritual values.

To end on a more general note, I should like to read you a short paper I wrote in 1977 for the Mainz Academy, of which I am proud to be a corresponding member. This institution was conducting a little inquiry into what it entitled "Literary Baggage" (*Literatur als Gepäck*).

Here is my reply:

To say baggage is to say voyage. . . . The journey we undertake without a travel agency, and without having chosen it. The journey that lasts a life-time. "Did you have a good journey?" It is the privilege of those whose baggage has been well packed to be able to answer yes. What will they have put into it? The thing that weighs the least, and whose name is: wisdom. It is vigilant, and it devours the kind of time that is always doing its utmost to prevent us from continuing our crossing: chronological time. Could there be another kind, then? Yes, that of childhood, of legend, the time of myths, of origins. *That* time has no weight, for it is a product of the Word. We have access to it when we listen to what was said in the beginning, the memory of which we have all retained in our innermost depths. *In illo tempore,* in that primordial time, which remains and does not pass, we were told truths which were soon written down, So the Word was consecrated by the Letter, and was called Legend—*that which is to be read.* All literature, whether sacred or profane, has its source in this ancient, mysterious process.

The sole "baggage" that helps us to conquer chronological time and to participate in the other, absolute time, is a bouquet of texts, an anthology which we are able to refer to at every moment of our existence. These texts may be of a different nature, but they nevertheless have the same far-distant origin. The *homo religiosus,* linked to the essential—if we admit his presence in every one of us—rebels against the lacerations produced by the succession of days, and seeks refuge in the time which knows neither succession nor laceration, that of the Word.

Light baggage, buzzing with words, which, ever since the world has been the world—and there are many legends that vouch for it—has ensured our passage, without let or hindrance, over on to the other bank.

This essay, translated by Barbara Wright, was delivered by Pinget at New York University for a conference on the New Novel, September 30, October 1 and 2, 1982.

First published in issue 3.2 (Summer 1983)

Some Aspects of the Short Story

Julio Cortázar

I find myself standing before you today in quite a paradoxical situation. An Argentine novelist makes himself available to exchange ideas on the short story, but his listeners and partners in the exchange, with few exceptions, know nothing of his work. The cultural isolation that continues to afflict our countries, added to the unjust current-day cutoff of communications with Cuba, have meant that my books, of which there are several by now, have not found their way, except here and there, into the hands of such willing and enthusiastic readers as yourselves. The problem is not just that you have had no opportunity to judge my stories, but that I feel a bit like a ghost coming to talk to you without that relatively soothing certainty of being preceded by the work one has done over the years. And this ghostly feeling I have must show, because a few days ago an Argentine lady assured me in the Hotel Riviera that I was not Julio Cortázar, and, to my stupefaction, she added that the genuine Julio Cortázar is a white-haired gentleman, a close friend of one of her relatives, and has never left Buenos Aires. Since I've been living in Paris for twelve years now, you can see how my ghostly nature has visibly intensified following this revelation. If I should suddenly disappear in midsentence, I won't be too surprised, and perhaps we will all be the better off for it.

It is said that a ghost's greatest desire is to get back at least a glimmer of substantiality, something tangible that will bring him, for a moment, back into his flesh-and-blood life. To gain a little substantiality in your eyes, I will sum up in a few words the general tendency and sense of my stories. I'm not doing this simply for the sake of information, for no abstract summary could replace the work itself; my reasons are more important. Since I'm going to be concerned with some aspects of the story as a literary genre, and it's possible some of my ideas may surprise or shock my listeners, it seems to me only fair to define the type of narrative that interests me, pointing out my special way of seeing the world. Almost all the stories I have written belong to the genre called fantastic, for lack of a better word, and are opposed to that false realism that consists of believing that everything can be described and explained, as was assumed by the optimism of nineteenth-century philosophy and science, that is, as part of a world governed more or less harmoniously by a system of laws, principles, cause-and-effect relations, well-defined psychologies, mapped-out geographies. In my case, the suspicion that there's another order, more secret and less communicable, and the seminal discovery of Alfred Jarry, for whom the true study of reality lay not in laws but in the exceptions to those laws, have been some of the guiding principles in my personal search for a literature beyond all naive realism. That's why, if in the ideas I set forth you find a predilection for everything exceptional about the short story, be it in thematics or in the forms of expression, I think this presentation of my own way of seeing the world will explain my stance and focus upon the problem. At worst, it can be said I've only spoken of the story as I write it, and yet, I don't think that's so. I feel sure that there exist certain constants, certain values that apply to all stories, fantastic or realistic, dramatic or humorous. And I think perhaps it's possible to show here those invariable elements that give a good story its particular atmosphere and qualify it as a work of art.

The opportunity to exchange ideas about the short story interests me for several reasons. I live in a country—France—where this genre has not held much of a place, though in recent years there has been a growing interest among writers and readers in this form of expression. At any rate, while critics continue to accumulate theories and maintain heated polemics about the novel, almost nobody takes an interest in the problems the short story entails. To live as a short-story writer in a country where this form of expression is almost an exotic product, forces one to seek in other literatures the sustenance lacking there. Gradually, in the original version or in translation, one gathers, almost spitefully, a vast quantity of stories past and present, and there comes the day to weigh it all in the balance, attempt an evaluative approach to this genre, so hard to define, so elusive in its many contradictory aspects, and in the last analysis so secret and turned in upon itself, a snail of language, a mysterious brother to poetry in another dimension of literary time.

But beyond this stopping-place that every author must reach at some point in his work, a discussion of the short story especially interests us because every Spanish-speaking country on the American continents is giving the short story a place of special importance that it had never enjoyed in other Latin countries like France or Spain. With us, as is only natural in young literatures, spontaneous creation almost always precedes critical examination; a good thing it is so, too. Nobody can try to say that stories should be written only after we know their laws. In the first place, there are no such laws; at most one may speak of points of view, of certain constants that structure this rather unbounded genre; in the second place, there is no reason theorists and critics should be the same people writing the stories, and they naturally would come on the scene only after there exists a body, a mass of literature that will allow for research into and clarification of its development and features. In America, in Cuba, just as in Mexico or Chile or Argentina, a great many short-story writers have been at work since the early years of the century, hardly knowing one another, at times coming across one another almost posthumously. Faced with this unwieldy panorama, where very few know one another's work well, I think it's useful to speak of the short story above and beyond particular national or international traits, because it's a genre that holds for us an ever-growing importance and vitality. One day the definitive anthologies will be drawn up—as they are in Anglo-Saxon countries, for instance—and we'll know how far we've come. For the moment it seems to me to make sense to speak of the short story in the abstract, as a literary genre. If we come up with a convincing idea of this form of literary expression, it can go toward establishing a scale of values for this ideal anthology yet to be. There's too much confusion, too many misunderstandings in this area. While writers plunge ahead with their task, it's time to speak of that task itself, leaving aside individuals and nationalities. We have to have a workable idea of what the short story is, and that's always hard because ideas tend to be abstract, to devitalize what they're about, while in turn life recoils in pain from being roped in by concepts in order to tie it down and classify it. But if we have no working idea of what a story is, our efforts will go for nothing, because a short story, in the last analysis, exists on that same human level where life and the written expression of that life wage a fraternal war, if you'll allow me the term; and the outcome of that war is the short story itself, a living synthesis and also a synthesized life, like water trembling in a crystal, a fleetingness within a permanence. Only via images can one convey that secret alchemy that explains the way a great story strikes a note deep within us, and explains as well why there are few truly great stories.

In trying to grasp the unique character of the short story, it's common practice to compare it to the novel, a much more popular genre with many precepts concerning it. It's pointed out, for example, that the novel unfolds page after page, and hence in the time it takes to read it, and need stop only when the subject matter is used up; the short story, on the other hand, starts with the idea of a limit, and first of all a physical limit, so much so that in France, when a story runs over twenty pages, it's then called a *nouvelle,* a genre straddling the short story and the novel proper. In this sense, the novel and the short story may be compared, using an analogy to cinema and photography, in that a film is in principle "open-ended," like a novel, while a good photograph presupposes a strict delimitation beforehand, imposed in part by the narrow field the camera covers and the aesthetic use the photographer makes of this limitation. I don't know whether you've heard a professional photographer talk about his art; I'm always surprised that it sounds so much as if it could be a short-story writer talking. Photographs as fine as Cartier-Bresson's or Brassaï's define their art as an apparent paradox; that of cutting out a piece of reality, setting certain limits, but so that this piece will work as an explosion to fling open a much wider reality, like a dynamic vision that spiritually transcends the camera's field of vision. While in cinema, as in the novel, catching that broader and more multiple reality is a matter of developing an accumulation of bits, not excluding, of course, a synthesis that provides the work's climax, in a photograph or great short story it works the other way, that is, the photographer or writer has to choose and delimit an image or event that's significant, not just in and of itself, but able to work upon the viewer or reader as a sort of *opening,* a fermentation that moves intelligence and sensibility out toward something far beyond the visual or literary anecdote the photo or story contains. An Argentine writer, very fond of boxing, told me that in that fight that takes place between an absorbing text and its reader, the novel wins a technical victory, while the story must win by knockout. It's true, in that the novel progressively builds up its effect upon the reader, while a good story is incisive, mordant, and shows no clemency from the first lines on. This shouldn't be taken too literally, since the good story writer is a very wise boxer, and many of his first blows may seem ineffectual when he's really tearing down his opponent's most solid defenses. Take any great story you prefer and analyze the first page of it. I'd be surprised if you found any gratuitous elements just there for show. The short-story writer knows he cannot work by accumulation, that time is not on his side; he can only work in depth, vertically, whether upwards or downwards in literary space. And this, which put this way sounds like a metaphor, expresses nonetheless the core of the method. The short story's time and space must be as if condemned, subjected to a spiritual and formal pressure to achieve that "opening" I spoke of. One need only raise the question why a certain story is bad. It isn't the theme that makes it bad, because in literature there are no good or bad themes, only good or bad treatments of a theme. Nor is it bad because the characters are uninteresting, because even a stone is interesting if a Henry James or Franz Kafka turns his attention to it. A story is bad when it's written without that tension that should be there from the first words or first scenes. And so we can anticipate that the notions of meaningfulness, intensity and tension will allow us, as we'll see, to come closer to the very structure of the story.

We were saying that the short-story writer works with material we may call meaningful. The meaningful element of the story would seem to lie mainly in its *theme,* in the choice of a real or imagined event that possesses that mysterious ability to illuminate something beyond itself, so that a commonplace domestic episode, as is the case in so many admirable stories of a Katherine Mansfield or a Sherwood Anderson, becomes the implacable summing-up of a certain human condition or the blazing symbol of a social or historical order. A story is significant when it breaks through its own limits with that explosion of spiritual energy that throws into sudden relief something going far beyond the small and sometimes wretched anecdote it tells of. I am thinking, for example, of the theme of most of Anton Chekhov's admirable stories. What is there but the drearily everyday, mediocre conformity or pointless rebellion? What's told in these stories is almost what we, as children, in the boring gatherings we had to share with the grown-ups, heard the grandparents or aunts talking about: the petty, insignificant family chronicle with its frustrated ambitions, modest local dramas, sorrows the size of a parlor, a piano, a tea served with sweets. And yet, the stories of Katherine Mansfield or of Chekhov are meaningful; something bursts forth in them as we read and offers us a sort of breakaway from the everyday that goes well beyond the anecdote summed up therein. You have seen that this mysterious meaningfulness does not lie only in the theme of the story, because indeed most of the bad stories we've all read contain episodes similar to those treated by the authors named. The idea of meaning makes no sense unless related to intensity and tension, therefore no longer concerning just theme but the literary treatment of that theme, the technique used to develop the theme. And here is where, suddenly, there's a division between the good and the bad writer. So let's pause carefully at this parting of the ways to see a little better that strange form of life, a story that works, and see why it's alive while others, apparently like it, are no more than ink on paper, made to be forgotten.

Let's look at it from the writer's point of view and in this case, necessarily, from my own version of the matter. A short-story writer is a man who suddenly, in the midst of the immense babble of the world, more or less involved in the historical reality around him, chooses a given theme and makes a story out of it. This choice of theme is not so simple. Sometimes the writer chooses, and at other times he feels as if the theme irresistibly imposed itself on him, pushed him to write it. In my case, by far most of my stories were written—how should I say this—beyond my will, above or below my reasoning awareness, as if I were no more than a medium through which an alien power were coursing and making itself seen. But this, which can depend on one's temperament, does not change the basic fact, and that's that at a certain moment *there is a theme,* be it voluntarily invented or chosen, or strangely imposed from a level where nothing can be defined. There is a theme, I repeat, and this theme will become a story. Before that happens, what can we say of the theme itself? Why that theme and not some other? What reasons consciously or unconsciously move the writer to choose a given theme?

To me it seems that the theme that gives rise to a good story is always *exceptional,* but I don't mean that a theme should be extraordinary, out of the common run of things, mysterious or unusual. Just the opposite; it can be a perfectly trivial, everyday anecdote. What's exceptional is a magnetlike quality; a good theme attracts a whole system of interconnecting links; for the author, and later for the reader, it "gels" a vast amount of notions, half-glimpsed things, feelings and even ideas that were virtually floating around in his memory or sensibility; a good theme is like a good sun, a star with an orbiting planetary system, that, often, goes unnoticed till the writer, an astronomer of words, reveals to us its existence. Or rather, to be both more modest and more modern, a good theme is somehow atomic, like a nucleus with its orbiting electrons; and all that, when it comes down to it, isn't it a proposal of life, a dynamic that urges us to come out of ourselves and enter into a more complex and beautiful system of relations? I've often wondered what it is about certain unforgettable stories; when we read them, they're in together with a lot of other stories, maybe by the same author. And here the years go by and we've lived through and forgotten so much; but those small, insignificant stories, those grains of sand in the vast sea of literature, stay with us, beating inside us. Isn't it true that each of us has his own collection of stories? I have mine, and I could give you some names. I have "William Wilson," by Edgar Allan Poe; I have "Ball of Lard," by Guy de Maupassant. The little planets keep their orbits; there's "A Christmas Memory" by Truman Capote, "Tlön, Uqbar, Orbis Tertius" by Jorge Luis Borges, "A Dream Come True" by Juan Carlos Onetti, "The Death of Iván Ilyich" by Tolstoy, "Fifty Grand" by Hemingway, "The Dreamers" by Isak Dinesen, and I could go on and on. . . . You'll have noticed already that these aren't all the standard anthology items. *Why* do they linger on in memory? Think of the stories you have never been able to forget and you'll see that they all have this in common: they bring in a reality infinitely vaster than that of their mere story line, and so they've influenced us with a power their seemingly modest content, their brief texts, don't even hint at. And that man who at a given moment chooses a theme and makes a story out of it will be a great short-story writer if his choice holds—sometimes without his awareness of it—that fabulous opening-out from the small to the great, from the individual and bounded to the very essence of the human condition. Every enduring story is like the seed in which the giant tree lies sleeping. That tree will grow in us, will cast its shadow across our memory.

Yet, this notion of meaningful themes needs further clarification. The same theme may be deeply meaningful for one writer and insipid for another; the same theme will strike a deep chord in one reader and leave another cold. In short, one can say there are no absolutely meaningless themes. What there is, is a mysterious, complex connection between a certain writer and a certain theme at a given moment, just as this same connection will later be struck between certain stories and certain readers. So, when we say that a theme is meaningful, as in the case of Chekhov's stories, this meaningfulness comes about partly through something beyond the theme in and of itself, by something that comes before and after the theme. What comes before is the writer, with his set of human and literary values, with his drive to create a work with meaning to it; what comes after is the literary treatment of the theme, the way in which the writer, faced with the theme, lays hold of it, forces it verbally and stylistically into shape, molds it into a story, and reaches beyond it toward something greater than the story itself. Here I see a chance to mention something that happens to me a lot, and that other story writers will be just as familiar with. Habitually in the course of a conversation someone tells of a funny, moving or strange episode, and then turning to the story writer at hand says, "*There's a great idea for a story; you can have it.*" They've given me tons of themes just that way, and I've always answered politely: "Thank you," and I've never written a story with any of them. Yet, once a friend was rambling on about the adventures a maid of hers had in Paris. While I was listening to her tale, I felt it could become a short story. For her, those episodes were just so many odd anecdotes; for me they suddenly took on a meaning that went far beyond their simple, even banal, content. So every time I've been asked how I distinguish an insignificant theme—however funny or exciting it might be—from a meaningful one, I've answered that the writer is the first to register that indefinable but overwhelming effect certain themes have, and that's why he's a writer. Just as for Marcel Proust the taste of a madeleine dunked in tea suddenly flung out a vast array of seemingly forgotten memories, so the writer responds to certain themes, just as his story, later, will get a response from the reader. All of which is set on course by the aura, the irresistible fascination, that the theme stirs in its creator.

So we get to the end of this first step in the birth of a story and come to the threshold of creation itself. Here we have the writer, who's chosen a theme using those subtle antennae that allow him to recognize those elements that later will become a work of art. The writer is faced with his theme, with this embryo that is by now a life, but has not yet taken on its definite form. To him this theme holds meaning, has a sense to it. But if that were the whole thing, it wouldn't get us much of anywhere; now, as the last phase of the process, as an implacable judge, the reader awaits, the final link in the creative process, the crowning or the downfall of the cycle. And that's when the story must be born as a bridge, born as an access route, take the leap that sends the first meaning, discovered by the author, clear to the other end, the more passive and less alert and often even indifferent end we call the reader. Clumsy writers are likely to fall into believing that all they need to do is write out, as is, a theme that touched them, to move readers as well. They're like the parent who naively imagines everyone else will find his son as beautiful as he does. With time, with failed attempts, the story writer who can get past this first naive stage, learns that in literature good intentions aren't enough. He discovers that to re-create in the reader the thrill that made him write the story, he needs a writer's craft, and this craft consists, among many other things, of achieving that climate found in every great story, that compels the reader onward, keeps him riveted, tears him away from everything going on around him, so that later, when he's finished the story, he can reconnect with his world in a new, richer, deeper or more beautiful way. And the only way to steal the reader temporarily away is with a style based on intensity and tension, a style where formal and expressive elements fit, seamlessly, the nature of the theme, give it the most penetrating and original visual and sound image, make it unique, unforgettable, and place it definitively in its time, in its setting, and in its core-most meaning. What I call intensity in a story means the elimination of all the ideas or situations that are neither here nor there, padding and transitions that the novel allows for and even needs. None of you has forgotten "The Cask of Amontillado" by Edgar Allan Poe. The extraordinary thing about this story is the sharp elimination of any description of the setting. By the third or fourth sentence we are at the heart of drama, present as revenge is implacably taken. "The Killers," by Hemingway, is another example of intensity won by eliminating all but what is essential to the drama. But now let's think about the stories of Joseph Conrad, of D. H. Lawrence, of Kafka. With them, each in his own way, intensity is a different matter, and I prefer to call it tension. It's an intensity that comes out in the way the author slowly leads us into the story line. We're still very far from knowing what will happen in the story; still, we can't tear ourselves away from its atmosphere. In the case of "The Cask of Amontillado" and "The Killers," the bare facts, with no buildup, leap out at us and capture us; but in the measured flow of a Henry James story—"The Lesson of the Master," for example—one immediately feels that the facts in themselves hardly matter, that it's all in the powers that unleash them, in the subtle net that was there before them and is still at work. But be it intensity of action or the story's inner intensity, it's the result of what I earlier called the writer's craft, and with this we come close to the end of this look through the short story. In my country, and just now in Cuba, I've been able to read stories by the most diverse authors: mature or young, from city or country, drawn to literature for aesthetic reasons or by the social needs of the moment, politically committed or not.

So, and even though it may sound like stating the obvious, whether in Argentina or here, the best stories are being written by writers who know their craft in the way I've been talking about. An Argentine example will help show what I mean. In our central and northern provinces there's a long tradition of oral tales, that gauchos pass on at night at fireside, that parents keep on telling children, and suddenly they leap into the pen of a local-color writer and, practically always, they're horrible stories. What happened? The tales themselves are a joy: they translate and sum up the experience, sense of humor, and fatalism of man out in the country; some even rise to poetic or tragic dimensions. Heard from an old man of old country stock, while sipping maté, they can wipe out time and one thinks this was how the Greek tale-singers told the adventures of Achilles to dazzle shepherds and travelers. But at that moment, when a Homer should come to make an *Iliad* or *Odyssey* out of this store of oral tales, in my country along comes a gentleman who finds city culture a sign of decay, for whom the short-story writers we all love are so many aesthetes who wrote for the trifling amusement of social classes whose star has gone out, and this gentleman realizes that, instead, to write a story all that's needed is to write down a traditional tale, keeping as much as possible of the tone of telling, country turns of phrase, grammatical errors, everything they call local color. I don't know whether this way of writing popular stories is cultivated in Cuba; I hope not, because in my country all it's given us is undigestible volumes that don't even interest people out in the country, who prefer to go on sipping their brew and *listening* to stories, nor do they interest city readers, who may well be jaded and decadent, but they have read the classics of the genre with care. On the other hand—and I'm still talking about Argentina—we've had writers like Roberto J. Payró, Ricardo Güiraldes, Horacio Quiroga and Benito Lynch who, also making frequent use of traditional themes heard from old-country elders like Don Segundo Sombra, have managed to bring out this material's potential and make it into a work of art. But Quiroga, Güiraldes and Lynch knew the writer's craft through and through, that is, they would only work with significant, nourishing themes, just as Homer must have discarded tons of war stories and magic tales to keep the ones that have come down to us through their enormous mythic power, the resonance of their mental archetypes, their psychic hormones, as Ortega y Gasset called myths. Quiroga, Güiraldes and Lynch were writers of universal scope, with no local, ethnic or populist prejudices: that's why, besides choosing the themes of their stories carefully, they pressed them into a literary mold, the only one that could convey to the reader all their values, all their ferment, their sweeping range both in depth and height. They wrote tensely, they showed intensely. There's no other way a story will work, hit the mark, and dig into the reader's memory.

The example I've given might well interest Cuba. It's clear that the possibilities the Revolution offers a story writer are almost endless. City, country, political struggle, work, various psychological types, ideological and personality conflicts, and how all this is heightened by the drive I see in you to act, to express yourselves, to communicate as you never before could. But all that, how will it translate into great stories, stories that reach the reader with due power and effect? Here's where I'd like to apply concretely what I've said on a more abstract level. Enthusiasm and willingness are not enough by themselves, just as writer's craft is not enough by itself to write the stories that will set forth literarily (that is, in our shared sense of admiration, in the memory of a people) the greatness of that Revolution in progress. Here, more than anywhere else, is needed a total fusion of these two forces, that of the man fully committed to his nation's and the world's reality, and that of the writer lucidly sure-handed in his craft. Nothing short of this will do. The more of a veteran and an old pro a writer is, if he lacks a deep-seated motivation, if his stories aren't born of core experience, his work will be no more than an aesthetic exercise. But the opposite will be even worse, because fervor and the urge to communicate a message are no good without the expressive, stylistic instruments that allow for that communication. At this moment, we are touching the crux of the matter. I believe, and I'm saying this after weighing at length all the elements involved, that to write for a revolution, to write within a revolution, means to write in a revolutionary way; it doesn't mean, as many believe, to be obliged to write about the revolution itself.

For my part, I believe the revolutionary writer is the one who fuses in himself, inseparably, awareness of his free individual and collective political commitment, and that other sovereign cultural freedom, that of the full mastery of his craft. If that writer, responsible and lucid, decides to write fantastic or psychological literature, or turn his writing toward past times, his act is an act of freedom within the revolution, and so it's also a revolutionary act even though his stories aren't concerned with the individual or collective forms the revolution assumes. Contrary to the narrow criterion of many who have literature mixed up with instruction, or literature with teaching, or literature with ideological indoctrination, a revolutionary writer has every right to address a much more complex reader, one who is much more demanding in spiritual matters than what's imagined by those writers and critics thrown into those roles by circumstances and convinced their personal world is the only world in existence, that the concerns of the moment are the only valid concerns. Let's repeat, with reference to what's going on around us in Cuba, Hamlet's admirable line: "There are more things in heaven and earth, Horatio, than are dreamt of in your philosophy." And let's think that a writer isn't judged only by the theme of his stories or novels, but by his living presence in the heart of the community, by the fact that the total commitment of his person is an undeniable guarantee of the truth and the necessity of his work, however foreign that work might seem to the circumstances of the moment. That work is not foreign to the revolution because it's not accessible to everyone. Just the opposite, it proves there exists a vast sector of potential readers that, in a certain sense, are much further separated than the writer from the final goals of the revolution, those goals of culture, freedom, full enjoyment of the human condition, that Cubans have set for themselves, to the admiration of all those who love and understand them. The higher they aim, those writers who were born for it, the higher will be the final goals of the people they belong to. Beware of the facile demagoguery of demanding a literature accessible to everyone! Many of those who push this line only do so because of their evident inability to understand literature of wider scope. They clamor for popular themes, never suspecting that often the reader, simple as he may be, will intuitively be able to tell a poorly written popular story from a more difficult, complex story that will force him for a moment out of the little world around him and show him something else, whatever it may be, but something different. It makes no sense to speak of popular themes, period. Stories on popular themes will only be good if they are built, like any other story, on that demanding and difficult inner mechanism that we've tried to show in the first part of this talk. Some years back, I had this proven to me in Argentina, in a gathering of country men where a few writers were present. Someone read a story based on an episode from our war of independence, written in deliberately simple style to place it, as its author said, "at the peasant's level." The story got a polite hearing, but it was easy to see it hadn't left its mark. Then one of us read "The Monkey's Paw," the justly famous story by W. W. Jacobs. The interest, the thrill, the fear and, at the end, the enthusiasm were extraordinary. I remember we spent the rest of the night talking about spells, witches, diabolical revenge. And I'm sure Jacob's story keeps on living in the memory of those illiterate gauchos, while the supposedly popular story, manufactured for them, with its vocabulary, its made-easy intellectual content and its patriotic interest must be as forgotten as the writer who manufactured it. I've seen the thrill simple people derive from seeing *Hamlet* on stage, a hard and subtle work if there ever was one, and an unending topic of scholarly study and infinite controversies. It's true those people can't understand many things that thrill specialists in Elizabethan theater. So what? Only their feelings matter, their awe and rapture at the tragedy of the young Danish prince. That proves that Shakespeare truly wrote for the people, in that his theme was deeply meaningful for anyone—on different levels, to be sure, but reaching each one—and the theatrical treatment of that theme had the intensity common to great writers, which breaks down the seemingly sturdiest barriers, and men recognize each other and become brothers on a level beyond any culture. Of course, it would be naive to believe that any great work could be understood and admired by simple people; it's not true, and can't be. But the wonder that Greek or Shakespearean tragedies evoke, as well as the passionate interest many stories and novels—not in the least simple or accessible—can flame, must raise the suspicion among advocates of mislabeled "popular art," that their idea of the people is slanted, unfair and, in the end, dangerous. It's not doing the people a favor to offer them a literature that can be taken in effortlessly, passively, like going to see a cowboy movie. What needs to be done is educate them, and that's a first step, a matter of instruction, not literature. It has been reassuring to me to see how in Cuba the writers I most admire participate in the revolution, giving the best of themselves, without offering up part of their possibilities on the altar of a supposedly popular art that will benefit no one. One day Cuba will have on hand a store of stories and novels containing—worked out on an aesthetic level, rendered eternal in the timelessness of art—the revolutionary adventure of today. But those works won't have been written out of obligation, following the slogans of the hour. Their themes will be born when the time is ripe, when the writer feels he must mold them into stories or novels or plays or poems. Their themes will carry a genuine, deep message, because they won't have been chosen in obeisance to a didactic, proselytizing norm, but from an irresistible force that will seize hold of the author, so that he, summoning all that his art and technique can offer, not sacrificing anything to anyone, will convey to the reader as fundamental things are conveyed: blood to blood, hand to hand, man to man.

This article originally appeared in Casa de las Americas, *Núms. IS16 (1962-1963). It is translated here by Naomi Lindstrom with the permission of the author.*

First published in issue 3.3 (Fall 1983)

Literature Pursued by Politics

Juan Goytisolo

In the course of recent international meetings of writers and artists—not only in Leningrad, Edinburgh or Florence, but also in
Formentor or Madrid—the relations between politics and literature, the concepts of art for art's sake vs. that of art serving a Cause,
have been the obligatory topic of discussion. A growing lack of confidence in the value of literature impels a considerable number of
writers to seek a justification of their work based on reasons extrin-
sic to art. Positions are defended with uncompromising rigidity and
the impartial spectator often has the feeling of attending a dispute
among deaf men. "Literature and politics are two different things,"
some say. "Literature, once it is published, is a social fact and, as
such, fulfills a political function," others answer. In reality, things
are not as clear-cut as they first seem, nor are they as simple. These
hastily formulated alternatives, these concepts of art-as-end or art-
as-means, are far from resolving the problems we intellectuals confront; rather, they avoid them and, perhaps, complicate them. It's
really a matter of superficial definitions that, instead of circum-
scribing and delimiting the topic, let it slither around and slip away
altogether, as well as a matter of apparent dilemmas that, if we examine them more closely, neither contain nor could contain any
truth or possibility of truth.

In a recent essay entitled "Literature Pursued by Politics," Alain
Robbe-Grillet criticized the politicization of the work of art in these
terms: "Writers are not necessarily political brains. And it's no
doubt normal for most of them to limit themselves, in this field, to short,
vague thoughts. But why do they feel such a need to express them in
public at every opportunity? . . . I believe, simply, that they're
ashamed of being writers and live in perpetual terror they'll be re-
proached with it, be asked why they write, what good they are, what
their role in society is. . . . The writer suffers, like everyone, over the
misfortune of his fellow human beings; it's dishonest to pretend he
writes to allay it. . . . The writer can't know what end he's serving.
Literature isn't a means he's to place at the service of some Cause."

The observations of the chief theorist of the *nouveau roman* are
relevant, beyond a doubt, but need some clarifications. To assess
them properly, it seems to me necessary, above all, to situate them
in their historical context as the concrete expression of the writer's

aspirations in a given society. In France, where freedom of thought and speech are a reality, and equality of political rights is no empty formula, the novelist's relation to the public is entirely different, for example, than the one existing in Spain and the Latin American countries. The reason is very simple.

When the social and economic conflicts that constitute the dynamic evolutionary force of a country can be freely aired through the natural outlets for the expression of conflicting interests, the writer's social responsibility to the public is not the same as in those other nations where the interests and aspirations of different pressure groups find no legal outlet for expression. The peculiar status of French society—rid of the anachronism of colonial wars, free of the "danger" of revolution thanks to the prodigious technical transformation brought about by neocapitalism, etc.—favors the growth of a literature that, to use Vittorini's formula, tends to move from the level of consolation, from the level of guiding awareness, to that of probing and seeking, that of fruitful answers, that of knowledge. On the other hand, in those countries either underdeveloped or in the preliminary stages of development—as Spain is today—literature strives to reflect political and social reality, and if this task were abandoned it would bring as an immediate consequence the writing of an imitative literature, a simple rehash of writing in those countries that, like England, Germany and France, have reached a higher political, cultural and economic level, only leaving out innovative literary technique, which leads, logically, to the growth of a literature that, confronting reality with old worn-out formulas, does so with an anachronistic focus, a holdover from our grandfather's naturalism. On this point Robbe-Grillet's insistence on pointing out the art-technique factor in itself seems to me valid, not only for the literature of his country, but for that of all those who, for different and sometimes opposite reasons, sacrifice artistic technique to reproduction—conventional and hence false—of reality.[1]

But Robbe-Grillet commits the sin of pride when, "with this nationalism inherent to French writers, who tend to confuse French literature with literature as such," as Bloch-Michel writes, he attempts to generalize his experience—product of the specific French situation—to countries whose political, social and cultural level is very far from fitting the pattern on which he bases his analysis. For better or for worse, the world can't be reduced to the cafés of St.-Germain des Prés, nor do the Tablets of the Law on the Rue Bernard Palissy have the universal validity that some believe.

When through an official push toward depoliticization—as is the case in Spain, or of total politicization serving the prime social objective of the State, as was the case in the Soviet Union under Stalin and, to a lesser degree, now, the press does not reflect the fruitful and contradictory dynamics of a society; when social groups—I'm referring to Spain—cannot air their feelings or defend their interests freely, the writer—poet, playwright, or novelist—becomes, in spite of himself, the spokesman for that dynamic, those feelings, those interests, playing a role that, in a way, resembles that of a safety valve.

On another occasion, I pointed out how the rigidity of Spanish censorship had forced novelists to respond to the public's hunger for information by transposing into their works the outline of a reality opposed to the unreality of the newspapers; that is, to perform the witness-bearing that would normally fall to the press. Robbe-Grillet's criticism of writers' involvement in politics loses, in this case, all its applicability. While in France political involvement grows out of the writer's free choice—given that the function of literature is less "consolation" than "seeking" and the writer, free of the impinging pressure of his readers, can forego reproducing immediate reality to concentrate upon the development of his art in terms of technique—in the Soviet Union and Spain, for different reasons, as we'll see, political involvement is predetermined by the particular situation of the artist within the society of these two countries and according to the needs—more or less formulated, more or less stated—of his public. Politics then lends its coloration to art, and the writer, willy-nilly, becomes spokesman for the forces that struggle in silence against the oppression of a social class or the monopoly of an ideology that has been turned into dogma. In this way, contemporary Spanish literature is a mirror of the obscure, humble, and daily struggle of the Spanish people for its lost freedom, just as the work of young Soviet poets channels the artistic rebellion of the new generations against the alienation engendered by Stalinism. Politics and literature end up sharing weapons in the same liberation struggle and, as with Monsieur Jourdain's prose, the writer is taking political action without realizing it.[2]

Lucien Goldmann recently analyzed the relation between the change in the form of the novel and the evolution of today's economy: the expression of free thought originated by the Reformation, reflecting the opposition created between man and society after the breakup of the medieval "civitas," the novel is thrown into crisis along with the individualism that was its basis. The decline and disappearance of the character, and the growing autonomy of objects—from Joyce, Kafka and Camus through Robbe-Grillet and the other representatives of the *nouveau roman*—would correspond, according to Goldmann, to the dissolution of the individual and individual life in the machinery of the economic structures of monopolistic capitalism of the first third of the twentieth century and of current-day neocapitalism, a process known in Marxist writing by the name of "reification." Following this line of thought, the work of Butor, Robbe-Grillet, Nathalie Sarraute, generally deemed formalistic, would express better than the nineteenth-century novel and behavioristic narrative the techno-industrial reality of our times (despite the fact it goes along with this reality rather than criticizing it).[3]

With the blessing of Goldmann, Robbe-Grillet defends what's almost an artisan's commitment to his craft—a commitment earlier called for by Michel Leiris—but, as soon as he adds "problems such as war, social awareness, etc.," they touch upon our lives, as citizens, "that begin at the moment we place our ballots in the box," and establishes a distinction between the citizen's commitment; this split cannot be applied to those countries where the lack of basic political freedoms—as is the case in Spain—or the adulteration of revolutionary ideology to serve a personality-style dictatorship—as it was in the Soviet Union after Lenin's death—forces the public to use literature as an escape valve and push the authentic writer to the fore of a struggle that, departing from the strictly literary, is, simply and plainly, one more episode in the unceasing struggle of peoples for their freedom.

What does it indeed mean for Spain or most of the underdeveloped countries of Latin America, this political involvement "at the level of writing," if illiteracy, social injustice, and the violence of power rule out the normal exercise of citizens' rights? If to demand publicly the freedoms granted by our conservative nineteenth-century governments constitutes a crime, who can speak, without blushing, of ballot boxes? When there is no political freedom, everything is politics, and the split between writer and citizen vanishes. In this case literature agrees to be a political weapon, or ceases to be literature and becomes an inauthentic echo of the literature of other societies situated at different levels (the proliferation of Spanish, Mexican, Portuguese or Argentine Robbe-Grillets, following upon hosts of Faulkners and Kafkas, is a good example of what I mean).

We have only to look around us to note that in three-quarters of the world literary work is condemned to remain, of necessity, at the level of consolation, of the guiding of consciousness, to be, as Pavese said during the Fascist regime, "a defense against the offenses of life." If Goldmann's analysis is correct—to my mind it's too unilateral and schematic—involvement at the level of writing would represent the advanced tendency of writers in the context of contemporary technological society, whether socialist or neocapitalist. But only the winning of public freedoms in Spain and almost all the

Third World countries, the end of artistic monopoly of so-called so-cialist realism and government pressure—that is, the return to the original form of Marxism—in the countries where the dictatorship of the proletariat is now in force, can allow, in the long run, for the universal validation of a literature of exploration and probing (of which the *nouveau roman* is but a small sample, and not the Tablets of the Law of a sacred art, exclusive birthright of a dozen-and-some-odd writers associated with Editions de Minuit), a literature that would reflect the many aspects of the alienation of man-as-object, a mere cog in the gigantic machinery of industrial organization, the preprogramming of every aspect of life, the tentacles of blind bu-reaucracy; this universe, so unattractive—yet for which we must fight—of present-day neocapitalism of the first stage of the building of socialism, a universe that is fated to be ours till the (unlikely) collapse of the West's economy or the (remote) advent of a truly communistic society in the USSR.

Thus it's not rash to prophesy that commitment in the future will be less political in nature than craftsmanly, at the level of writing and technique, and that for a reason that stems from the very nature of the literary work: for while political commitment is always ambigu-ous and dependent on circumstances, commitment to craft is well suited to the ambivalent nature of an art whose prime exigency is not to exclude the opposite exigency. Conceived, simultaneously, as experience and utopia, as action and escape, literature plays a real political role insofar as it is the source of an entire set of options and projects that modify and transform the face of the earth, but this role rests, in reality, on a misunderstanding. As Maurice Blanchot said: "He [the writer] writes novels, these novels imply certain po-litical statements, so he seems to become involved with a Cause. The others who have embraced this cause directly tend to see in his work the proof that the Cause is indeed their cause, but, as soon as they proclaim it . . . they realize the writer has not become involved, that the game is being played only with himself, that what interests him in the Cause is his own workings." The overlap between litera-ture and politics is annihilated at the very instant when the factors that bring it about—political oppression, artistic dogmatism, etc.—cease, unless, as often happens, in the West as well as the East, the writer abandons literature and throws himself heart and soul into pseudoliterary panegyrics for the cause he embraces. But then we're no longer talking about a writer but about a pen wielder, and his "merchandise" has nothing to do with literature.[4]

For the moment—whether Robbe-Grillet likes it or not—we Spanish writers, like Soviet ones and those from almost the world over, will live pursued by politics. To pretend otherwise would be, as

Bloch-Michel says about the theorists of the *nouveau roman,* "to mistake their national drop of water for the world's ocean and their own fatigue for the desperation of humanity."

NOTES

[1]In a penetrating and suggestive essay entitled "Industry and Literature," Elio Vittorini, after analyzing the effect on the human imagination of the newness of the things we live among, owing to the last industrial revolution, concluded: "The industrial world that by work of man has replaced the natural one is a world we do not yet possess." For Vittorini, almost all European, Soviet and American writers who present in their works the new human relations that have arisen in factories and businesses, do so within literarily preindustrial limits. That is: applying an old form to a new theme, they produce a bastard work that neither captures the essence, nor characterizes the universe they describe.

[2]The socialist state's intervention in literary creation cannot be historically supported by anything in Marx and Engels. The Marxist theory of the superstructure is anything but systematic in matters of art, and in the *Introduction to the Critique of Political Economics* Marx writes of Greek art: "Certain periods of great artistic development have no direct link either with the general development of society, or with the material basis and the framework of its organization." As Edmund Wilson very correctly observes, such intervention, motivated by circumstances derived from the nineteenth-century Russian tradition, only occurred after Lenin's death.

[3]Goldmann's article was later included by the author in the volume *Pour une sociologie du roman,* one of the most closed and narrow works of criticism to appear in France in recent years; a phenomenon I will deal with at a later time.

[4]In the propagandist and his audience there develops that double error that Octavio Paz denounces in *The Bow and the Lyre:* the former thinks he's speaking the language of the people, the latter, that it's hearing the voice of poetry. The deterioration of poetic art, so frequent in the vast output of Neruda, constitutes in this regard an illuminating example. Let us recall his elegy upon the death of Stalin and that delicious line:

> But Malenkov now will continue his work . . .
As the great bard of the fifteenth century sang:
> Mais où sont les neiges d'antan?

This essay originally appeared in Goytisolo's El furgón de cola *(Paris: Ed. Ruedo Ibérico, 1967). It is here translated by Naomi Lindstrom by permission of the author.*

First published in issue 4.2 (Summer 1984)

The Novel as Concept

Camilo José Cela

I

On occasion, I have compared the process of making a novel with the process of having a child. The concept is not really original and may even be pedestrian, vulgar, and commonplace. I don't say it isn't. Still, to have a child, just as to *have* a novel, to write it, a set of circumstances must occur, for without them neither child nor novel can be produced. Savants, those who pass their idle hours combining substances in retorts or staring through a microscope or pouring over blurred palimpsests, have children in the same way as foremen on cattle ranches, the same as stevedores or bus drivers. If anyone proposed to make an analysis of a child and determine its desirable parts for combination in a laboratory, who knows what would result? Perhaps stock for soup, or shoe polish, or even dynamite, but as for a child, not likely . . .

It's the same with the novel. If a Spaniard, a German, a Russian can put together the necessary ingredients, count on the required circumstances which no one can enumerate, and put their minds to the task, they can produce novels, perhaps magnificent novels. If they were to imitate the savants, they would be lost; the laboratory technician may not engender a viable child, but he can turn out utilitarian objects; novelists-à-la-savant can only produce aberrations.

The life of a child, however short it lasts, completes a cycle: the child is born, grows, dies. In addition, it cries, laughs, sucks a teat, wets itself . . .

In a letter, a friend tells me: "A novel is the description of a complete circle, an enclosed horizon of life, with no void spaces, just as there are none around us." This friend is quite right: the cycle may be closed—by the death of the child or the end of the novel—but it cannot be interrupted.

To speak of the novel is like speaking of the sea. The novel simply needs to be written. Dogmatic pronouncements are useless.

There is no point in trying to fit it into a Procrustean bed. And no one should forget its inexhaustible sources—of action, of aesthetic beauty, of sustained interest—sources with names like Balzac, Dickens, Dostoyevsky, Stendhal. Divagations and lucubrations are of little value here.

Proust wrote: "*Une oeuvre où il y a des théories est comme un objet sur lequel on laisse la marque du prix.*" Proust knew whereof he spoke: it would be frightful to give birth to a child who, instead of causing a fuss and setting up a din, as natural law requires, stood up in his cradle and pontificated: "O parents and brothers: the economic theory of free competition . . ." Such a child would deserve capital punishment.

A novel has no business expressly defending anything, absolutely anything at all. It will inevitably be seen that it plays some part in life, but those novels which are known to be, before they are opened, intent on defending this or attacking that, are devoid of any importance whatsoever.

The nursery of proletarian novelists which the Communist Party nurtured with a view toward overawing the Western world came to a sterile end, a blasted crop, even though the Russians are exceptionally gifted for developing the genre. The great writers of the nineteenth century, who developed and came to fruition under the twin scourges of persecution and imprisonment, a very poor environment indeed for the production of luxury goods like the novel, were never bettered or even equaled by the Soviet hacks whose names are already forgotten—not even by Gorky, the best of the lot.

The concept of the novel must come from within, like the taste of a pear or the odor of a flower or of the sea. It cannot be severed, separated, or cast aside like an orange peel or a banana skin, for therein lies the danger: that the whole will be thrown away with the parings.

It is difficult indeed to conceal the scaffolding of a book from its reader. But it is a necessity. In the novels of Pío Baroja, if we take as an example the most noteworthy and most universal of modern Spanish novelists, we never stumble on the joints or the scaffolding, however much we turn the work about, hold it up to the light, or sniff around in general. For the body of Don Pío's work is like a seamless tunic, without stitching. It is spawned—just as a boy-child or a girl-child is born—altogether and once and for all.

In contrast, let us mention Valle-Inclán, Don Ramón with his goat's beard. His plots are more obvious than protruding ribs. What about this plank sticking out here? That board is Barbey, the French writer. And this other protrusion? That belongs to Casanova, the gentleman-writer. And so on . . . The fact that Don Ramón manages to emerge triumphant simply implies genius, something a bit apart from the point we are making.

The novel requires a gut truth, a whole-bodied verity, one which has been digested and redigested by the author. The novelist by rights should have four stomachs, like oxen. Thus equipped, he would constantly be ruminating his gut truth, and his book would always be well born.

Balancing acts are not permissible in the making of a novel, because if the author ever loses his balance, he falls into the abyss and breaks his neck. The great lacuna in the history of the Spanish novel, which stretches from the time of the writers of the Generation of '98 until . . . until when, O Lord? . . . is filled with castaways who tried balancing acts.

II

> A starving man is more sound in his reasons than a hundred men of letters.

It would be convenient to know, so as not to lose ourselves in a labyrinth whose secret key we do not possess, something about the function of literature. It would also not be amiss to find a way of weighing the worth of literary ingredients, of determining the soundness of the building materials with which we are working. While we are about it, why not plumb, within reasonable limits, the rarefied nature of the writing profession itself? We might then be in a position to guess whether the art of the novel is some kind of scientific paradox or if it is instead a manifestation of wondrous chance—of a pure, if truncated, kind of stern destiny.

To Carlyle's way of thinking, writing is the greatest miracle of man's imagining—perhaps simply a miraculous curse. For Goethe, it seems a laborious way of relaxing, perhaps a form of relaxation which will let us die wearing the frightful grimace of a person succumbing to overwork.

A writer's singular office may be compared to a disappointing game of blindman's buff: the principal actor dances in desperation before a chorus of invisible and phantasmagoric spectators. "To write is to arouse interest, but the interest we manage to arouse may be no more than a tiny bell tinkling in a great desert waste, and it may make us forget the blindfold around our eyes and prevent us from properly assessing the materials with which we will have to work: that is, the prose which will give only a poor idea of things, and the poetry which will yield only an inexact notion." Thus spoke that tormented and blindfolded Spaniard, Ángel Ganivet, who committed suicide in the Dwina River.

And to write novels, to "novelate"? To novelate is to die step by step on a dusty road leading nowhere. And to go down smiling, the better to please the world's lurid tastes, the better to endure its mockery, all the while being beaten while fending off the Tyrians, who play with a stacked deck because they are not allowed to lose, and taking additional blows from the Trojans, who jump into the ring bearing arms forbidden by all codes of honor because, according to the laws promulgated by themselves, their side must always win.

To write novels is to uproot oneself, to venture forth carrying one's roots in the air above one's head, and to let oneself be cut down by the first fool one encounters without a show of resistance and in the full knowledge of one's own ignominy.

Today it is not enough to possess a purely artistic understanding of the hara-kiri involved in novelating. A genius may raise his particular science to the heights of art, but the artist lacking genius may be merely a fraud, a dealer in contraband. It's for the likes of the latter that literary prize contests are organized: fraudulent novelists write novels with a thesis—proletarian novels, inspirational novels, redemptive novels, sex novels—and the host of nonsense books that are invented for the stultification of man, who was once called, in happier times, the measure of all things.

The novelist does not know where he is going. The same is true of the north needle on a compass. The novelist allots himself a certain amount of terrain, applies the technology he has mastered, and awaits to see what he produces: if it's a boy he'll know by its lap, likewise if it's a girl; if it's bearded he can call out San Anton, if not, he can speak of an Immaculate Conception.

Science, like life or death, does not allow subterfuge. Art, like love, does. Thus, for the latter, fraud is a distinct possibility. The point is to avoid, with a measure of precision, concepts as such, and also to avoid confusing love with alterations in the nervous system. No novelist would ever think "to tell a book by its cover," and neither would he confuse an underground tuber with its leaves, for he must begin by knowing what leaves are and what a tuber is. George Santayana affirmed that the function of literature is to convert events into ideas. This conversion or transformation, be it understood, cannot be attained by exclusively artistic means, or by purely intuitive, nondeliberated means, which would amount to the same. The present crisis in literature is due to the inability of the novelist to dominate modern technical means. Beyond Faulkner's interior monologue, for example, which can be carried on through talent alone, there rises, like a giant mountain, the terra incognita of strict objectivity. Objectivity in itself is a difficult bone to gnaw, especially with the teeth provided by art. Nevertheless, if the novelistic genre is not to atrophy, science must sooner or later sink its teeth into the matter.

Today's novelist should surely give up his affair with the likes of

Madame Bovary and turn his attention to a Lazarillo, the archetypal picaro of the picaresque. The novel should no longer concern itself with the amusements of featherbrained housewives, maudlin dreamers who whore around, in body or soul, at the far corners of provinces. Such things as hunger and bad faith are still prevalent, as is the wretchedness of the servant with a hundred masters.

To rejuvenate themes grown old and to revivify the eternal myths: that is the business of the contemporary novelist, assuming he does not want to go into cold storage, where, as with multicolored cats at night, all things are a monotone.

If it's all a matter of killing time—a role assigned literature by all its detractors and a goodly number of those who cultivate it—everything we have said is superfluous. Still, something greater may be involved, though it have so many names we dare not name it with any one name.

The art of novelating is clearly, more clearly each day, seen to be an affair of two or three world novelists who work with energy and faith above and beyond the orbit of art. In physics, the same was true with Planck, Schrödinger, Heisenberg, and even true before them.

Ortega's figure of a divine somnambulist no longer serves. That time is done. In the field of the novel, the seer exchanges his walnut wand for a radar installation.

All this does not mean the death of the genre. It may represent its birth. In Galdós's time the novel was still in its intrauterine stage.

Translated by Anthony Kerrigan

First Published in issue 4.3 (Fall 1984)

Reflections on the Novel: Address to the Colloquium on the New Novel, New York University, October 1982

Claude Simon

Before beginning, I would like to be forgiven if the talk that I am going to give lacks a certain rigor and lets fly in a number of different directions. For reasons "beyond my control" (as we say), I only knew that my visit here would be authorized twelve days before my departure, which left me very little time to try to put the notes I had made while thinking about this colloquium into some kind of order, and to hastily draft a text that would doubtless have gained from being more condensed. But I am not to blame for that . . .

And firstly, by way of a preamble, I must warn those who have come to listen to me that they have before them just a self-taught writer whose literary knowledge does not go beyond an amateur level.

Most of you, whether teachers, critics, or students, certainly know a good deal more than I do about the novel, drama, or poetry, as well as literary theories, semiology, or linguistics, which makes me sometimes wonder, as a matter of fact, whether contrary to what Barthes thought, Jakobson did not in this instance give to literature a poisoned offering, as others may have done in some respects with sociology or psychoanalysis.

But after all, perhaps it is written that art must periodically navigate between the redoubtable reefs of scientism. For example, at the end of the last century, a painter whose name we would certainly have otherwise forgotten, Paul Sérusier, worked out a "theory of complementary colors" as attractive as it was unusable at a practical level, and, not to be outdone, we have seen, in recent years, writers toiling away and exhausting themselves in the construction of texts relying entirely upon dreary sequences of anagrammatical acrobatics more or less inspired by Saussure or again by a celebrated psychoanalytical guru.

It is not that I want to throw out the baby with the bathwater, but apparently, just as Lenin denounced the "infantilism" of left-wing communism (which nevertheless seems to continue), there is a chronic illness of art and literature which may be infantile, or senile for all I know, but which scientists of all persuasions are diligently engaged in aggravating, not curing.

As far as I am concerned, my cultural equipment is that of a dilettante. When I was young I was pushed toward mathematics (which, alas, I have forgotten), and I do not even have my baccalaureate in philosophy. The little I know has been acquired by chance—in reading, traveling, walking round museums and going to concerts, always in a rather desultory way, without ever worrying about studying a subject in depth, obeying solely the rules of pleasure. It was for example necessary that I be taken prisoner (I think that one of the lucky aspects of my existence has been to have lived the first part of it in a somewhat troubled Europe, which enabled me, by getting involved willingly or unwillingly in certain events, to learn, I think, other things than can be learned in books) . . . it was necessary, therefore, that I be taken prisoner in order for me to read Kant and Spinoza, not by choice, but, once again, because that was what happened to be there. I experienced then, moreover, something doubly instructive: the discovery first of all that in a space surrounded by barbed wire and where it was strictly forbidden to possess anything beyond the absolute minimum required for the most elementary form of survival, it was possible to find almost anything, from women's suspenders to *Das Kapital* via obscene photographs and the Acts of the Apostles; then, that if Kant and Spinoza were not of any practical or even moral and intellectual use to a starving man (they did not in any way help me to accept my abject state), these books nevertheless offered, even to one as philosophically profane as I am, the possibility of the kind of stimulation reading procures—purely gratuitous in a sense, but irreplaceable because of its very gratuitousness, like music or painting.

So much then for my intellectual formation, or, if you prefer, my "cultural baggage," constituted for the most part of lacunas and contained in the kind of colander that is my brain, retaining here and there a few scraps of knowledge, at least consciously, for after all it is possible that the ingurgitation of Kant and Spinoza, as with mathematics, forcibly as it were, and of which I do not have a very clear recollection either, may, without me knowing it, have contributed to shaping it, in the same way (albeit negatively) as the books I have never had the desire to open again, like for example *La Princesse de Clèves, Les Liaisons dangereuses, Lucien Leuwen,* or again those which I never managed to finish so much did they bore me, whether it be *La Cousine Bette, L'Education sentimentale,* and, I must admit, the majority of nineteenth-century novels of that kind, as well as their twentieth-century counterparts, whose characters, with their too predictable and too rational destinies (as against those, for example, of Dostoyevsky) make me think of the bulls so prized by matadors and which, in bullfighting slang, are called "ferrocarrils," that is, "mounted on rails," because they charge in a straight line, quite predictably, toward their prey. (In passing, and since I have just alluded to Dostoyevsky, I must say how surprised I am, each time I hear someone talk about what is described as "the traditional novel," that Balzac, Stendhal, or Zola is automatically invoked, forgetting about one of the two or three greatest writers in the history of literature, as if he had not existed, and to whom, precisely, we owe fictions that are the opposite of the univocal novels turned out in such quantities in the nineteenth century, giving not a reassuring picture of the world but that eminently unsettling one about which Robbe-Grillet talked yesterday.)

To come back to myself, if I am asked the ritual question "Why do you write?", well, to tell the truth, I have to admit, to my great shame, that I have never been touched, however lightly, by the ambitious motives of some: it has never occurred to me (and I have never asked myself if it might be the case) to write against the established order, or to challenge it. If I have written (and if I continue to do so), it is because, very prosaically and doubtless very selfishly, I was simply driven (like anyone, I think, working within his field) by a certain need to "make something," and if I am still asked why I have "made things" in the domain of literature rather than elsewhere, and if I want to be sincere, I will reply: "Because I was not capable of doing anything else."

In my youth I was rather lazy, and at the same time, like all young people, rather romantic (which is perhaps, on reflection, a kind of laziness), and these two failings led me to throw myself into various experiments like, for example, painting, or for a while, revolutionary action (which my incurable amateurishness made me abandon fairly rapidly and which nevertheless always costs me all sorts of annoying problems each time I have to visit this country).

There remained the possibility of writing, which I thought easier than painting or revolution, and, naturally, of writing what seemed to me to require the least specialization or discipline, that is the kind of holdalls that are novels, a genre whose rules (if there are any!) are not at all well defined, and which one thinks, when beginning, one is going to be able to do just about anything with, and put just about anything into.

I did not, unfortunately, realize that for this as well I lacked the real gifts that allow one to produce books that are liable to interest people. In choosing my pleasure alone as my guide, as with my reading, I thought, naively, that this pleasure would be transmissible and that I would be able to procure some of the same pleasure for those who might read me. In spite of my various experiences as revolutionary and amateur warrior (for war, in the circumstances in which I made it, that is in open country, on horseback and armed with a sabre and a rifle against planes and armored vehicles, even if it was horrifyingly murderous, almost bordered on caricature) . . . in spite of my various experiences, therefore, I did not know that the general public (the one dreamed of by all writers) has a tremendous vested interest in the proceedings (like in a card or dice game where money is staked), in other words that the pleasure or rather the "profit" which it expects from a novel is either escapist, allowing it to forget itself for a few hours in order to identify with an exemplary hero or heroine conforming to some archetype (of either virtue or evil), or didactic, bringing knowledge that will offer a solution to the problems preoccupying it, whether it be those concerned with social or amorous and sentimental relationships, the meaning of life or of History, even without the capital H, as, for example, in a detective story, by revealing the name of the murderer.

In view of this, I resigned myself pretty quickly to the admission that I would never be a true professional in this area either. In actual fact, if I average out the profits I have made from my books over thirty years, I think that they must come to roughly what someone gets on the dole, and lacking, furthermore, the erudition and the talents that would have enabled me to earn my living writing articles or teaching in a university (but teaching what?), I certainly wonder how, if I had not had the good fortune to benefit from a small inheritance, I would ever have managed to clothe and house myself, or even just feed myself, and remain in that marginal situation thanks to which, without making any financial or opportunistic concessions, I can write and say just what I like.

By some miracle (or perhaps some misunderstanding), I had the good luck, in spite of the small number of my books printed, to find, in the course of my life, a first, then a second, and finally a third publisher who turned out to be also the publisher of some other writers none of whose work, with the exception of Samuel Beckett, I had yet read, but which, however, certain people assured me was oriented in the same direction as mine (perhaps again as a result of a misunderstanding), which was very nice of them, and flattering for me, but which, I must admit, did not stand out all that clearly to me when I became acquainted with their works, unless, just as in my case, the period of a certain form of novel seemed to them to have come and gone, a form that had become unbearable even, and that like me they were seeking to do "something else."

Unlike my new friends, however (and as anyone can see, in any case, from the highly contradictory declarations each one of us made during a colloquium held some ten years ago which brought us together and where we had our knuckles rapped by a severe schoolmaster) . . . unlike my new friends, therefore, I had never reflected theoretically upon the problems posed, or on the way to solve them, and I proceeded in a groping fashion, so that I rather had the impression of being a kind of Monsieur Jourdain to whom his grammar instructor explains that he is writing prose without knowing it. For example, I read in the press (*Le Monde,* January 1982) that during another more recent colloquium our mutual friend Robbe-Grillet had concluded that he and Nathalie Sarraute were the spiritual heirs of Jean-Paul Sartre, something that he confirmed last evening, and which was moreover approved by Michel Rybalka. Of course, I know nothing about the laws of genetics, but I must admit that however hard I examine myself, I discern nothing in me that might permit me to claim such a strange paternity—unless on that point too I am still like Monsieur Jourdain.

Because as far as I am concerned, whether it be thirty years ago or now, I used to work, and still work, in a totally empirical way, taking—to begin with—what suited me, and rejecting what did not suit me in one or other of the authors I liked to read, such as Dostoyevsky, Conrad (whose astonishing preface to *The Nigger of the Narcissus* still appears, to my surprise, to have been forgotten), Joyce, Proust, Faulkner, and I made my way forward (and still do so) like a blind man, never knowing when I start a text what it will be like at the end of the day (eventually, it is always completely different from the vague initial project so much modified along the way that generally not much is left of it), and I know even less what the text "ought to be" in order to obey certain canons.

I must add to this that I am rather afraid that it might be as a result of another misunderstanding that I find myself here today, a bit confused and embarrassed at having crossed the Atlantic in order, finally, to disappoint those who invited me, for I have little else to formulate than some amateurish reflections—made after the event—about my work, accompanied by a few very down-to-earth remarks.

This is why I feel quite at ease in asking those listening to me not to consider the remainder of my remarks to be at all a formal lecture on the novel, and that I would gratefully welcome objections or even observations pointing out my errors, which would be for me an opportunity to learn something and to enrich my knowledge. Thank you, therefore, in advance.

And since I have just spoken of misunderstandings, it would perhaps be best to begin with those revealed by certain questions I was asked, a little more than a year ago, when my last novel, *The Georgics,* came out, and which show rather well how the majority of readers continue today to conceive of and to receive the novel, fiction, and in a general way, literary texts.

Two things struck me in particular: First of all, many of my interlocutors insisted on the fact that the characters in the novel had, as they said, "existed," that they were "real" characters (some critics even believed they could identify them), and then (this was said, incidentally, without any unkind intention) . . . then, therefore, that one was presented (still in the novel) with phenomena of "fragmentation" and "discontinuity," phenomena which, according to some, are characteristic of "modernism" in the sense (to quote word-for-word one of my interviewers) that "the writing incessantly frustrates the narrative drive," statements which, it seems to me, bear witness to a certain confusion and even to the disarray which has led, today, to the conflict between, on the one hand, old reading habits, and on the other, certain maximalist theories, to a greater or lesser extent deluded and smelling strongly of intellectual terrorism, which have become fashionable in recent years.

The reply that one is spontaneously tempted to make to this kind of observation is: "narration" *of what?* "fragmentation" and "discontinuity" *of what?*

I am not going to launch myself here into a critical analysis of the "realist" novel such as it imposed itself in France during the nineteenth century (and such as it continues today to serve as a model for many people), but in a few words, what strikes me in this kind of novel (and doubtless what bores me so much) is less the expulsion from the established order of the "wrong-thinking" hero about whom Robbe-Grillet talked yesterday, than its pedagogical and literary pretensions. And what strikes me again is that, based as it is upon the model of the fable, the parable, and the philosophical tale, and conceived of as a demonstration of some moralizing thesis, whether in the social or the psychic domain (a "social lesson," Balzac said), this type of novel offers precisely all the characteristics of fragmentation and discontinuity.

Contrary to its claim to describe "objectively" what it calls "reality," it is very evident that not being materially able to say *everything,* the realist novel restricts itself to putting fragments of a story into a sequence whose discontinuity is only concealed from the reader's eyes by the assurance given by the writer that he is reporting there "the essentials."

Other people besides me have maliciously underlined all the ways in which the notion of what is "essential" is arbitrary and debatable, and others, by setting on two parallel abscissae the scales of what they call "referential" time (clock-time) and "literal" time (that of the text), have not had much trouble showing how, in the latter, the former is submitted to a constant process of dilatation (when the text lingers on such and such an event or description) alternating with astounding compressions (when the text skims over events considered to be "minor," only just mentioning them) or is often even annulled (when the author decides, and as he will indeed sometimes write, that during an hour, a day, or a few days, nothing "important" happened), or, again, is inverted, as the narrative returns, in flashbacks, to tell what happened, as the expression has it, "during that time."

The principle governing the composition of this kind of novel, whose author hides behind a screen of false objectivity (thus the most stinging condemnation of realism is indeed Baudelaire's remark: "Nature, as if I were not there to tell of it") . . . the principle, then, governing the succession of reported events in the text is that of *causality,* a chain of causes and effects leading the characters and the reader to the famous climax which Emile Faguet described as the "logical consummation" of the novel, the characters being therefore narrowly *determined.* In the same way, another critic, Henri Martineau, declared for his part that Stendhal, on starting to write *Le Rouge et le noir,* already knew how Julien Sorel had to "end up," which is moreover accurate since we know that Stendhal wrote the novel (as did Flaubert with *Madame Bovary*) on the basis of an incident reported in a gazette, which confirms once again that this type of novel has the status of a fable: it is not because a wolf devours a lamb that "might is always right," it is quite the reverse, for it is in order to demonstrate the axiom that the fabulist constructs a little fiction at the end of which an allegorical wolf devours a no less allegorical lamb. In the same way, in order to justify the pistol shot fired by Julien at Madame de Rênal, or Emma's suicide by arsenic, Stendhal and Flaubert had previously to fill hundreds of pages with psychosocial observations that lead their hero and heroine, respectively, to these actions.

Happily (and this must be said straight away), between these intentions seemingly flaunted by these authors and what they have given us to read, there exists, for the salvation of literature, something more, which does not in any way go along with such laborious "teachings," and in which lie, in fact, their respective geniuses, even if they would have perhaps considered this "something" to be "inessential." (And I stress the "perhaps," for when one reads the many "scenarios" Flaubert composed with a view to writing *Madame Bovary,* one notices, as a matter of fact, that they are made up *for the most part,* of notations of smells, colors, noises, and sensations of all kinds, to the extent that one is led to wonder whether, anticipating by eighty years the view that Tynianov will put forward later, and in spite of the famous caricature representing him brandishing Emma's heart, dripping with gore, on the end of a scalpel, Flaubert did not consider his *fable* to be above all the *pretext* for an accumulation of descriptions.)

When it comes to "modernity" (or rather to our modernity—for each period has its own, and there are no great writers, painters, or musicians who have not been innovators) . . . when it comes, therefore, to our modernity, which without any doubt marks an important break (one of the most spectacular, no doubt, since Giotto's break with the hieratic style of Byzantine art), I think, for my part, that we would have to date it from the end of the last century and the beginning of the one in which we are living

I know that it is always perilous to risk making comparisons and parallels between different art forms, and I am no more a specialist in the history of painting than in that of literature, but even so, it seems to me, if I am not mistaken, that the decisive break took place as a result of pressure not from writers but from painters who, quite openly (and I mean "openly" since the "subject" in painting was no longer anything more than an alibi) questioned the principles (or rather the dogma) of realism and said aloud that their work was concerned not with pictures of the "real" world but only (and it is a very different thing) with the *impressions* they received from it. Putting it another way, from this moment on, it will no longer be a question of "Nature, as if I were not there to tell of it," but of the world as perceived through me, of the partial, deformed, and personal vision that I have of it.

And this is the context in which Cézanne intervened. He objected to the word "impression," preferring to it "sensation." "We *know,*" said Jakobson, "but we cannot *see.*" And it was in relentlessly purging himself of the ready-made knowledge which comes between our real sensations and our minds that Cézanne entirely transformed painting, and doubtless much else also.

To explain what I mean, I shall say that two things above all strike me in the contribution he made: On the one hand, that he left paintings that were apparently "incomplete" (I say "apparently," for the question of the "completeness" of a work, its "finished" state, whether it be written or painted, is in itself a whole problem that requires to be gone into more deeply) . . . on the one hand, therefore, Cézanne left behind him apparently incomplete paintings in which only the "strong points" of the motif are retained, that is to say that here and there, on the virgin and neutral surface of the canvas, there are only a few lines and a few patches of color whose relationship the spectator's eye is asked to grasp, confronting them without going through any intermediate process of filling out.

What is more, always anxious to pin down his sensations exactly, he realized that (I quote) "the planes override each other" and he will even say to Jochim Gasquet (I quote again) that "objects penetrate each other," which is what characterizes, if we think about it, our way of perceiving the visible world, in a kind of imprecision or indistinctness, just like our perception of the world as a whole (forms, colors, smells, sounds, etc.), as much in the present as in our memory where recollections, images, and emotions ceaselessly slide over and into each other, are superimposed, brought together by associations, and penetrate each other.

And it was from this starting point (that is to say, the view that we only really apprehend things as discontinuous fragments that overlap and combine *to form what is, in contrast, a continuous emotional or sensorial sequence in our minds*) . . . it was from this starting point that the cubists were subsequently led to elaborate, in an initial phase, what has been called "Analytical Cubism," which, following Cézanne's example, was *an architecture against a neutral background,* a few lines (horizontal and oblique) and a few patches of color—or rather, a few color modulations—then, in a second phase, in 1913, "Synthetic Cubism," which, *without any break in continuity therefore,* and without any other principle than their qualitative affinities (shapes, colors, rhythms) make fragments of represented or sometimes even "real" objects (like pages from newspapers, pieces of material, imitation wood, etc.) stick together, collide, and mingle *just as we really perceive them* . . . until later, after Picasso's collages and sculptures, artists like Schwitters, Louise Nevelson, or Robert Rauschenberg conceive vast compositions or assemblages executed with the aid of a variety of materials: planks, tarred paper, fragments of furniture or machines, runs of paint poured straight from the tin onto the canvas, etc. So that if the word "realism" were not so devalued today, we could say that this was indeed a true realism in the double sense that starting from a meditation upon the simultaneously chaotic and very coherent nature of our perception and our memory, objects which seek their reality only in themselves are constituted.

If I had to sum up in a trenchant and necessarily oversimplified phrase the change that took place in this way, I would venture to say that in place of the principle of the establishment of relationships justified by *causality* and necessitating a kind of totalizing inventory (an illusory one, moreover), the principle of the establishment of, above all, *qualitative* relationships was installed.

And if I have insisted, in a way that some may find a little pedantic, upon the year 1913, it is because at the same moment Proust and (although to a lesser extent) Joyce (for *Ulysses* still wants to load itself with more or less esoteric meanings) undertake to construct on their own behalf texts in which, as a matter of priority, considerations of quality will govern the linking, or, if you prefer, the confrontation of elements.

And then, just as the cascades of cause and effects linking the different episodes in a story and supposedly demonstrating the excellence of some moral principle or thesis might appear debatable or arbitrary, so the way in which this *new* vision associates two events in a text with no view to proving anything seems to me to impose itself in an irrefutable way. I still think, in spite of what Balzac wants me to believe, that César Birotteau might just as well have been unable, despite his honesty, to ever recover from having been ruined: I may well think that it is as a result of a series of very strange coincidences that Fabrice del Dongo commits the murder which will cause him so many problems and reveal to him the mechanism of power and the intrigues of the powerful; I can remain skeptical (if not stunned) when Faulkner writes, in a projected introduction to *The Sound and the Fury:* "I saw that they had been sent to the pasture to spend the afternoon to get them away from the house during the grand-mother's funeral, *in order that* the three brothers and the nigger children *could look up* at the muddy seat of Caddy's drawers,"[1] but on the other hand I cannot doubt that the unevenness of a paving stone creates an association between the courtyard of the Hôtel de Guermantes and two flagstones in the Baptistry of San Marco; I cannot doubt, so self-evident does it strike me as being, that the juicy savor of the fruit she is thinking of buying at the market leads Molly Bloom into an erotic daydream: I cannot doubt either that the word "caddy" shouted by the people playing golf makes Benjy scream with pain; and it appears to me that on this basis, on this principle, Proust, Joyce, or Faulkner erects constructions whose solidity, trustworthiness, and *continuity* seem to be far more determining, if one can use such a word, than a fortuitous encounter between two characters or two animals in a fable, for these other kinds of meetings, if they are dictated by associations between impressions or images, are also (like the impressionists' brush marks) inseparable from the raw material (that is to say, language, which, as it has been very well said, "speaks before we do," speaks through what we call its "figures," its tropes [metaphors, metonymies] and through its own dynamism [sometimes phonetic effects alone], itself bringing about meetings, associations, and *transports* [should I remind you that the word μεταφορά is to be found written, in Greece, on lorries?]).

There exist, it seems to me, two excesses (or if you prefer, two maximalisms, two terrorist attitudes) whose effects are equally negative. Just as Valéry said that the world was ceaselessly menaced by two dangers—order and disorder—so one could say that language is ceaselessly menaced by two dangers: on the one hand, that of being considered only a vehicle for meaning; and on the other, as only a structure, for it is always *at the same time* one and the other, and it is indeed in this twin potential, and their perpetual collisions, that the marvelous ambiguity that grants it such formidable powers seems to me to reside.

To those, therefore, who claim to bend it to the sole imperatives of expression and representation, we can reply with Lacan (but already also with Proust: let us not forget that the last part of *Du côte de che Swann* has as its title "Noms de pays: le nom"), we can therefore reply that the word is not only a "sign," but a "knot of meanings," or again, as I wrote in my preface to *Orion aveugle,* a "crossroads of meanings," that is to say, that like the elements of a cubist painting or assemblage, it is *in itself* a reality, and that if it naturally suggests the image or the concept of the object that it names, it calls up at the same time a great many other concepts, and other images, those of objects sometimes very distant in the measurable time and space dimensions of the "real" object, and with which it is immediately put in contact, so that in *the present of the writing* a multitude of propositions are made, which, when taken into consideration, are going to twist considerably the prior intention of the author to such an extent that it could be said that he who works with language is at the same time worked upon by it, which naturally entails a drift of meanings which are not therefore "expressed," as the conventional formula has it, but are *produced.*

As for the pure hard-line terrorists in the other camp, who fearfully keep away from any notion of meaning or "reference," their declarations always make me think of a little apologia written by an art critic who noticed that when the impressionists started out and were not yet admitted into the fold, and the public could only see "formless daubs" in their paintings, their few defenders, at the time, said to people (for example before Monet's *Nymphéas*): "Move back, get further away, and you'll see that it represents something!", whereas a few years ago, at the time of the tachist vogue, the defenders who were looking for respectable ancestors for them said to people they brought to see the same *Nymphéas:* "Come along, get closer, and you'll see that it doesn't represent anything!"

I was asked to speak particularly here about my latest novel, *The Georgics,* and I only have a little time left, although, in fact, I have been doing more or less that for more than half an hour now.

It is naive to believe, as I heard it said by an essayist whom as a rule I respect (it was at a colloquium on Proust organized by New

York University at the Ecole Normale in Paris, as it happened) . . . it is naive to believe that through some unthinkably perverse act a novelist fragments a totality in order to assemble the pieces as the mood takes him, and as I remarked earlier, this kind of suspicion would only be found to be solidly based by examining the methods employed by the so-called "realist" writers.

As with my other projects for novels, the initial idea for *The Georgics* was extremely vague. As I have already had occasion to stress, I am neither a philosopher ("Luckily for you!", Merleau-Ponty said to me one day, "If you were, you would be quite incapable of writing your novels!"), nor a moralist, nor a believer. Because of this, I have nothing special to reveal on the great questions that men ask, about sex, the meaning of History, life, evil, or good. Naturally, like everyone, I have a few ideas about these things, but finally they are too confused and sometimes too contradictory for me to judge them worth printing.

The question that faced me was not "What have I to say?", but rather, "What might I manage to *do* with?" a pile of old papers left by one of my ancestors, a member of the Convention, then a general during the French Revolution, and finally a general during the First Empire.

I am no more a historian than I am a philosopher, and I did not therefore have the ambition to write about this person's life, going digging into dossiers in official archives in various ministries to find documents that might have enabled me to complete the information I had, for despite the abundance of papers that had come into my possession (letters, memoranda, travel diaries, roughs of speeches, and a great quantity of military orders), enormous gaps, or if you prefer, enormous "black holes" remained in the story of his life.

All the same, and in spite of these blanks, the mass of images that these documents aroused in me was more than sufficient to constitute a stimulant that made me want, without looking any further, to make "something" with them, together with others, other images of war, other images of revolution that I had retained from personal experience.

For if there was indeed *discontinuity* in the fragmentary information I possessed, it appeared to me that it possessed on the other hand an astonishing *continuity* (I think that thematics are out of fashion at the moment and are condemned in certain university circles, but that's too bad) . . . I found, then, a troubling relationship, to the extent that time seemed on occasion to have been abolished, between events that had happened some one hundred years earlier and those I had witnessed in Barcelona in 1936, and in Belgium in

1940, or again in George Orwell's account of his Spanish adventure, a narrative that is itself, from the very first page, a model of a story that proceeds by omissions, of a more or less deliberate kind, and is therefore itself full of holes.

What I was therefore seeking was a way of assembling all this scattered material into a composition which would owe its coherence to those qualitative principles I evoked a moment ago, by linking together the themes as in a fugue, by developing variations, etc. I have said elsewhere how much my work makes me think of the first lesson introducing the study of higher mathematics, and which is entitled "Arrangements, Permutations, Combinations," and I cannot explain why I have the feeling that just as there exist syntactic laws governing the coherence and the ordering of the sentence into main, relative, and subordinate clauses, so there must exist also, although uncodified, an internal logic of language which demands a syntactic order for the text as a whole, from the first to the last line, and that if one manages to follow these hidden laws, then "something" will *be said,* whereas in the opposite case all discourse is only conventional chatter. "If one could only make people understand that language and mathematical formulae are alike," wrote Novalis nearly two centuries ago, ". . . they constitute a self-contained world, interplay only amongst themselves, convey nothing but their own wondrous nature, and it is precisely for this reason that they are so expressive—precisely for this reason that the strange interplay of relations between them is reflected in them."[2]

And naturally, from these discontinuous fragments of history, thus ordered and related to each other in a way which seemed to me appropriate to the formation of something continuous, from this *composition,* no "message," no "moral," no "fatality" emerges which would, as was once pompously stated, "introduce Greek tragedy" into the novel, and no derision either: all in all, no "teaching" of any kind, beyond the sole statement of the thematic or simply emotional "correspondences" (and for this I ask forgiveness from the ruthless scourges of "humanism").

And nothing allowed me to set these events into a progression leading up to a climax which would have constituted what Faguet calls a "majestic and logical conclusion," for in fact, after facing all the dangers a man can be exposed to in the course of a lifetime, the General "L.S.M." dies very prosaically by his fireside; "O," for his part, only escapes through sheer luck from the N.K.V.D. agents who are mercilessly tracking him down in Barcelona, as are his comrades in the P.O.U.M.; and the great-great-grandson of the General comes out of the massacre into which the French generals sent the cavalry in 1940 without a scratch.

After this, do I have to bring to your attention the fact that in speaking of these various personages I have been using the *present indicative?*

Must one underline, after all I have just said, that they only existed (took on a "real" existence) while the text was in the process of being written? Or that "L.S.M." is made of words and of images and cannot be a portrait of General Lacombe Saint-Michel, that in the same way "O." is not George Orwell (who in any case was himself not George Orwell since his real name was Eric Arthur Blair), that the old lady is not my grandmother, that the great-great-grandson of the General, *a character in this novel in just the same way that the others are,* only has distant and partial connections with me?

Of course, these characters borrow many of their features from beings who have "really existed," and in this respect they are different from the allegorical characters that one usually finds in France in fictional works, purpose built and ready cast, and given the task of showing by their behavior and their adventures what happens to the miser, the liar, the prodigal, the ambitious individual, or other such conventional classical "characters." Neither the life nor the death of "L.S.M." proves anything at all and no "moral" is brought out from his existence, any more than from "O." 's adventure, or from the activities of the other characters who appear in the novel. What is more, too many unknowns remain, too many contradictions, too many doubts. Hence, in *The Georgics,* as in my other novels and with the risk of tiring the reader, the profusion of words like "perhaps," the abundance of questions asked, and of questions that remain unanswered . . .

And it is doubtless this uncertainty, over and beyond our divergent views, which creates the solidarity existing between myself and my friends in the "New Novel" movement, a movement which has given rise to a fair amount of misunderstandings, many outrageous statements, many hasty and superficial commentaries, but where I think a common feeling brings us together, a feeling that one is never quite sure of anything and that we are forever advancing on shifting sands.

Thank you for your patience.

Translated by Anthony Cheal Pugh

NOTES

[1]William Faulkner, "An Introduction to *The Sound and the Fury,*" in *A Faulkner Miscellany,* ed. James B. Meriwether (Jackson: Univ. Press of Mississippi, 1974), 159. Also quoted in *Faulkner: A Biography,* Joseph L.

Blotner (London: Chatto and Windus, 1974), 568. Claude Simon quotes from *Oeuvres romanesques* (Coll. Pléiade, vol. 1), trans. Michel Grenet. "Si on avait envoyé les enfants passer l'après-midi dans le pré pour qu'ils ne restent pas à la maison . . . c'était *afin que* les trois frères et les petits noirs *puissent* lever les yeux vers le fond souillé de la culotte de Caddy grimpée dans l'arbre" (Claude Simon's emphasis).

[2]"Wenn man den Leuten nur begreiflich machen könnte, dass es mit der Sprache wie mit den mathematischen Formeln sei— Sie machen eine Welt für sich aus— Sie spielen nur mit sich selbst, drücken nichts als ihre wunderbare Natur aus, und eben darum sind sie so ausdrucksvoll—eben darum spiegelt sich in ihnen das seltsame Verhältnisspiel der Dinge." Novalis, *Schriften,* Das philosophische Werk, ed. Richard Samuel (Darmstadt: Wissenschaftliche Buchgesellschaft, 1965), 672 ("Monolog"). Claude Simon originally quoted a French translation in *Les romantiques allemands* (Paris: Desclée de Breuwer) but also gave the following reference: Novalis, *Fragmente III* (Heidelberg: Lambert Schneider, 1957), 203-4.

First published in issue 5.1 (Spring 1985)

Introduction to Aren't You Rather Young to Be Writing Your Memoirs?

B. S. Johnson

It is a fact of crucial significance in the history of the novel this century that James Joyce opened the first cinema in Dublin in 1909. Joyce saw very early on that film must usurp some of the prerogatives which until then had belonged almost exclusively to the novelist. Film could tell a story more directly, in less time and with more concrete detail than a novel; certain aspects of character could be more easily delineated and kept constantly before the audience (for example, physical characteristics like a limp, a scar, particular ugliness or beauty); no novelist's description of a battle squadron at sea in a gale could really hope to compete with that in a well-shot film; and why should anyone who simply wanted to be told a story spend all his spare time for a week or weeks reading a book when he could experience the same thing in a version in some ways superior at his local cinema in only one evening?

It was not the first time that storytelling had passed from one medium to another. Originally it had been the chief concern of poetry, and long narrative poems were best-sellers right up to the works of Walter Scott and Byron. The latter supplanted the former in the favours of the public, and Scott adroitly turned from narrative poems to narrative novels and continued to be a best-seller. You will agree it would be perversely anachronistic to write a long narrative poem today? People still do, of course; but such works are rarely published, and, if they are, the writer is thought of as a literary flatearther. But poetry did not die when storytelling moved on. It concentrated on the things it was still best able to do: the short, economical lyric, the intense emotional statement, depth rather than scale, the exploitation of rhythms which made their optimum impact at short lengths but which would have become monotonous and unreadable if maintained longer than a few pages. In the same way, the novel may not only survive but evolve to greater achievements by concentrating on those things it can still do best: the precise use of language, exploitation of the technological fact of the book, the explication of thought. Film is an excellent medium for showing things, but it is very poor at taking an audience inside characters' minds, at telling it what people are thinking. Again, Joyce saw this at once, and developed the technique of interior monologue within a few years of the appearance of the cinema. In some ways the history of the novel in the twentieth century has seen large areas of the old territory of the novelist increasingly taken over by other media, until the only thing the novelist can with any certainty call exclusively his own is the inside of his own skull: and that is what he should be exploring, rather than anachronistically fighting a battle he is bound to lose.

Joyce is the Einstein of the novel. His subject-matter in *Ulysses* was available to anyone, the events of one day in one place; but by means of form, style and technique in language he made it into something very much more, a novel, not a story about anything. What happens is nothing like as important as how it is written, as the medium of the words and form through which it is made to happen to the reader. And for style alone *Ulysses* would have been a revolution. Or, rather, styles. For Joyce saw that such a huge range of subject matter could not be conveyed in one style, and accordingly used many. Just in this one innovation (and there are many others) lie a great advance and freedom offered to subsequent generations of writers.

But how many have seen it, have followed him? Very few. It is not a question of influence, of writing like Joyce. It is a matter of realising that the novel is an evolving form, not a static one, of accepting that for practical purposes where Joyce left off should ever since have been regarded as the starting point. As Sterne said a long time ago:

Shall we for ever make new books, as apothecaries make new mixtures, by pouring only out of one vessel into another? Are we for ever to be twisting, and untwisting the same rope? For ever in the same track—for ever at the same pace?

The last thirty years have seen the storytelling function pass on yet again. Now anyone who wants simply to be told a story has the need satisfied by television; serials like *Coronation Street* and so on do very little more than answer the question "What happens next?" All other writing possibilities are subjugated to narrative. If a writer's chief interest is in telling stories (even remembering that telling stories is a euphemism for telling lies; and I shall come to that) then the best place to do it now is in television, which is technically better equipped and will reach more people than a novel can today. And the most aware filmmakers have realised this, and directors such as Godard, Resnais, and Antonioni no longer make the chief point of their films a story; their work concentrates on those things film can do solely and those things it can do best.

Literary forms do become exhausted, clapped out, as well. Look what had happened to five-act blank-verse drama by the beginning of the nineteenth century. Keats, Shelley, Wordsworth and Tennyson all wrote blank-verse, quasi-Elizabethan plays; and all of them, without exception, are resounding failures. They are so not because the men who wrote them were inferior poets, but because the form was finished, worn out, exhausted, and everything that could be done with it had been done too many times already.

That is what seems to have happened to the nineteenth-century narrative novel, too, by the outbreak of the First World War. No matter how good the writers are who now attempt it, it cannot be made to work for our time, and the writing of it is anachronistic, invalid, irrelevant, and perverse.

Life does not tell stories. Life is chaotic, fluid, random; it leaves myriads of ends untied, untidily. Writers can extract a story from life only by strict, close selection, and this must mean falsification. Telling stories really is telling lies. Philip Pacey took me up on this to express it thus:

Telling stories is telling lies   is telling lies about people
       is creating or hardening prejudices   is providing an
alternative to real communication not a stimulus to communication
and/or communication itself   is an escape from the challenge
of coming to terms with real people.

I am not interested in telling lies in my own novels. A useful distinction between literature and other writing for me is that the former teaches one something true about life: and how can you convey truth in a vehicle of fiction? The two terms, *truth* and *fiction,* are opposites, and it must logically be impossible.

The two terms *novel* and *fiction* are not, incidentally, synonymous, as many seem to suppose in the way they use them interchangeably. The publisher of *Trawl* wished to classify it as autobiography, not as a novel. It is a novel, I insisted and could prove; what it is not is fiction. The novel is a form in the same sense that the sonnet is a form; within that form, one may write truth or fiction. I choose to write truth in the form of a novel.

In any case, surely it must be a confession of failure on the part of any novelist to rely on that primitive, vulgar and idle curiosity of the reader to know "what happens next" (however banal or hackneyed it may be) to hold his interest? Can he not face the fact that it is his choice of words, his style, which ought to keep the reader reading? Have such novelists no pride? The drunk who tells you the story of his troubles in a pub relies on the same curiosity.

And when they consider the other arts, are they not ashamed? Imagine the reception of someone producing a nineteenth-century symphony or a Pre-Raphaelite painting today! The avant-garde of even ten years ago is now accepted in music and painting, is the establishment in these arts in some cases. But today the neo-Dickensian novel not only receives great praise, review space and sales but also acts as a qualification to elevate its authors to chairs at universities. On reflection, perhaps the latter is not so surprising; let the dead live with the dead.

All I have said about the history of the novel so far seems to me logical, and to have been available and obvious to anyone starting seriously to write in the form today. Why then do so many novelists still write as though the revolution that was *Ulysses* had never happened, still rely on the crutch of storytelling? Why, more damningly for my case you might think, do hundreds of thousands of readers still gorge the stuff to surfeit?

I do not know. I can only assume that just as there seem to be so many writers imitating the act of being nineteenth-century novelists, so there must be large numbers imitating the act of being nineteenth-century readers, too. But it does not affect the logic of my case, nor the practice of my own work in the novel form. It may simply be a matter of education, or of communication; when I proposed this book to my publisher and outlined its thesis, he said it would be necessary for me to speak very clearly and very loudly. Perhaps the din of the marketplace vendors in pap and propaganda is so high that even doing that will not be enough.

The architects can teach us something: their aesthetic problems are combined with functional ones in a way that dramatises the crucial nature of their final actions. *Form follows function* said Louis Sullivan, mentor of Frank Lloyd Wright, and just listen to Mies van der Rohe:

To create form out of the nature of our tasks with the methods of our time— this is our task.

We must make clear, step by step, what things are possible, necessary, and significant.

Only an architecture honestly arrived at by the explicit use of available building materials can be justified in moral terms.

Subject matter is everywhere, general, is brick, concrete, plastic; the ways of putting it together are particular, are crucial. But I recognize that there are not simply problems of form, but problems of writing. Form is not the aim, but the result. If form were the aim then one would have formalism; and I reject formalism.

The novelist cannot legitimately or successfully embody present-day reality in exhausted forms. If he is serious, he will be making a statement which attempts to change society towards a condition he conceives to be better, and he will be making at least implicitly a statement of faith in the evolution of the form in which he is working. Both these aspects of making are radical; this is inescapable unless he chooses escapism. Present-day reality is changing rapidly; it always has done, but for each generation it appears to be speeding up. Novelists must evolve (by inventing, borrowing, stealing or cobbling from other media) forms which will more or less satisfactorily contain an ever-changing reality, their own reality and not Dickens's reality or Hardy's reality or even James Joyce's reality.

Present-day reality is markedly different from say nineteenth-century reality. Then it was possible to believe in pattern and eternity, but today what characterises our reality is the probability that chaos is the most likely explanation; while at the same time recognising that even to seek an explanation represents a denial of chaos. Samuel Beckett, who of all living is the man I believe most worth reading and listening to, is reported thus:

What I am saying does not mean that there will henceforth be no form in art. It only means that there will be a new form, and that this form will be of such a type that it admits the chaos, and does not try to say that the chaos is really something else. The forms and the chaos remain separate . . . to find a form that accommodates the mess, that is the task of the artist now.

Whether or not it can be demonstrated that all is chaos, certainly all is change: the very process of life itself is growth and decay at an enormous variety of rates. Change is a condition of life. Rather than deplore this, or hunt the chimera of stability or reversal, one should perhaps embrace change as all there is. Or might be. For change is never for the better or for the worse; change simply *is*. No sooner is a style or technique established than the reasons for its adoption have vanished or become irrelevant. We have to make allowances and imaginative, lying leaps for Shakespeare, for even Noël Coward, to try to understand how they must have seemed to their contemporaries. I feel myself fortunate sometimes that I can laugh at the joke that just as I was beginning to think I knew something about how to write a novel it is no longer of any use to me in attempting the next one. Even in this introduction I am trying to make patterns, to impose patterns on the chaos, in the doubtful interest of helping you (and myself) to understand what I am saying. When lecturing on the same material I ought to drop my notes, refer to them in any chaotic order. *Order* and *chaos* are opposites, too.

This (and other things I have said) must appear paradoxical. But why should novelists be expected to avoid paradox any more than philosophers?

While I believe (as far as I believe anything) that there may be (how can I know?) chaos underlying it all, another paradox is that I still go on behaving as though pattern could exist, as though day will follow night will follow breakfast. Or whatever the order should be.

I do not really know why I write. Sometimes I think it is simply because I can do nothing better. Certainly there is no single reason, but many. I can, and will, enumerate some of them; but in general I prefer not to think about them.

I think I write because I have something to say that I fail to say satisfactorily in conversation, in person. Then there are things like conceit, stubbornness, a desire to retaliate on those who have hurt me paralleled by a desire to repay those who have helped me, a need to try to create something which may live after me (which I take to be the detritus of the religious feeling), the sheer technical joy of forcing almost intractable words into patterns of meaning and form that are uniquely (for the moment at least) mine, a need to make people laugh with me in case they laugh at me, a desire to codify experience, to come to terms with things that have happened to me, and to try to tell the truth (to discover what is the truth) about them. And I write especially to exorcise, to remove from myself, from my mind, the burden having to bear some pain, the hurt of some experience: in order that it may be over there, in a book, and not in here in my mind.

The following tries to grope towards it, in another way:

> I have a (vision) of something that (happened) to me
>   something which (affected) me
>   something which meant (something) to me
>
> and I (wrote) (filmed) it
> because
> I wanted it to be fixed
>   so that I could refer to it
>   so that I could build on it
>   so that I would not have to repeat it

Such a hostage to fortune!

What I have been trying to do in the novel form has been too much refracted through the conservativeness of reviewers and others; the reasons why I have written in the ways that I have done have become lost, have never reached as many people, nor in anything like a definitive form. "Experimental" to most reviewers is almost always a synonym for "unsuccessful." I object to the word *ex-*

perimental being applied to my own work. Certainly I make experiments, but the unsuccessful ones are quietly hidden away and what I choose to publish is in my terms successful: that is, it has been the best way I could find of solving particular writing problems. Where I depart from convention, it is because the convention has failed, is inadequate for conveying what I have to say. The relevant questions are surely whether each device works or not, whether it achieves what it set out to achieve, and how less good were the alternatives. So for every device I have used there is a literary rationale and a technical justification; anyone who cannot accept this has simply not understood the problem which had to be solved.

I do not propose to go through the reasons for all the devices, not least because the novels should speak for themselves; and they are clear enough to a reader who will think about them, let alone be open and sympathetic towards them. But I will mention some of them, and deal in detail with *The Unfortunates,* since its form seems perhaps the most extreme.

Travelling People (published 1963) had an explanatory prelude which summed up much of my thinking on the novel at that point, as follows:

Seated comfortably in a wood and wickerwork chair of eighteenth-century Chinese manufacture, I began seriously to meditate upon the form of my allegedly full-time literary sublimations. Rapidly, I recalled the conclusions reached in previous meditations on the same subject: my rejection of stage-drama as having too many limitations, of verse as being unacceptable at the present time on the scale I wished to attempt, and of radio and television as requiring too many entrepreneurs between the writer and the audience; and my resultant choice of the novel as the form possessing fewest limitations, and closest contact with the greatest audience.

But, now, what kind of novel? After comparatively little consideration, I decided that one style for one novel was a convention that I resented most strongly: it was perhaps comparable to eating a meal in which each course had been cooked in the same manner. The style of each chapter should spring naturally from its subject matter. Furthermore, I meditated, at ease in far eastern luxury, Dr. Johnson's remarks about each member of an audience always being aware that he is in a theatre could with complete relevance be applied also to the novel reader, who surely always knows that he is reading a book and not, for instance, taking part in a punitive raid on the curiously-shaped inhabitants of another planet. From this I concluded that it was not only permissible to expose the mechanism of a novel, but by so doing I should come nearer to reality and truth: adapting to refute, in fact, the ancients:

Artis est monstrare artem

Pursuing this thought, I realised that it would be desirable to have interludes between my chapters in which I could stand back, so to speak, from my novel, and talk about it with the reader, or with those parts of myself which might hold differing opinions, if necessary; and in which technical questions could be considered, and quotations from other writers included, where relevant, without any question of destroying the reader's suspension of disbelief, since such suspension was not to be attempted.

I should be determined not to lead my reader into believing that he was doing anything but reading a novel, having noted with abhorrence the shabby chicanery practised on their readers by many novelists, particularly of the popular class. This applied especially to digression, where the reader is led, wilfully and wantonly, astray; my novel would have clear notice, one way or another, of digressions, so that the reader might have complete freedom of choice in whether or not he would read them. Thus, having decided in a general way upon the construction of my novel I thought about actually rising to commence its composition; but persuaded by oriental comfort that I was nearer the Good Life engaged in meditation, I turned my mind to the deep consideration of such other matters as I deemed worthy of my attention, and, after a short while thus engaged, fell asleep.

Travelling People employed eight separate styles or conventions for nine chapters; the first and last chapters sharing one style in order to give the book cyclical unity within the motif announced by its title and epigraph. These styles included interior monologue, a letter, extracts from a journal, and a film script. This latter illustrates the method of the novel typically. The subject-matter was a gala evening at a country club, with a large number of characters involved both individually and in small groups. A film technique, cutting quickly from group to group and incidentally counterpointing the stagey artificiality of the occasion, seemed natural and apt. It is not, of course, a film; but the way it is written is intended to evoke what the reader knows as film technique.

The passage quoted above was deliberately a pastiche of eighteenth-century English, for I had found that it was necessary to return to the very beginnings of the novel in England in order to try to re-think it and re-justify it for myself. Most obvious of my debts was to the black pages of *Tristram Shandy,* but I extended the device beyond Sterne's simple use of it to indicate a character's death. The section concerned is the interior monologue of an old man prone to heart attacks; when he becomes unconscious he obviously cannot indicate this in words representing thought, but a modified form of Sterne's black pages solves the problem. First I used random-pattern grey to indicate unconsciousness after a heart attack, then a regular-pattern grey to indicate sleep or recuperative unconsciousness; and subsequently black when he dies.

Since *Travelling People* is part truth and part fiction it now embarrasses me and I will not allow it to be reprinted; though I am still pleased that its devices work. And I learnt a certain amount through it; not least that there was a lot of the writing I could do in my head without having to amass a pile of papers three feet high to see if something worked.

But I really discovered what I should be doing with *Albert Angelo* (1964) where I broke through the English disease of the objective correlative to speak truth directly if solipsistically in the novel form, and heard my own small voice. And again there were devices used to solve problems which I felt could not be dealt with in other ways. Thus a specially-designed type-character draws attention to physical descriptions which I believe tend to be skipped, do not usually penetrate. To convey what a particular lesson is like, the thoughts of a teacher are given on the right-hand side of a page in italic, with his and his pupils' speech on the left in roman, so that, though the reader obviously cannot read both at once, when he has read both he will have seen that they are simultaneous and have enacted such simultaneity for himself. When Albert finds a fortune-teller's card in the street it is further from the truth to describe it than simply to reproduce it. And when a future event must be revealed, I could (and can; can you?) think of no way nearer to the truth and more effective than to cut a section through those pages intervening so that the event may be read in its place but before the reader reaches that place.

Trawl (1966) is all interior monologue, a representation of the inside of my mind but at one stage removed; the closest one can come in writing. The only real technical problem was the representation of breaks in the mind's workings; I finally decided on a stylized scheme of 3 em, 6 em, and 9 em spaces. In order not to have a break which ran-on at the end of a line looking like a paragraph, these spaces were punctuated by dots at decimal point level. I now doubt whether these dots were necessary. To make up for the absence of those paragraph breaks which give the reader's eye rest and location on the page, the line length was deliberately shortened; this gave the book a long, narrow format.

The rhythms of the language of *Trawl* attempted to parallel those of the sea, while much use was made of Trawl itself as a metaphor for the way the subconscious mind may appear to work.

With each of my novels there has always been a certain point when what has been until then just a mass of subject-matter, the material of living, of my life, comes to have a shape, a form that I recognise as a novel. This crucial interaction between the material and myself has always been reduced to a single point in time: obviously a very exciting moment for me, and a moment of great relief, too, that I am able to write another novel.

The moment at which *The Unfortunates* (1969) occurred was on the main railway station at Nottingham. I had been sent there to report a soccer match for the *Observer,* a quite routine League match, nothing special. I had hardly thought about where I was going, specifically: when you are going away to report soccer in a different city each Saturday you get the mechanics of travelling to and finding your way about in a strange place to an almost automatic state. But when I came up the stairs from the platform into the entrance hall, it hit me: I knew this city, I knew it very well. It was the city in which a very great friend of mine, one who had helped me with my work when no one else was interested, had lived until his tragic early death from cancer some two years before.

It was the first time I had been back since his death, and all the afternoon I was there the things we had done together kept coming back to me as I was going about this routine job of reporting a soccer match: the dead past and the living present interacted and transposed themselves in my mind. I realised that afternoon that I had to write a novel about this man, Tony, and his tragic and pointless death and its effect on me and the other people who knew him and whom he had left behind. The following passage from *The Unfortunates* explains his importance to me:

To Tony, the criticism of literature was a study, a pursuit, a discipline of the highest kind in itself; to me, I told him, the only use of criticism was if it helped people to write better books. This he took as a challenge, this he accepted. Or perhaps I made the challenge, said that I would show him the novel as I wrote it, the novel I had in mind or was writing: and that he would therefore have a chance of influencing, of making better, a piece of what set out to be literature, for the sake of argument, rather than expend himself on dead men's work.

The main technical problem with *The Unfortunates* was the randomness of the material. That is, the memories of Tony and the routine football reporting, the past and the present, interwove in a completely random manner, without chronology. This is the way the mind works, my mind anyway, and for reasons given the novel was to be as nearly as possible a re-created transcript of how my mind worked during eight hours on this particular Saturday.

This randomness was directly in conflict with the technological fact of the bound book: for the bound book imposes an order, a fixed page order, on the material. I think I went some way towards solving this problem by writing the book in sections and having those sections not bound together but loose in a box. The sections are of different lengths, of course: some are only a third of a page long, others are as long as twelve pages. The longer ones were bound in themselves as sections, or signatures, as printers call them.

The point of this device was that, apart from the first and last sections which were marked as such, the other sections arrived in the reader's hands in a random order: he could read them in any order he liked. And if he imagined the printer, or some previous reader, had selected a special order, then he could shuffle them about and achieve his own random order. In this way the whole novel reflected the randomness of the material: it was itself a physical tangible metaphor for randomness and the nature of cancer.

Now I did not think then, and do not think now, that this solved the problem completely. The lengths of the sections were really arbitrary again; even separate sentences or separate words would be arbitrary in the same sense. But I continue to believe that my solution was nearer; and even if it was only marginally nearer, then it was still a better solution to the problem of conveying the mind's randomness than the imposed order of a bound book.

What matters most to me about *The Unfortunates* is that I have on recall as accurately as possible what happened, that I do not have to carry it around in my mind any more, that I have done Tony as much justice as I could at the time; that the need to communicate with myself then, and with such older selves as I might be allowed, on something about which I cared and care deeply may also mean that the novel will communicate that experience to readers, too.

I shall return shortly to readers and communicating with them. But first there are two other novels, and they represent a change (again!) of direction, an elbow joint in the arm, still part of the same but perhaps going another way. Perhaps I shall come to the body, sooner or later. The ideas for both *House Mother Normal* (1971) and *Christie Malry's Own Double-Entry* (1973) came to me whilst writing *Travelling People* (indeed, I discussed them with Tony) but the subsequent three personal novels interposed themselves, demanded to be written first. I also balked at *House Mother Normal* since it seemed technically so difficult. What I wanted to do was to take an evening in an old people's home, and see a single set of events through the eyes of not less than eight old people. Due to the various deformities and deficiencies of the inmates, these events would seem to be progressively "abnormal" to the reader. At the end, there would be the viewpoint of the House Mother, an apparently "normal" person, and the events themselves would then be seen to be so bizarre that everything that had come before would seem "normal" by comparison. The idea was to say something about the things we call "normal" and "abnormal" and the technical difficulty was to make the same thing interesting nine times over since that was the number of times the events would have to be described. By 1970 I thought that if I did not attempt the idea soon then I never would; and so sat down to it. I was relieved to find that the novel did work, on its own terms, while not asking it to do anything it clearly should not be trying to do. Each of the old people was allotted a space of twenty-one pages, and each line on each page represented the same moment in each of the other accounts; this meant an unjustified right-hand margin and led more than one reviewer to imagine the book was in verse. House Mother's account has an extra page in which she is shown to be

the puppet or concoction of a writer (you always knew there was a writer behind it all? Ah, there's no fooling you readers!)

Nor should there be.

The reader is made very much aware that he is reading a book and being addressed by the author in *Christie Malry's Own Double-Entry,* too. The idea was that a young man who had learned the double-entry system of bookkeeping started applying his knowledge to society and life; when society did him down, he did society down in order to balance the books. Form following function, the book is divided into five parts each ended by a page of accounts in which Christie attempts to draw a balance with life.

I do not really relish any more description of my work; it is there to be read, and in writing so much about technique and form I am diverting you from what the novels are about, what they are trying to say, and things like the nature of the language used, and the fact that all of them have something comic in them and three are intended to be very funny indeed. When I depart from what may mistakenly be extracted from the above as rigid principles it is invariably for the sake of the comic, for I find Sterne's reasons all-persuasive:

. . . 'tis wrote, an' please your worships, against the spleen! in order, by a more frequent and a more convulsive elevation and depression of the diaphragm, and the succussations of the intercostal and abdominal muscles in laughter, to drive the *gall* and other *bitter juices* from the gall-bladder, liver, and sweet-bread of his majesty's subjects, with all the inimicitious passions which belong to them, down into their duodenums.

For readers it is often said that they will go on reading the novel because it enables them, unlike film or television, to exercise their imaginations, that that is one of its chief attractions for them, that they may imagine the characters and so on for themselves. Not with my novels; it follows from what I have said earlier that I want my ideas to be expressed so precisely that the very minimum of room for interpretation is left. Indeed I would go further and say that to the extent that a reader can impose his own imagination on my words, then that piece of writing is a failure. I want him to see my (vision), not something conjured out of his own imagination. How is he supposed to grow unless he will admit others' ideas? If he wants to impose his imagination, let him write his own books. That may be thought to be anti-reader; but think a little further, and what I am really doing is challenging the reader to prove his own existence as palpably as I am proving mine by the act of writing.

Language, admittedly, is an imprecise tool with which to try to achieve precision; the same word will have slightly different meanings for every person. But that is outside me; I cannot control it. I can only use words to mean something to me, and there is simply the hope (not even the expectation) that they will mean the same thing to anyone else.

Which brings us to the question of for whom I write. I am always sceptical about writers who claim to be writing for an identifiable public. How many letters and phone calls do they receive from this public that they can know it so well as to write for it? Precious few, in my experience, when I have questioned them about it. I think I (after publishing some dozen books) have personally had about five letters from "ordinary readers," people I did not know already that is; and three of those upbraided me viciously because I had just published the book that they were going to have written.

No, apart from the disaster of *Travelling People,* I write perforce for myself, and the satisfaction has to be almost all for myself; and I can only hope there are some few people like me who will see what I am doing, and understand what I am saying, and use it for their own devious purposes.

Yet it should not have to be so. I think I do have a right to expect that most readers should be open to new work, that there should be an audience in this country willing to try to understand and be sympathetic to what those few writers not shackled by tradition are trying to do and are doing. Only when one has some contact with a continental European tradition of the avant-garde does one realise just how stultifyingly philistine is the general book culture of this country. Compared with the writers of romances, thrillers, and the bent but so-called straight novel, there are not many who are writing as though it mattered, as though they meant it, as though they meant it to matter.

Perhaps I should nod here to Samuel Beckett (of course), John Berger, Christine Brooke-Rose, Brigid Brophy, Anthony Burgess, Alan Burns, Angela Carter, Eva Figes, Giles Gordon, Wilson Harris, Rayner Heppenstall, even hasty, muddled Robert Nye, Ann Quin, Penelope Shuttle, Alan Sillitoe (for his last book only, Raw Material indeed), Stefan Themerson, and (coming) John Wheway; (stand by): and if only Heathcote Williams would write a novel. . . .

Anyone who imagines himself or herself slighted by not being included above can fill in his or her name here:

. . . .

It would be a courtesy, however, to let me know his or her qualifications for so imagining.

Are we concerned with courtesy?

Nathalie Sarraute once described literature as a relay race, the baton of innovation passing from one generation to another. The vast majority of British novelists has dropped the baton, stood still, turned back, or not even realised that there is a race.

Most of what I have said has been said before, of course; none of it is new, except possibly in context and combination. What I do not understand is why British writers have not accepted it and acted upon it.

The pieces of prose (you will understand my avoidance of the term *short story*) which follow were written in the interstices of novels and poems and other work between 1960 and 1973; the dates given in the Contents are those of the year of completion. None of them seem to me like each other, though some have links and cross-references; neither can I really see either progression or retrogression. The order is that which seemed least bad late on one particular May evening; perhaps I shall regret it as soon as I see it fixed.

Make of them what you will. I offer them to you despite my experience that the incomprehension and weight of prejudice which faces anyone trying to do anything new in writing is enormous, sometimes disquieting, occasionally laughable. A national daily newspaper (admittedly one known for its reactionary opinions) returned a review copy of *Travelling People* with the complaint that it must be a faulty copy for some of the pages were black; the Australian Customs seized *Albert Angelo* (which had holes justifiably cut in some pages, you will remember) and would not release it until they had been shown the obscenities which (they were convinced) had been excised; and in one of our biggest booksellers *Trawl* was found in the Angling section. . . .

First published in issue 5.2 (Summer 1985)

Dangerous Words

Luisa Valenzuela

The task of writing is at the same time heartrending and joyful. It is the discovery of one's own imagination, of the associations and the creative powers implicit in language, and a meticulous confrontation with something so denigrated and surprising as words can be.

The word is our tool and our enemy at the same time, it is the sword of Damocles sometimes suspended over our heads when we feel incapable of expressing it, of hitting on the key word, the Open Sesame that will allow us to enter into a new text. That is why I often say that literature, the production of literature, is a full-time curse. And not only because doubt springs up with each step or because the skepticism regarding the usefulness of writing is stated on each page, but also because it tears at the other side: the guilt, or the terror of not writing, of not writing each and every hour of life as is demanded by a certain dark desire so opposed to the other dark desire which pushes us out into the world and to that other thing we call life.

The distance isn't far between the chair where I have the idea and the desk where I will write it; it's insurmountable.

It's the same distance that lies between wanting to say it and not being able to say it. It's the resistance offered by words at being trapped as such. And we writers, with a butterfly net, always running after the blasted words, no longer with the intention of affixing them with a pin driven into the text, rigidly, but the intention of maintaining them alive, fluttering and changing, so that the text will have the necessary iridescence—perhaps called ambiguity—that will allow the reader to reinterpret it. As Barthes said: "The objective of literary work (of literature as work) consists of the reader no longer being the consumer but the creator of a text."

And in the literary puzzle, what I write isn't as interesting as how I write it (Felisberto Hernández and James Joyce insisted on the idea). In the articulation between the narrated anecdote and the style of narration is where the secret of the text resides and where we can witness the bewilderment of the word that can alternately assume the role of a faithful dog, a knife or dice.

An apparently innocent word acquires splendor and transforms itself thanks to the intention with which it is hurled from afar, thanks to that bed which has been prepared for it with piles of other words that precede it. And let's not speak about the silences, which are impossible to speak about anyway. What goes unsaid, that which is implied and omitted and censured and suggested, acquires the importance of a scream.

Inflexible semiologists talk about the "contamination" of the word when they speak of polysemy, meaning the disconcerting synonyms, the analogies, the varied connotations which disrupt the nature and functioning of every word.

As writers, we have our harvest with these so-called contaminations; we sharpen them, shine them, present them in the best way possible so that the light of the reading will bring out all its facets, even the most hidden ones, those most ignored by us and, as such, most delightful—the ones that elude our self-censorship, our internal repressions.

The Fruits of Summer

I'm at the marketplace and I'm peddling my merchandise. She comes to warn me, precisely me who never stepped into the convent, comes toward me and tells me, "Take care, my child." And I continue hawking my merchandise, as if I hadn't heard her, "Come, touch, touch, feel them, you'll never ever find others as round, as firm." With hands on my hips and with a fixed eye on the grapefruit, I don't look at her and she goes on reprimanding me. "This isn't the way, my child, the vendor's cry is different, everything you say degrades the market, it belongs somewhere else, it isn't the right way to say it."

And I just go on as if I hadn't heard, "Here is the reddest pulp, the softest skin." I'm referring to the tomatoes, of course, the fruits of the summer. She only detects in me a malicious seed, she doesn't care for the fruit.

I saw the large gate of the convent open on the other end of the marketplace and I saw her come out and I knew unwittingly that this singular, incredible violation of her monastic life was dedicated to me. How dismal. I don't mess with anybody, I only look around and sometimes hawk my merchandise. The other vendors also look around and hawk their merchandise but it seems that I do it with greater intensity and better results, not necessarily louder. She, who never leaves the convent—that is why she bothered to drag some of the best of us behind those doors—, came out to confront me. She still has hopes? I was the only one who escaped from her without really escaping, just by simply not paying attention to her words. They say that her words were as radiant as the summer sun and reverberated on the snow. That was one winter. It seems that the others curled up against the warmth of those words—salvation, she would say, apparently, and eternal love—and they let themselves be trapped forever. I was into something else. I waited for words with another warmth within them, not a rigid warmth, but a changing, twinkling warmth. And they only spoke colorful words and talked to me with fireworks. Her color was white, how boring. I now proclaim the sweetness of my fruit, its brilliant pulp. In this marketplace, almost a public square, where everything is crowded together, I try to make my stall different and my merchandise special, and that is why she seeks me out. After having forgotten me for many years, now she deigns to stand in front of me to reproach me. "Don't say that, that shouldn't be said," she warns me, and I know damn well what can be said and what should be said underneath this awning that protects my stall, among perfumed mangos and guavas. The sweetest and most fragrant to melt in the mouth, for the special caresses of the tongue. An exquisite pulp. The deliquescence, the pleasure of the olfactory. "Smell, caress, taste. If you taste it, you take it." And for her I mumble between clenched teeth: "You pretend to know what really can be said, that doesn't exist." I then cry out, "They are bursting with milk," while I offer a pair of coconuts, real hairy.

  She makes a quick about-face, and, without hiding her anger, she retraces her steps. On my account she has left the convent and returns there because of me. Dressed in white and her hair also white. I don't hurl the coconuts at her, I hurl these words that she perhaps had come for without admitting it. "Slut," I yell at her, "traitor, worse than the worst bitch," I shout, and the market turns against me because they think she's a saint and what do I care, she came to my stall to defile my words. Take a look at this pulp, how juicy, how shiny, I want to proclaim once more but it doesn't come out. Thief, thief, the insult reaches her when she is about to enter the convent and then never again. But just before the convent gate closes after her steps, I manage to yell at her: "You prickly pear full of thorns, dry papaya." And I belong once more to the marketplace and all the fruits of the summer smile at me.

Translated by Cynthia Ventura

First published in issue 6.3 (Fall 1986)

Dirty Words

Luisa Valenzuela

Good girls can't say these things, neither can elegant ladies or any other women. They can't say these things or other things, for there is no possibility of reaching the positive without its opposite, the exposing and exposed negative. Not even the other women, the ones that aren't so ladylike, can utter these words categorized as "dirty." The big one, the fat ones: *swearwords*. These words that are so delicious to the palate, that fill the mouth. *Swearwords.* These words that completely spare us from the horror gathered in a brain almost ready to explode. These are cathartic words, moments of speech that should be inalienable and that have been alienated from us from time immemorial.

During childhood, mothers or fathers—why always blame women—washed our mouths with soap and water when we said some of these so-called swearwords, "dirty" words, when we expressed our truth. Then came better times, but those unloving interjections and appellatives remained forever dissolved in detergent soapsuds. To clean, to purify the word, the best possible form of repression. This was known in the Middle Ages, and in the darkest regions of Brittany, France, until recently. Witches' mouths—and we are all witches today—are washed with red salt in order to purify them. Substituting one orifice for the other, as Margo Glantz would say, the mouth was and continues to be the most threatening opening of the feminine body: it can eventually express what shouldn't be expressed, reveal the hidden desire, unleash the menacing differences which upset the core of the phallogocentric, paternalistic discourse.

No sooner said than done, from the spoken word to the written word: just one step. Which requires all the courage we can muster because we believe that it is so simple; however, it isn't because writing will overcome all the abysses and so one must have an awareness of the initial danger, of the abyss. We must forget the washed mouths, allow the mouths to bleed till we gain access to the territory in which everything can and *should* be said. Knowing that there is so much to explore, so many barriers yet to be broken through.

It is a slow and untiring task of appropriation. A transformation of that language consisting of "dirty" words that was forbidden to us for centuries, and of the daily language that we should handle very carefully, with respect and fascination because in some way it doesn't belong to us. We are now tearing down and rebuilding; it is an arduous task. Dirtying those washed mouths, taking possession of the punishment, with no room for self-pity.

Among us, crying is prohibited. Other emotional manifestations, other emotions no, but crying yes, prohibited. We can, for example, give estrus free reign and be happy. Jealousy, on the other hand, we must maintain under strict control, it could degenerate into weeping.

Why so much fear of tears? Because the masks we use are made of salt. A stinging, red salt which makes us beautiful and majestic but devours our skin.

Beneath the red masks, our faces are raw and the tears could well dissolve the salt and uncover our sores. The worst penitence.

We cover ourselves with salt and the salt erodes us and protects us at the same time. Red salt, the most beautiful of all and the most destructive. Long ago, they scrubbed our mouths with red salt, wanting to wash out our shamelessness. Witches, they yelled when something disturbed the acquiescent order established by them. And they scrubbed our faces with red salt of infamy and we remained branded forever. Witches, they accused us, they persecuted us, until we learned how to take possession of that salt and we made beautiful masks for ourselves. Iridescent, skin toned, translucent with promise.

Now if they want to kiss us—and sometimes they still do—they have to kiss the salt and burn their lips. We know how to respond to kisses and we don't mind being burnt with them from the other side of the mask. They/us, us/they. The salt now joins us, the sores join us and only weeping can bring us apart.

We mate with our masks on, and sometimes the thirsty come to lick us. It is a perverse pleasure: they become more thirsty than ever and it hurts us and the dissolution of the masks terrifies us. They lick more and more, they moan in desperation, we moan with pain and fear. What will become of us when our stinging faces outcrop? Who will want us without a mask, in raw flesh?

They won't. They will hate us for that, for having licked us, for having exposed us. And we wouldn't have even shed a tear nor allowed ourselves our most intimate gesture: the self-disintegration of the mask thanks to the prohibited weeping that opens furrows in order to begin again.

Translated by Cynthia Ventura

First published in issue 6.3 (Fall 1986)

For Prizewinners

Harry Mathews

to Joseph McElroy

I intend to talk to you seriously.

Before coming here today, I considered several possibilities of what to say to you, especially to the prizewinning writers who are being honored on this occasion. I first thought of warning all of you who plan to write professionally what a bleak future lies ahead of you, in the manner of Virgil Thomson, whom I once heard address the commencement audience at a music school so eloquently that each new graduate must have left in search of a plain steady job—anything rather than a musical career. I then told myself that, after all, the world gives writers an easier time than musicians, since they do not require organized performances to make themselves heard, and their audience can be reached in bedrooms and subways rather than in public halls. I next turned to the possibility of entertaining you, of cheering you with funny and edifying tales of the writing life, so that you could go home warmed by the prospect of a delightful as well as worthwhile future. Conscientiousness nipped that idea. I had gradually been coming to recognize this occasion as too large for mere entertainment: I felt that I would be remiss in not taking advantage of the opportunity it was offering to make myself genuinely useful, which I have since decided means this: to make available to you as appropriately as possible what I have learned from my own experience as a writer. So I intend to talk to you seriously, perhaps at times even thornily.

Even if you are not musicians, I shall start with a warning: if any of you expects that being a writer will give you a better or happier life than you would otherwise have, forget it. "Being a writer"—proclaiming writing as your livelihood, thinking of yourself as "being a writer" when you go to bed at night and get up in the morning—will make no difference in your life; at least, none that matters. Being a writer will bring you some minor privileges. Out of either respect or mistrust or both, most people will keep a distance from you when they find out what you are: you will thus acquire a certain safety. (When someone asks me what I do, I usually say that I sell insurance. This sets both of us at ease.) Being a writer will also cloak you in a rather spurious authority. You may be asked to express yourself publicly on the fate of the snail darter more often than other citizens, not because you know anything, simply because you're a writer; you will also from time to time be offered the pleasure of lecturing captive audiences. Finally, you may get occasional recognition: "See that guy? He's a writer." "A writer? A *real* writer?" ("Help! I'm an insurance salesman!") This will sometimes enable you to make money. I'm actually being paid to tell you what I think because I "am a writer."

Being a writer intermittently and unreliably brings you safety, authority, and recognition—values oriented toward the public world and that, perhaps because of this, give little private satisfaction. No one will deny that their satisfaction is small, that this kind of safety, authority, and recognition add little to our capacity for happiness or liveliness or wisdom. I do not call these values bad, merely disappointing. If you are to spend several hours each day with pencil, pen, typewriter, or word processor, you will want more satisfaction than these values can give—you will want satisfaction in fact. Otherwise the effort looks pointless. And I—someone who enjoys society at least as much as solitude, who persistently daydreams of finding occasions for working with others—I spend several hours every day closeted with pencil and typewriter. What satisfaction do I expect? Do I get it?

First of all, I assert that satisfaction in every activity can be accurately defined as residing in the private counterparts of safety, authority, and recognition: that is, in power, knowledge, and love. For convenience, let's think of power as the ability to create energy over and over; of knowledge as the awareness of things as they exactly are (neither information nor theory); of love as whatever you say it is.

If you cannot find power, knowledge, and love in the condition of "being a writer" (only their public substitutes), the one place you can then look for them must be the act of writing itself. The act of writing: taking words and setting them down, reading what you have written, and then of course rewriting that, and rereading and rewriting it again and again. Here our questions begin to look interesting—they begin to look like questions: because, leaving writing for the moment aside, I have always—almost always—found the power, knowledge, and love that bring satisfaction to be made available through participation. Participation means engaging in collaborative activity with others, whether in work, play, conversation, lovemaking. I wish right now that instead of me speaking and you listening we were having a discussion. That would satisfy me more; and if I haven't proposed it to you, that is only because we would then need a day or two to work our way through our subject. All of you doubtless have experienced satisfaction through participation in work, in sports, in performing with others whether on stage, playing musical instruments, or singing together; you know what I'm talking about. If we can agree that satisfaction finds expression in participation, we are faced with the inevitable question: how can you be satisfied in the act of writing, sitting alone at your desk? How can you participate? What can you participate in? Whom do you participate with?

To the last of these questions the answer must take the shape of that legendary beast, The Reader. Let me remind you of something you have probably found out for yourselves: the writer has no communication with his actual readers (aside from himself). To elaborate the point: for a number of reasons, we cling to the notion that the writer communicates with the reader the way a speaker communicates with a listener, or a letter writer with a correspondent. These analogies can only mislead us. When I speak to you in conversation, I can tell I am communicating with you by your response (or by your lack of response, which is only another kind of response). I can expect an answer to a letter I write; the answer will validate my communication. A writer never receives this validation from his readers, no matter how strongly they feel about what he has written. They provide no feedback, without which direct communication, since it depends on a two-way relationship, disappears. You may point out that readers can tell me about what I have written in conversation, letters, reviews. These apparent exceptions only confirm the rule, because they always come hopelessly late—weeks, months, or years after the moment when I was writing my poem or story or essay. These comments have lost all relevance, and they almost always embarrass more than they please me. My reader is discussing an event that lies dead and buried in the past. I invariably feel that I'm being told how beautiful my ex-wife is.

The question of how to participate with your reader therefore remains an urgent one. Solving it—and understanding how it may be solved—means replacing our intuitive notion that the writer is "saying something" to the reader with a new conception of their relationship. I suggest that in order to guarantee his participation with the reader, a writer does two things. First, he gives up his claim to be the one in the relationship who creates. Second, to establish a space in which participation can take place, he chooses as the innermost substance of what he is writing a terrain unfamiliar to both the reader and himself. You may find these two points obscure; I mean to spend the rest of this talk making them clearer.

The first of the points—the relinquishing by the writer of his role as creator—is the easier to grasp. A simple analogy can indicate why this needs to happen. Imagine that I am a victim of multiple disasters and in utter despair because of them. I now decide to communicate my feelings to the young lady in the first row, whose name is? Sharon. If I rush up to her, grasp her hands, squeeze them furiously, burst into tears, and start screaming, I'll certainly be expressing my feelings; and no less certainly I shall destroy in her all interest in finding out what they are. The only thing Sharon will want to do is get out of the room. If on the other hand I supply her dispassionately with the facts—that the IRS has just confiscated my house, my car, and my savings; that my wife and children died this morning in a horrible accident; that tomorrow I must enter the hospital to have my head amputated—if I supply her with these facts and give her a chance to add them up, she can start imagining what my feelings may be: she can re-create my feelings and eventually respond to them. (She may head for the nearest exit all the same; that's life.) Similarly, if in writing, I do all the work on my reader's behalf, explaining everything, painting a picture in which nothing is left out, the reader, having nothing to do, will not even read what I have written. Like Sharon, he will go elsewhere. The writer must take care to do no more than supply the reader with the materials and (as we often say nowadays) the space to create an experience. That is all the creating that takes place: of writer and reader, the reader is the only creator. This is how reading can be defined: an act of creation for which the writer provides the means. The writer's privileges are restricted to choosing the means and, more important, to becoming his own first reader. He becomes a creator to the same extent as any of his other readers. This is the first way writer and reader participate with one another; in creating the experience for which the writer has provided the means.

The second thing a writer does to open up the possibility of participation is harder to explain. As I said before, the writer chooses, as the substance of his writing, matter unfamiliar both to his reader and to himself. What I say now may appear to contradict that first assertion almost absurdly: the unfamiliar matter the writer chooses is nothing else than his own story.

How can someone's own story be unfamiliar to him? Proust's remarks on the subject may help. He writes that the true, essential book does not need to be "invented by a great writer—it exists already inside him—but it has to be translated by him." He goes on to compare the writer's task of translating the symbols within him to the deciphering of hieroglyphs. Proust thus sees the story within not as readily available but as something to be decoded. Our own stories belong to us, but we cannot easily read them.

I suggest that the apparent contradiction between "one's own story" and "something unfamiliar" comes from confusing our real stories with the stories we tell *about* ourselves (and not only to others: each to himself): publicity stories, explanations of ourselves. Such explanations generally assume one of two forms. Either: "My parents are awful to me, my boss (or my teacher) is a jerk, nobody understands me, I don't stand a chance, no wonder I feel so bad." Or: "My parents are wonderful to me, I'm successful at what I do, I have nothing to complain about, how come I feel so bad?" Have you noticed how rarely anyone tells you how much she enjoys life? If the person doesn't feel bad about himself, he will point out the near and distant disasters rampant in our world—if nothing else, he will remind you that the forces of evil are once again ganging up on the snail darter. Stories such as these can never escape the category of versions or interpretations of what is happening. And all the while we know that something quite different is going on inside and around us, and the difference, we also know, amounts to the difference that separates life from the pretense of life, from the renunciation of life.

How can we win access to our real stories, to what is truly happening in our lives? We have three places where we can look for the decipherable hieroglyphs Proust refers to. First, we have our personal history, the sum of inner and outer events that have made up our lives. Even as we plunder this domain for our publicity stories, we realize how much of it we neglect; this material can be explored at length and in depth. Second, we have our bodies, which are packed (in case you didn't know it) with meanings and indeed with words. Your shoulders are bursting with nouns, your knees with verbs. An insatiable "but" is locked into your right wrist. All these words are held there by force and are waiting to be released. The third place we have to look for our stories I shall call our consciousness; let me define my use of this word straight off. By consciousness I do not mean your feelings, or your ideas, or your imagination; I mean what you feel *with,* what you have ideas *with,* what you imagine *with.* Not the voice chattering in the back of your head telling you what's right and wrong, rather what enables you to hear that voice, and also what enables you to hear yourself listening to that voice. Not your experience: your awareness of experience.

A new question arises: how does a writer go about looking for his story in these three places? In regards to our personal history, the answer is simple enough. The act of writing itself works the necessary wonders. As far as each of us is concerned, personal history means what we can remember, and it so happens that because language is inextricably bound up with the act of remembering; a deliberate use of language inevitably fishes up memories. To explore your history, you need only begin writing about it. As you write, you will discover things about yourself that you did not know you knew. Don't take my word for it: try it. I recently asked my mother to write down all she could remember about certain people she had known as a child. Before starting, she told me that with luck she might fill a few pages. She now expects to be busy for months, at least.

Next, what of the body? How can the body be persuaded to release those words it holds in store? Although we might exploit a number of techniques -for instance, those practiced by actors—to unlock our muscles and bones, I propose for a start resorting to a rather ordinary notion: words are commonly released from our bodies through our breath; that is, if words are to emerge they have to be spoken; so writers should make a point of keeping what they write in touch with how they speak. Here lies a clue to why so many writers find it useful to read what they have written out loud: it gives the body a chance to show up what is phony in their writing. As a second valuable habit, I recommend taking your actual everyday speech as the starting point for what you write. A minute of reflection will convince you that when you talk to your friends there is nothing you know which you cannot communicate to them. (Although you may have to repeat and rephrase, sooner or later you will get your meaning across.) Even if such direct communication is impossible with a reader, that ability to communicate looks like a good place in which to begin writing. Here is a way to do just that. Before setting down a sentence on paper, imagine yourself sitting in a coffee shop with a friend. How would you tell him what you have to say in that next sentence? Write it down. What you have to write down may strike you as chaotic, vulgar, and undignified. This makes no difference—you can clean it up later; in the meantime you will not have resorted for words to the information dump inside your head; you won't be running away from yourself in order to hide behind the not-so-impressive bastions of culture; and you will have started down the path to discovering your own voice in writing. Let me give you one small example of what such a procedure can produce. Last year I asked my students to translate a passage from *Brideshead Revisited* into their own speech. One sentence in the passage read: "The evening passed." How would you tell your friend in the coffee shop that "the evening passed"? One student rendered it perfectly: "It got late." The translation of course evoked another world: his world.

Finally, what about the third place where we can look for our stories, the domain of consciousness? Like the body, consciousness—what you think and feel *with*—generates a profusion of words and meanings. Unlike the body, however, it does not contain or withhold meaning; and consciousness itself has no meaning at all. More accurately, we might say that consciousness generates not meaning but the power to create meaning. It does not produce a particular meaning—it produces no conclusions. Instead, it has the capacity of creating meaning again and again, one meaning after another. We could also describe it as an infinite potentiality of meaning.

Let me once again use an analogy to suggest the way consciousness works. My analogy is the night sky, the star-filled sky. From the first Babylonian shepherd down to our own age, the night sky has been looked on as a vision that must be deciphered, as if it were a text so fascinating that we feel obliged to read it, so obviously significant that it inspires us with a passion for understanding it. While interpretations of the sky have changed many times and are still changing, what has not changed is this desire to understand. Every explanation of the sky, from mythical constellations to present-day theories of the creation of the universe, turns out to be inadequate. (As things are going now, the ultimate explanation of what constitutes the cosmos—like that of the irreducible substance of subatomic matter—seems bound to be definable as neither more nor less than: nothing.) Whatever formulations the long process of explanation may have yielded strike me as not mattering much when they are confronted with the overwhelming desire for knowledge that the night sky never fails to inspire. This desire is expressed as speculation—a word that etymologically signifies mirroring. What the night sky mirrors is ourselves, and it will serve as a mirror of what I have called our consciousness. What we long to know in our speculations about the stars surpasses merely something: we long to know everything. And in fact the consciousness is capable of exactly that: of knowing not only anything but everything.

How can this capacity for engendering infinite meaning, this capacity for absolute knowledge, be drawn upon in writing? What must the reader do so that this domain can be made accessible to writer and reader?

The writer cannot content himself, as he does with his history and his body, with providing something—he cannot provide "things" at all. Somethings are what consciousness produces—its residue— and so consciousness must never be equated with particular things: while consciousness generates particularities, it is never limited to them. Doesn't the answer to our last questions stare us in the face? If providing somethings will not do, the writer must provide nothings. I am not playing with words. A little observation will show you that writers do nothing else. They make the experience of consciousness available through nothings—absences, negations, voids.

To put it another way, writing works exclusively by what the writer leaves out.

(Let me return in passing to an earlier point. The nothingness the writer offers the reader opens up space—a space that acknowledges that the reader, not the writer, is the sole creator. Providing emptiness, leaving things out, gives the reader exactly the space he needs to perform his act of creation.)

To show you that I am not babbling about an idea that I happen to be fond of, let me read you parts of the opening pages of a classic realistic English novel, Jane Austen's *Northanger Abbey*. The book begins:

No one who had ever seen Catherine Morland in her infancy would have supposed her born to be an heroine. Her situation in life, the character of her father and mother, her own person and disposition, were all equally against her.

The rest of the long first paragraph lists all the qualities Catherine Morland does not possess: she is declared to be not an orphan, not poor, not mistreated, not misunderstood, not beleaguered by ill-health, not beautiful, not feminine (i.e., not physically weak), not sensitive, not exceptionally gifted, not stupid, not pathetically submissive, not artistic, not particularly good, and not particularly bad. With one exception, to which I shall return presently, what we learn about Catherine is all the things she isn't; as a result of having her introduced to us in this fashion, we, the readers, are invited to think up what she is. The opening sentence—"No one who had ever seen Catherine . . . would have supposed her born to be an heroine"—of course obliges us to think, "There's our heroine."—The method resembles that of telling someone "Don't think of a white horse" when you want to make them think of a white horse. We are less insistently encouraged to imagine Catherine through the description of what she is not; we nevertheless inescapably find ourselves creating her, or at least creating what she may be. (For those of you who know the book, I cannot resist pointing out that its climactic scene—Henry Tilney's visit to Catherine at her parents' house, one of the most affecting scenes I have read—is also narrated by not describing it: in place of what happens between Henry and Catherine, we are told about Mrs. Morland's search for the volume entitled *The Mirror*.)

I hope that this example has persuaded you to accept, at least provisionally, the possibility that the first step a writer takes to ensure participation in the domain of consciousness is to supply the reader with negations and absences. As you might guess, he must do more than that. The reason he must do more can be expressed in the question: so then what? The writer provides a void, the reader fills it up, and now you have a something. As soon as a particular meaning (a something) is produced, consciousness wants to move on. So the writer provides a new emptiness, the reader creates a new something to fill it, and this process must be maintained to the end of the work (and perhaps beyond). In other words, the second step a writer takes to engage consciousness is to initiate and maintain movement. You may think of this as a kind of action, but you should realize that such movement or action bears no resemblance to narrative action. The movement I am discussing sustains narrative (or the progression of the poem or essay); it does not manifest itself as a feature of narrative.

To understand this kind of movement better, let's return to Jane Austen. I mentioned that in the opening paragraph of *Northanger Abbey* one attribute of Catherine Morland was presented in positive rather than negative terms. That item reads:

. . . [The Morlands] were in general very plain, and Catherine, for many years of her life, as plain as any. She had a thin awkward figure, a sallow skin without colour, dark lank hair, and strong features;—so much for her person . . .

Remember, this is virtually the only one of her qualities that we are not allowed and invited to imagine for ourselves, the one thing we are *told*. It is also the last thing we want to hear. We have been happily concocting a heroine of our own; we had no intention of giving her "a thin awkward figure," and so forth. The fact sticks in our craw; for my own part, I simply pretended it had never been said (it still stuck in my craw). Then, in the next paragraph, something remarkable happens. First we read:

Such was Catherine Morland at ten. At fifteen, appearances were mending: she began to curl her hair . . . ; her complexion improved; her features were softened by plumpness and colour, her eyes gained more animation, and her figure more consequence.

What a relief! We can at last begin to swallow those earlier remarks about her plainness. And *then* . . . Listen:

. . . she had now the pleasure of sometimes hearing her father and mother remark on her personal improvement. "Catherine grows quite a good-looking girl, — she is almost pretty today," were words which caught her ears now and then; and how welcome were the sounds! To look *almost* pretty, is an acquisition of higher delight to a girl who has been looking plain the first fifteen years of her life, than a beauty from her cradle can ever receive.

Catherine feels exactly the way we do. The fact of her plainness has been sticking in her craw, and when that plainness goes she experiences a relief like our own. For a moment, without warning, and of course *without* being told, we become Catherine. She and I are briefly the same person. As a result, I am propelled head- and heartlong into her story. How can I help feeling concerned about Catherine? She is me: naturally I want to know how my own story turns out. Since, moreover, I can usually manage to forgive myself for anything, I shall follow Catherine through thick and thin, and no stupidity or injustice on her part will dent my loyalty to her.

The movement of consciousness illustrated in this example occurs precisely at the moment in which I identify myself with Catherine. I invite you to notice that this extraordinary moment is woven out of the purest illusion. We are in this moment thoroughly, beautifully conned. Catherine does not exist (we have barely started inventing her) or, if you prefer, she need not exist. The effect of the moment in no way depends on Catherine, on this particular story, on this scene. The effect could belong to a story about Eskimos; Catherine could be a middle-aged man called Schwarzenberg, or a dog named Minnie—why not? The effect is produced by a formal device (so sure, one is tempted to find a place for it among the tropes of rhetoric) that precedes and remains independent of any specific material assigned to it. The effect belongs to the realm of what might be called form; however, since that word raises the eyebrows, dander, and hackles of many sincere people, I shall call the special aspect of form that engages the movement of consciousness—not process, although I might use that word, or procedure, or progression, or prosody—I shall call it syntax. Clearly the ordinary sense of the word *syntax* has to be stretched slightly to accommodate the meaning I am now giving it; but only slightly. To the sense "the way in which words are put together to form phrases and sentences" must be added the sense of "the way in which sentences are put together to form stanzas and paragraphs." With that modification, I think I can claim that syntax is what engages my consciousness in an action of shifting, of discovery, at the moment when I recognize that Catherine and I are one and the same person.

To show how truly syntactic the operation of this expanded syntax can be, I have prepared a demonstration for you using as material a complete and unabridged work by a modern master: a very short short story by Franz Kafka. My demonstration demands a certain patience, since you must listen to and reflect on three texts: that of the short story itself and, in addition, those of two revisions or rewritings of the story. Here, first of all, is the story. It is entitled "The Truth about Sancho Panza":

Without making any boast of it Sancho Panza succeeded in the course of years, by feeding him a great number of romances of chivalry in the evening and night hours, in so diverting from himself his demon, whom he later called Don Quixote, that this demon thereupon set out, uninhibited, on the maddest exploits, which, however, for lack of a pre-ordained object, which should have been Sancho Panza himself, harmed nobody. A free man, Sancho Panza philosophically followed Don Quixote on his crusades, perhaps out of a sense of responsibility, and had of them a great and edifying entertainment to the end of his days.

(Trans. Willa and Edwin Muir)

Let me interrupt my argument to say a few words about the matter of the story, not to define or limit it, only to indicate its general scope and give those of you who have never read it a chance to become aware of the topics involved. As you noticed, the two characters in this very short story are taken from another very long work of fiction. We might suspect from this fact alone that "The Truth about Sancho Panza" involves fiction as its subject in some way or other; and our suspicion is corroborated by what takes place—by the "plot." The narrative, quantitatively minimal, presents us with the original and, in its implications, vast proposition that Sancho Panza, the skeptical, realistic servant of Don Quixote, was his master's creator—that he was, in other words, responsible for the invention of one of the most extravagant characters in the history of literature. Sancho Panza's act of creation is presented, however, as anything but an extravagance, rather as the sober means by which he preserved himself from terrible suffering, by which he actually transformed that suffering into an "edifying entertainment." We can reasonably deduce that Sancho Panza is to be identified with Cervantes; more interestingly, we can guess that this story of Kafka's proposes a general view of fiction: that, at least on occasion, fiction can serve to make the most oppressive aspects of reality bearable, even entertaining, not by describing them "realistically," not by denying or running away from them, but by "masking" them—by pretending that one has made them up, or by making something else up to take their place. Kafka makes his point clear by following the precepts implicit in his view in this very story, which is thus transformed into an elegantly economical metaphor illuminating both itself and the practice of the art of which it is an example.

I shall now read you my two rewritings of "The Truth about Sancho Panza," which I shall henceforth refer to as translations. In my first translation, while I have kept the vocabulary and phrasing of the original, I have divided the two sentences of the original—the first long, the second much shorter—into five sentences of less disproportionate length:

Without making any boast of it, Sancho Panza succeeded in diverting his demon from himself—the demon he later called Don Quixote. What he did was feed him a great number of romances of chivalry and adventure in the evening and night hours. As a result, this demon set out, uninhibited, on the maddest exploits; but since they lacked a preordained object, which should have been Sancho Panza himself, they harmed nobody. Sancho Panza thus became a free man. Perhaps out of a sense of responsibility, he philosophically followed Don Quixote on his crusades and had of them a great and edifying entertainment to the end of his days.

In the second translation, I have kept the two sentences of Kafka's story intact; on the other hand, I have replaced all its nouns with other nouns chosen with no consideration for the meanings of the original ones (this choice has been made in a way that I need not explain to you except to say that it leaves virtually nothing either to personal fancy or to chance*):

"The Tub about Sancho Panza"

Without making any bobbin of it Sancho Panza succeeded, in the courtship of yellowness, by feeding him a great numskull of romantics of chloroform and advertisement in the evil and nil housings, in so diverting from himself his demonstrative, whom he later called Don Quixote, that this demonstrative thereupon set out, uninhibited, on the maddest exports, which, however, for lack of a preordained objurgation, which should have been Sancho Panza himself, harmed nobody. A free manager, Sancho Panza philosophically followed Don Quixote on his cruxes, perhaps out of a sensitiveness of restaurants, and had of them a great and edifying enticement to the endlessness of his dead.

Putting it simply, one can describe what has been done in the two translations by saying that in the first the sense of the original is kept and its structure altered, in the second the sense is altered and the structure kept. If you agree to this description, it may strike you as a waste of time if I ask you which of the two translations best preserves the meaning of the original. Obviously, you have already concluded—who wouldn't?—that the translation that keeps the sense of the original must best preserve the original's meaning. (Let me hasten to add that I have no intention of using the distinction

---

*The method followed, known as S+7 or N+7, was invented by Jean Lescure for the Oulipo; see Oulipo, *La littérature potentielle* (Paris: Gallimard, 1973), 143 ff. The *Concise Oxford Dictionary* was the dictionary used in this instance.

between sense and meaning in any but the most ordinary way.) If, furthermore, the little story is indeed a metaphor, the second translation has without doubt destroyed—in addition to the literal sense of each phrase and sentence—any possibility of engendering the metaphorical content that I found so enlightening. How, you may wonder, can the second translation even begin to be taken seriously?

Let me reread the original and the two translations—the translations twice each.

Two developments, you will notice (and I observe that you *are* noticing), have begun taking place. The first translation (unlike the original) is growing steadily more boring; the second translation is making more and more sense—or, at least, we seem more,and more to be expecting it to make sense; and much of the sense we are persuading ourselves to discover sounds, while in no way replicating that of the original, like a kind of commentary on it. "A great numskull of romantics of chloroform and advertisement" can certainly be read as a respectable gloss on the character of Don Quixote; calling one's demon a "demonstrative" fits—our demons, alas, compel us to demonstrate ourselves; exploits are often for export (cf. "advertisements" above); Sancho Panza most definitely becomes the "manager" of the situation. (As for the "sensitiveness of restaurants": imagine what most of us would be thinking about if *we* were traveling through Spain. . . .)

Little by little, the "meaningless" second translation is accumulating an appearance of meaning. I suggest that this is no accident, and that the meaning of the second translation has its source in the original. I suggest that this meaning can certainly not be found in what the translation has changed—its vocabulary—but in what it has left intact: the structure and rhythm of Kafka's story. I claim that the essential meaning of the story is produced by the contrast between the long, complex, almost teeteringly clumsy first sentence (so exquisitely preserved by the Muirs in *their* translation) and the short, forthright, satisfyingly balanced concluding sentence. That contrast embodies the moment of discovery, the moment in which confusion gives way to clarity, the moment in which Sancho Panza learns how to exorcise his demon, in which whoever is telling this story perceives the usefulness of writing fiction, perhaps the moment in which Franz Kafka sees the possibility of truth in writing a story called "The Truth about Sancho Panza." This movement of discovery and resolution irresistibly survives the travesty of sense perpetrated by the second translation, just as it irresistibly succumbs to the "faithful" rendering of the translation, in five sentences. You should notice in conclusion that this embodiment in the contrast between the two sentences, of what I called action empowers the reader to create, using the sense of the words made available to him, the experience of discovery that is the substance of the story. Syntax makes the metaphor work; and we may conclude that meaning is to be equated not with content but with what makes content produce its effect. Here, as so often in Kafka, the nominal sense of the words gives only indirect clues as to what is really going on. Syntax and syntax alone delivers the goods.

To those of us who write, the consequences of this demonstration offer one notable advantage. Once you accept that the movement or action embodied in syntax provides the *essential* meaning of what you write, you will find it easier to get off the hook on which most of us so painfully dangle—the notion that subject matter gives writing its significance. If you can even hypothetically entertain the possibility that the meaning of what you write does not depend on what you write about, you will be spared needless hours and days of frustration. I suggest, incidentally, that this possibility corresponds to the experience of our non-writing lives. Don't you already know that to get into an argument, any subject will do? that to express love for someone, almost no words will do? You may argue with murderous violence about politics or the superiority of Babe Ruth and Hank Aaron, in every case your meaning remains: I want to argue with you. As for telling someone you love them, the difficulties often look insurmountable. For instance: "You never tell me you love me!" "Oh, sure—uh—I love you." At such a moment, neither party experiences very much satisfaction. The moment might nevertheless be redeemed by a bout of dancing.

You are free to write about anything—whatever you find necessary to tell your story. You are free to pick material that you are drawn to, remembering that you may be drawn to what is strange or frankly appalling. Do not resist that appeal, no matter how disgraceful or unreasonable it may look. In a talk a few weeks ago Italo Calvino said that all his books began with problems that he knew he never could solve. Plainly he is attracted to insoluble problems. Why? They allow him to make discoveries. Choose your subjects so that you can discover what you didn't know you knew. You cannot, after all, *start* with syntax. When you sit down to write, you will probably have no more than an inkling of where your syntactical strength is to be found; it will be part of what you discover in the process of working. Perhaps that is why rewriting is always so crucial a part of writing; why reading must be the locus of participation. There, where you have become a reader among readers, you at last begin to *know:* the community of your readers participates in an act of discovery that you have made accessible, to yourself no less freshly than to any of your fellows.

I realize that you think the world is a mess and that you have a responsibility to do something about it. The world *is* a mess, one of our very own making. Two points, nevertheless. First, all the solutions to the world's problems have already been written down, and this fact continues to make very little difference—the problems do not go away. We might even say that the problems are so mired in words that we can rarely manage to approach them directly, and that most of the time writing about them only stirs up other people's mud. Perhaps you may deal with them more usefully, if less obviously, by writing a romance about a butterfly and a lollipop-if that is what you feel like doing. Second, no one yet knows who you are—not the you whose secret story can be re-created in the medium of the written word. There lies the extraordinary contribution you can make to the world, and I recommend that you give yourself the chance to make it. Write about the things that attract you. Choose your subjects the way you used to choose your toys: out of desire. You have the universe for your toy shop now. The time has come for you to go out and play.

An address delivered in May 1982 at Queens College, New York.

First Published in issue 7.3 (Fall 1987)

French Version

Claude Ollier

That every sign contracts as soon as it is written, in the very moment it is written, losing contact with the present, incapable of anchoring the present or of capturing the instant, inscribing itself only as already caught in the nets of narratives and the networks of texts, dislocated from the moving instant, however minimal the gap; and that, simultaneously, the gesture of tracing this sign lets the body float more than ever in the swollen substance of the moment: this is a paradox of the action of writing, of an act, a posture that everyone assumes daily or almost daily, and where is fleetingly enunciated, as though in its nascent state, between the minimal oscillation of the wrist and the tracing of a pen stroke, the major question mobilizing our books for some time—the contradiction between writing and narration.

That this dislocation, this initial gap, has been experienced as a conflict, and probably for quite a long time, is attested to by many texts from the past. This conflict is more or less manifest, depending on the period in question: more or less silenced, latent, or, most often, relegated to the background. But it is in our time that it has overtly occupied the scene, that it has defined itself, proclaiming what animates it. Thus we live this conflict today; we think and write it. It is from within it that we write: in a contradiction between writing and narration.

It would seem that such has not always been the case concerning this sundering, or the extent to which it has been remarked; it would seem that we have here a sign of the times, a significant sign, a current symptom of a serious dissociation: between the subject and society, between writing and society. It is probably the lot of the writer in our century, particularly since the end of the Second World War, to have been alerted here and there, by the new disposition of this gap, of this conflictual hiatus, and to have more or less obstinately sought to discern its effect in the currents of narrative invention—to have watched for it, or rather to have listened for it. To have listened to it vibrating in the hollow of the sentence, or rather the crucible, since from time to time we hear here the word "laboratory" used in respect to our books—and not always in order to credit the chemist with the prestige of the research. But care must be taken here; if there exists one day a science of writing, it will have to take into account the perception of this interval and of the rending which resounds there.

Whence the necessity sensed by some writers in the forties to take things back to their foundations in this domain, to dwell on this nascent state of listening, to dwell on the friction, the pulsation of this dissociation between the gesture and what is given to be read by the gesture. And whence the necessity to become attentive to the "present" of writing, a present which is corrosive in its relation to any narrative, any story, and thus to the economy, cultural environment, and development of our society in all its trials of violence and in its mute, spasmodic, hidden transfers. It is the contribution of what our *lettres françaises* have registered as a New Novel, to have taken the novel back to its foundations after its having been submerged in recent years under layers of an "American-style" narration, in which the valorous models were too highly charged with moral imperatives. Which is not to say that these New Novels owed nothing to Faulkner or Dos Passos, but rather that one must also listen for the interval in *their* works, as in the work of Kafka, Joyce, Roussel, or Michaux, in which the relations between different materials are inscribed with force on a scale echoing the fierce "catastrophes" of Mahler, Webern, Stravinsky, and Cage: a whole algebra!

What does this rally consist of, this new attitude, which Beckett soon extended to the radical level of a "word by word" narrative when he chose the French language in order to see more clearly, by force of its greater grammatical constraint, and thus to better localize and designate the gap? After the decline of the narrative practices in favor at that time, following upon the national disaster and the blurring of the values that subtended the novelistic edifice, this rally consisted essentially in rearranging the relations between two types of materials. It consists in reanimating their imbrication, in raising their stakes: on the one hand, there are those materials provided and arranged by vocabulary and syntax; on the other hand, there are those materials delivered up by the body's functioning, and by that mysterious, negatively defined entity which psychoanalysis has, according to Freud's simple formula, "inserted between the physical and what has been called until now the psychic." A scandalous, a capital insertion, and one which has gone far in putting these matters back in play. It was thus in some respects a question of connecting in a different way those relations between vocabulary, verb tense, narrative pronouns, effects of metaphor and of the transfer of meaning, tempo, pace of narration, scansions, and cuts. And in other respects it was a question of sensations, perceptions, lines and surfaces, full or empty volumes; of a feeling of distances and durations; of relations fixed upon a gesture, a step, an object; of trajectories of sight or hearing; of impressions of silence or movement, inertia, ephemeral apprehensions, bodily sensations drawn in graphisms like networks of nerves and blood; it was a question of a persistence on the retina and memory paths, the birth of events, pulsations of space and of places of origin, memory. . . . Narratives of the present place and of memory, where the contradiction passes and is felt with violence, for memory is also writing; it frames, isolates, evacuates, differentiates, blinds, masks, and thwarts the narrative. What must be made clear here, when we speak of contradiction, is that it is not a question of a theoretical view (formulated in anticipation of some later conceptual elaboration) concerning a practice which is, finally, more playful than morbid, despite what is said of it here and there. It is a question, rather, of a daily phenomenon (and these notes have no other goal than to localize, describe, and emphasize this phenomenon) experienced emulously, the whole duration of the narrative effort, in effects of uneasiness, of reticence, of inability to "push" the narrative attempt beyond an instant of inscription that the hand reaches out imperatively to retain, to block, to divide, to close, to drown in a white blankness. Effects of submersion, of effacement, of fading, of rupture. Of stuttering. Of censorship and stoppage. Of the impossibility of continuing to recount or constitute even a minimum of narrative or fable lifted from the rut, rescued, sounding just the right note as it is drawn out from the tight unwinding of a phrase, a fable risked at the edge of the reef and sometimes kept, recopied, stored away— to what end? "It's done on conviction," a friend of mine, a filmmaker, said one day about an American film—a great "spectacle"—whose merits he was trying in vain to explain. . . . Narrative fragments wrenched away from physical constraint, from the torment of a cramp or of a contraction which is projected upon the page and marked abruptly in the drawing of lines, in the scrawl of signs: a stop at line's end, at the inaccessible end of the line. Word-by-word invention of a new narrative; emergence of an overstepping into the aleatory; the changing of a terrorized, scattered, routed guard.

Can this new narration be called a novel? For a time we called it "fiction," this product of contradiction made manifest. It is a product which must certainly harbor some innovation, since simple oppositional systems have tried in vain for the last twenty years to take account of it. At first it was called "objective" or "objectal." As this didn't help matters much, it was later called "subjective" as well. All one or all the other: an irrelevant opposition if ever there was one, contributing nothing but increased confusion. Then it was dubbed "textual" or "scriptural," and the term "non-realistic" was opposed to the "realistic" or the "ordinary" in an attempt to demonstrate that the criteria was one of a textual generation purified of any external sources or any prior input, a generation purified of any preconstituted link with the social, economic, or biographical fabric. Or, if links do exist, they did not intervene in the initial tracing of lines and should not be taken into account by the analysis. But what is the value of such an analysis of a narrative inventoried in all its excesses, its "abysses," its degenerations, its losses, its wars, its transmutations, its subsidences; what is the value of this analysis when the narrative is cut off—by a decision which strongly resembles an idealist a priori, transforming the text into an entity in itself, an absolute—from the determinations of a given era, with its excesses of war, its economic catastrophes, its historical losses, its social transmutations, its racist "abysses," its ideological subsidence, its colonial occultations? Certain people have spoken of writing and narration; it has been said that the writing produces the narration. This is not absolutely false; at a certain point it is partially true, but one fails thereby to delimit the exact site of the struggle. The conflict is restricted; it is not conceptualized in the complete disposition of its practices, and especially not in time, well before the first trace of text, where biographical memory and linguistic symbolization operate—by all sorts of schemas and organizations previously derived from determinations of childhood, of adolescence, of education, of formation—a complex process of selection where narration and writing already confront each other, mutually wounding, molding, and sharpening each other. Is it not remarkable that the two avant-garde movements which have shared for several years the field of theoretical reflection on questions of contemporary prose and poetry have, on the one hand, put the accent on writing alone (with a disconcerting opportunism: *Tel Quel);* and on the other hand *(Change:* with greater competency and seriousness), on narration alone? Is it not remarkable that each has thus curiously incarnated, in its publications and quarrels, one of the two terms, which is then lived and conceptualized as functioning according to an opposition rather than in a conflictual, antagonistic play—in other words, a dialectic?

For this process of the constitution of fiction in its successive stages *is* dialectical before, during, and after the actual work on the text. Any investigation of modern fiction which does not propose to get back to this movement, lodging itself in the wake of that violent, constant magnetization and renewing contact with the crises of the text in order to untangle its components; any discourse which excises, dissects, extirpates, and exhibits separately, as surface rather than as volume, the elements of the contradiction at work, delivers up from this work only a dead letter—though it may be a literal one.

And in so doing, it bypasses what is important above all: not only the real comprehension of what has been the practice of elaboration and the impulse that animated it, but also, and especially, whatever traces that elaboration may have left, in every turn of a phrase, to be discerned by reading, and which result in the reader being impelled to read, espousing the movement of invention in all its uncertainties, its emotions, its perils. A book like *S/Z* exposes everything except what is essential. Hypnotized by the most striking contours of the "structure," it is powerless to show how it was that the text's inventor changed one structure into another as he wrote, in the process of an overstepping, a "going beyond" which branded the life of that text with indelible marks that can be perceived by a careful listening: by listening to the conflicts, not by observing the spectacle of structural oppositions. These marks are the impasses, the returns, the abandonments, the resumptions, the steps scaled, the catastrophic passages which give a text its pulse and a fiction its *suspense.* This latter is a term that structuralist criticism has been unable to "come to grips with," to incorporate into its lexicon, and has let slip through its nets. But the suspense is precisely the story in the process of inventing itself, the story of the text in its precarity, its refusals, its élans, its derailments, its weak spots, its breaks, its illuminations. And this has nothing to do with the chronology of the events recounted, as has often been said, nor, certainly, with dis-chronology: an irrelevant opposition, here too, miles away from the real question. But there does exist a chronology of fiction, and this one is completely independent of any eventual chronology of occurrences; it is the chronology of the germinating process in all its freezes and blockages, its starts, its revivals. And this chronology of fiction goes back well before the first trace of the text.

Here resides the great problem of "creativity" in contemporary fictional invention. The future of the *word* has been assured in recent years, but it is as if the word, placed as an exergue, has hidden the phenomenon itself. And the major point to clarify would be, to begin with: how biographical givens are dealt with by memory; that is, how the contradiction already operates at this stage, the contradiction between narration (the givens lived as a narrative and always doubled by a second narrative which is continually resumed, delivered up, remodeled) and writing (the memory framing the "flashes" of this narrative, fixing their traces in space and time, loosening them, surrounding them with white, inserting intervals, producing snapshots, both positive and negative, to be exhibited, repressed, developed). Throughout these trials a first fictionalizing is articulated: sensations, emotions, discourses, dreams, projects, chosen scenes, recurrent gestures, readings, multiple texts from the socio-cultural environment. Then other fictionalizings intervene, like so many "turns of the screw," in the form of narrative seeds, schemas, outlines of itineraries, prefigurations of greater or lesser precision that are often geometrical or arithmetic in nature and based on sketches, maps, number games. The fiction itself, occurring much later, is constructed "only" upon this long, meticulous, copious, and prior selection which privileges certain traces at the expense of numerous others, eliding points of reference, overdetermining sets of signs, operating strict choices, trying out different "pages," provoking collisions and frictions which have for a long time shaken the whole system of relations between the two types of materials defined earlier. A whole grill of "symptoms" is set in place, as well as repetitions and resurgences crossed by effects of language or narrative rhetoric instilled willingly or by force and later endowed with fictional indices operating a veritable symbolization of the biographical in certain crucial points of which the text takes possession. And it is not an exaggeration to say that what is subsequently written in black on white, on the page this time, is already a *re-writing*—whence the pleasure *(jouissance),* felt at this instant, of a resumption, a renewal, a going beyond. What Stevenson said at the end of his life is so true: "It's marvelous when someone else breaks the ground for you, allowing you the luxury of tasting the only real pleasure of writing: rewriting."

These are indeed facts of exploration, the staking out of paths, adventures. . . . The word "itinerary" has often been spoken in respect to these books and several other more recent ones—fictions constructed upon a peregrination and its obstacles, its ambushes, its shortcuts, its twists and turns, even its "trials," for those who wanted to link the new narrative to the novel of apprenticeship (there was even the inevitable, debilitated spiritual variant). And a number of these books do, in effect, partake of an aesthetic of the steeplechase which has proven itself, whether in the detective story or elsewhere. But has it been noticed that the first obstacles on the itinerary were precisely these inaugural schemas, which have always existed whether they be structured or not, and which shore up the fictional effort? For this is the central point: the decisive stage of textual inscription is that of the destruction of the initial prefigurations; what is written "produces" the fiction, if you will, but through "sublation" of these schemas, of this first organization which thereby finds itself subjected to violence—fissured, dislocated. This sublation is more often than not unexpected, unanticipated; its result is surprising. In reality, a transmutation of the project results from the very attempt to realize the project: writing against narration. And this transmutation is apparently a necessary condition. But this is not the last stage: often the new organization devours itself halfway through, or at the end of its itinerary; it opens onto something unheard-of, something hurried and sometimes chaotic—a sort of cacaphonic "stretto," which can also announce the "suite," like a filigree, across narrative caesuras and liquidations. If in the classical narrative the itinerary was heavy with psychological evolution, bearing in itself both social insertion and metaphysical closure, and if it found its justification in this same historical weightiness, then *here* it is a question of something entirely different. Here, the itinerary is a vector of the process of the unfolding of the fictional text. And the dialectical itinerary is not reversible. If there is something non-reversible in any fiction, it is not the chronology of events nor the "evolution of the character" which is ordinarily connected with that chronology, but rather the setting into motion of the productive mechanism. It is therefore an authentic mutation of the novelistic itinerary that we have witnessed for the last two or three decades; this mutation was itself due to the decisive fact that it was no longer possible (since when? since the beginning of the century? at least since the end of the Second World War, at any rate) to elaborate the schema of a story or a plot the way it was done before, except by replaying the old mode of novel writing, with a linear story and characters with "qualities." As if nothing had happened, as if nothing had radically changed in our geographical and cultural territory, on the map of the relations of force existing between society and economy; as if the problem of European identity, for example, could still be posed in terms of the same narrative synthesis. As if the idea of a "story to tell" could raise no questions as to its foundations or its future. It is because one can no longer knowingly constitute, for a whole number of historical reasons, such inaugural schemas that the writing of novels has found itself shaken from top to bottom, and that the latent conflict between writing and narration has been revealed—a secret force—in all its power, if not yet in the full light of day. A brutal discontinuity, a narrative catastrophe, occurred in the forties, proclaiming voicelessly that our society could no longer recount in that old manner; it could no longer double itself with the same type of stories it had always used, and used precisely by means of *genres*— genres constituted, pedagogically instituted, and functioning correctly as reservoirs for narratives and as recognizable structures. Those narrative figures founded on the recognition of mechanisms that had long been taught and assimilated, those remarkable figures of fictional rhetoric that are very commonly admitted, categorized, and imposed by the use of a cultural "baggage" standing the test of time, found themselves on false ground, in disequilibrium, with their superstructures out of gear. Certainly, attempts were made to rework them, to redeploy them, to modernize them. But these attempts at renewal by massive injection of "American-style" forms only emphasized their inability to articulate the new ties between society and narrative: an economy of words, an economy of social signs. It was at this moment that a new narrative tried itself out on the decline of the novelistic genre—by skirting its rules, misappropriating its myths, obscuring its paths, crossing its fingers, and recoding its signals. Certain of those new fictions thus appeared to be travesties of one or more genres, such as the detective novel, the mystery, the colonial adventure, the romantic novel, the war epic, the psychological novel, the novel of quest or of apprenticeship, the spy novel. Subsequently, narrative forms underwent other transformations: disintegrating, fragmenting themselves to the extreme, playing on discontinuity, division, and the impossibility or the refusal to constitute a narrative totality; applying themselves to provoking frictions between an ordinary (economic) order and a fictional ("mythic") one, with combustions overactivating the effect of "ordinariness," the "documentary" effect, and maintaining a permanent tension between "document" and "fiction"—but not by substituting for the "ordinary" a "scriptural" whose own nature would be covertly mythical. It would be interesting, along this line, to study the transitions, in these books, between the two poles, along with the modes of passage, especially when the passage is made in the course of a sentence; this would provide one way, among others, of surprising contradiction at work.

It would at any rate be more valid, in my opinion, than posing the question of current fiction in terms of "representation" or "expression," even in order to endow these terms with a negative exponent. Indeed, it seems that these terms belong to the vocabulary of an outmoded problematic—that of the so-called traditional novel, and that fiction considered in this way (at least its analysis) is based on the pure and simple reversal of an outdated opposition, an irrelevant perpetuation of its questioning rather than a radical decentering of perspectives.

This decentering takes place, gradually, in the field of a new economy: that of the inscription of the conflicts between subject and language, between language and society, between subject and society, culture, environment. This economy is characterized by its means (different for each "author") of inscribing the biographical through symbolization of its chosen givens, which take on the value of *documents*. Or one might say that this economy is characterized by the way in which it registers the biographical overdetermination of each of its particular, successive contradictions, all of which have worked, in their succession, upon the fundamental contradiction, present at each stage, between elements of writing and elements of narration. It is the traces of those struggles that are given to be read, as they are arranged on the page in their specific occupation of space, their distribution, their disposition of intervals and scansions, their play of precise *minimal differences* between signs: words, punctuation, silences; delays, anticipations; reversals, caesuras. Rhythms. The flow of signs. Nietzsche long ago brought attention to this last point, in *Ecce Homo,* in the chapter entitled "Why I Write Such Excellent Books": "To communicate by signs— and by the *tempo of* these signs—a state, or the internal tension of a passion. . . ."

Thus a directive: not to make mistakes as to signs, or as to the tempo of these signs. And to leave live traces, as scrupulous and irrefutable as possible, in the wake of each line—traces to be replayed, revived, reanimated by a reading sympathetic to those signs, to their movement, and to their power of resonance.

A new reading, and thus also, consequently, new gestures of reading, ones which are attentive to metamorphoses. It is not in the least surprising that some readers find this task arduous at times, or that they call these books difficult or—why not?—unreadable. This is an old problem echoing in our post-war world. It is our society that is no longer readable. Like its "literature." For "literature" is a media invention, at least since the advent of printing. As for the writer, he knows only the curious position described earlier: one of vigilance in *correctly setting down his legacy.*

Translated by Cecile Lindsay

First published in issue 8.2 (Summer 1988)

"Once More unto the Breach, Dear Friends, Once More": The Publishing Scene and American Literary Art

George Garrett

> Literary mores no longer place as much stock in the hieratic model of the winner, which is just as well. Unless one is good at self-sacrifice, is endowed with an iron will and a genius-sized gift, it's likely to be a defeating thing to insist on producing Art or nothing.
> —Theodore Solotaroff,
> *A Few Good Voices in My Head*

Once upon a time, not so long ago, trade books published in America were conveniently divided (*segregated* might be a better word for it) by publishers into two basic categories—"popular" and "serious." It was those terms, as much as anything else, Saul Bellow was fighting against when he coined his own opposite poles—"public" and "private." We are talking about, roughly, thirty years ago: the War over with, replaced, of course, by other, smaller wars without ceasing; the last of the original millions of veterans, who had crowded the campuses as never before on the G.I. Bill and changed American education (among other things) for better and for worse forever more, gone off into their long deferred "real" lives at last; the paperback revolution which had furnished the affordable textbooks of that era and which had, for a time, revitalized the dozing, yawning American publishing business with the double whammy of fresh new money for the taking and the up-to-date sweaty greed to go out after it. About thirty years ago we had even had a little literary revolution, too, one of those once in a century or so (maybe) overturnings of the statues and monuments of the Literary Establishment and their replacement with a new set of heroes and icons. (I suppose the nearest thing to it was in seventeenth-century England when the Roundheads finally managed to kick ass on the Cavaliers and shut down all the theaters as part of what they hoped was a final solution. Of course, half a century later the theaters were back in business, but utterly different. The old Shakespearean stage as long gone and forgotten.) In our own revolution, for example Faulkner, Fitzgerald, Hemingway and even Steinbeck, none of whom could be said to have prospered greatly, either in rewards or reputation in the years before the War, were now suddenly declared to be the Old Masters of the first half of this century. (You want to see how highly regarded they were during that first half-century? Go and pick up any old *New York Times Book Review* or *Herald Tribune* or *Harper's* or *Scribner's* or any other literary magazine between, say, 1920 and 1945, and you'll see who the Updikes and the Oateses of the time were, and they were sure not Faulkner, Fitzgerald, Hemingway or Steinbeck. Wolfe, maybe, but his time was brief, brief.) Needless to say, certain publishers began sifting through their backlists looking for old-timers and unknowns who maybe could be resurrected to the cheerful music of the cash register. And, do not forget, for the first time ever, courses in modern and contemporary literature were now being offered at American colleges and universities. There was going to be some good money there, too, for these lucky or clever publishers who could get their snouts up close to the edge of the trough. "Serious," or to use another synonymous term of the period, "prestige" writing just might pay off in the long run after all.

It is an important condition of modern and contemporary literary art that the most prominent and active American publishers of our times have had, at least as a secondary or "spin off" goal, the desire to be not only successful but also socially respectable. Money alone could not purchase or confer that reward. It was necessary to publish something not merely worthwhile, but *recognized* to be worthwhile, at least within the precincts of the New York City where they lived and worked and prospered. See Theodore Solotaroff's essay "What Has Happened to Publishing," in *A Few Good Voices in My Head* (1987), where he writes "of Jewish newcomers using family money to establish houses that conformed to their desire and drive to play an important cultural role in New York, much as their counterparts were doing in Vienna, Berlin, and London." We could make too much out of the special limitations, partly self-imposed, both ethnic and regional in American commercial or "mainstream" publishing. But there is a tension there and a different purpose. Insofar as Solotaroff's observation is accurate—and there is no good reason to question his authenticity—it depicts a curious cultural and social scene, at once strictly regional and of small space, and international. Looking not west of the Hudson to the huge area and population of the nation itself (which appears to figure chiefly in their calculations, *dream* if you prefer, as a source of raw materials, including writing, and of potential customers, *natives* if you would rather, caught in a classically colonial paradigm), but east, across the Atlantic to the example of European urban culture. This particular upward social mobility is not, then, an example of the *American* dream and has only a commercial need to be in touch with the larger and wider American dreams and aspirations. He said it, I didn't; but in large part it helps explain how the inordinate influence of the New York City community (as it sees itself, of course) on serious American literature came to pass.

In the meantime "popular" literature, preferably best-sellers, could keep the old cash flow flowing, pay the piper and take care of overhead—which latter included the salaries and expense accounts of people employed in the business who, if they weren't getting rich, were at least living comfortably.

It all seems so sweet and innocent and so very long ago. So long before the arrival of the "Blockbuster," and the chain bookstores and all the latest, improved means of persuasion and advertising and publicity, of the conglomerates which could afford to pay for all this. Before, also, the sudden upsurge of "creative writing" in hundreds of institutions, which soon led to hundreds of jobs for poets and fiction writers, who could be modestly supported by the patronage of the colleges and universities, provided they published and in places with enough "visibility" to bring credit on themselves and their patron institutions. And provided that they picked up enough good reviews in the right places. The "right places" being mainly and chiefly the media centered in and around New York, thus, in a serious sense, making these American educational institutions, coast to coast, curiously dependent on the good will and attention of one particular region with its own mindset and special interests. And there was also an exponential increase in the number and variety of possible grants, awards, fellowships and prizes able to be acquired if not exactly earned by writers.

Along with all of this came, hand in glove, the social twins who always arrive to accompany awakening ambition—corruption and conflict of interest. What had once, and recently enough, been a lonely and savage struggle for simple survival was radically altered, at least for some, becoming the perhaps even more ruthless and brutal battle for the fruits of personal ambition. The poets turned out to be the worst of the lot. No surprise there. They had endured the toughest times. Only the well-to-do could really afford to write poetry. Those who were not rich enough by inheritance or, by privilege, firmly set (like Williams and Stevens, for instance) in a lucrative profession, went under. Like poor old Maxwell Bodenheim. But now you could earn a half-decent salary as a teacher with a prospect of maybe tenure or even, maybe, an endowed chair someday, provided you minded your p's and q's, acted more or less the way a poet is supposed to act, and picked up enough outside support and recognition to justify your very existence. Given the prospect of comfort and a kind of junior executive security for poets, it is hardly surprising (though not in the least praiseworthy, either) that the poets in large numbers began to behave towards each other in ways which would have embarrassed Iago and to pull insider tricks and stunts which would make Ivan Boesky blink and blush. The fiction writers were only marginally better behaved, perhaps because there was/is more scrutiny devoted to them. They still had some readers and the prospect of reaching a few more. Some of them are doing rather well. Ann Beattie, for example, who only teaches from time to time when she really has to, is quoted in *Publishers Weekly* (December 25, 1987) in a statement which less than a decade ago (and even allowing for inflation) would have aroused some hearty horse laughter among the brotherhood and sisterhood of working writers: "If I tried to support myself solely by writing short stories, I'd have an annual income of under $10,000 a year." It has been at least half a century in America since anybody came close to making that kind of money from writing short stories. The poets didn't even read each other (not even when judging or reviewing each other's work), so who cared what they did or didn't do? Those among the poets who had (somehow, as much to their own surprise as anyone else's) arrived at the top of the little heap were willing to live with things just as they are. If people started to *read* them, who knows?, they might easily be toppled from eminence and replaced by others whose names and whose works were mostly unknown. To them at least.

By now, you will have guessed, we are already located in the big middle of the here and now. And we are supposed to be talking about the publishing scene, not writers. Problem is, *truth* is, most of the writers (practically anybody you have ever heard of) are involved in a close symbiotic relationship, cosy you might say, with the publishing world. Without the acquiescence and tacit support of the writers (especially the most successful ones) the whole creaky system might collapse. They can fool you, though, the writers. Take PEN for example, forever using our dues to battle against some forms of overt censorship here and there, against racial separation and segregation in South Africa if not, say, Kenya or Ghana, firmly committed against torture everywhere in the world except in certain Eastern Bloc nations, and mostly keeping their own mouths shut tight about the inequities and injustices, trivial and profound, perpetrated on the American public by the same folks who give them their advances against royalties and publish their books. Whatever their price is, it doesn't include a vow of silence or even very much self-sacrifice.

The writers are far from blameless and they must take a good share of the blame, not only the publishers, that there is so little place for genuine experimental writing in America. By Americans. If you happen to come from another country and have to be translated out of another language and into English, you are *expected* to be a little bit off the wall.

What has happened most recently within the old system of American trade publishing is a series of slight but significant changes, chiefly during the past five years. One item is a new category, a new usage—*literary,* as in "a literary novel." A literary work has no pretensions (or hope) of somehow becoming a Blockbuster; possibly, though, it may become a best-seller. Blockbusters, the ultimate best-sellers, are the bread and butter, meat and potatoes of contemporary commercial publishing. The whole system is organized around the Blockbuster. But a great many of the type, widely advertised and expensively promoted, given every chance, have proved to be duds. Nothing is more costly or absurd than a Blockbuster which has arrived on the scene with all the excitement of a soggy firecracker. For a little while the routine was to try to line up several potential Blockbusters per season and hope that one or two caught on. This proved to be very wasteful; and whereas American commercial publishing is nothing if not widely wasteful, it was too much so for the limited resources of most publishers. Over the past few years the publishers have tended to spend more time and money and planning on fewer potential Blockbusters. For the rest of their line, many have discovered that a "literary" book will do just fine. You get a lot more attention and review space (which, at least, can be considered as a form of cheap advertising; like the publication of poetry, for instance); more so than before, because reviewers, given a choice, prefer to review literary works rather than most of the Blockbusters which don't need to be reviewed, anyway. A true Blockbuster can't be helped much by good reviews. And bad reviews? Think of Samuel Goldwyn's famous reaction to criticism: "It rolls off my back like a duck." More to the point, the literary book is, almost always, more economical. Doesn't call for an enormous advance. If good things develop, fine and dandy. If bad things accrue, why the publisher can quickly dump it, cutting losses (and they are usually *minimal* losses anyway) at a dead run. And once in a while, it is believed, a genuinely literary work can, in fact, achieve a noteworthy financial success. Can even become a bona fide best-seller. On November 30, 1987, the *Washington Post* book critic Jonathan Yardley took positive note that serious writers were beginning to show up on the best-seller lists. He cited Gail Godwin, Toni Morrison, Tom Wolfe, and Scott Turow. He did not mention some others whose books had, earlier in 1987, found places on the various best-seller lists, writers like Philip Roth, Saul Bellow, Gore Vidal, John Gregory Dunne, Walker Percy, Larry McMurtry, Kurt Vonnegut, and Pat Conroy. Important thing to keep in mind is that (surprising as it may be), from the point of view of most "mainstream" publishers and the national book critics and reviewers, these writers are all equally "serious" and "literary." One should also be aware that the term "literary" has been stretched, perhaps to its extreme, to include even such things as movies, widely distributed and advertised feature films. For example, the *New York Times* (January 7, 1988) discussed *Broadcast News* as an example of the type—"The Making of a 'Literary' Film."

In some ways the fact that writers, who at least began their careers as "serious" and "literary" artists, can now produce profitable work for commercial publishers has had a negative impact on contemporary writers. The positive values, if only as a vague source of hope and of good morale, are obvious. But in many cases these people are merely the token literary artists on the publishers' lists. Which is to say there is usually not a whole lot of room left on those lists, or in the publishers' special mindset, for many new people. Or for any *rediscoveries.* The latter is, ironically, the most difficult category of all, because the publishers have by now established a deep and serious interest (it's their investment, after all) in keeping the accepted Literary Establishment intact, as firmly settled as can be. Just as, at the end of World War II, rediscovery and revisionist history were worthwhile (therefore almost inevitable) in practical, pure and simple financial terms, so from now on it would be a serious problem, in those same terms and for an entire linked chain of beings living off the literary plankton—publishers, their stables of writers, reviewers and literary journalists, critics and academics— if the Establishment were, at any point, threatened with any significant change.

Because of what happened to Faulkner, Fitzgerald, Hemingway, Steinbeck, etc., a whole generation of American writers came along believing that nothing in literary history is carved in stone, set in concrete. They learned the wrong lesson from their own immediate past; for now nothing seems so solid, secure, and untouchable as the literary pantheon as it is perceived by its supporters. The sense of revision and rediscovery has been transferred away from the contemporary scene and turned onto the redefinition of the Canon. (For a popular discussion of this, see "U.S. Literature: Canon under Siege," *New York Times,* January 6, 1988, p. 12.) The motives here are, of course, political and social as well as personal. (The personal element is for feminist and minority critics, for example, to find things to write about and to build profitable careers upon. And it is always somewhat easier to be an instant, natural-born gender or ethnicity expert than to be the master of an extensive and approved canon.) Thus, in terms of revisionism Hawthorne and Melville and Cooper are far more vulnerable than, say, Carver or Barthelme or Beattie. These latter are, at this time, contemporary mid-list authors. That is, they do not lose a great deal of money for their sponsoring publishers; but, at the same time, they do not, not directly at least, make much for the publisher either. Their star status is partly a matter of acknowledged quality and excellence and partly a matter of publicity and promotion. The ratio of these characteristics to each other would be an interesting subject for debate if there were any place (other than this one) for even discussing such things. Never mind. I expect most readers are willing to grant those three, and others, a measure of literary excellence even if they do not necessarily take them all to be self-evidently head and shoulders above, superior to any number, a goodly number, of others among their contemporaries. The most interesting thing, here, is that unlike Roth, Bellow, Walker Percy, etc., who somehow (though not without support and supporters) earned their status in the hierarchy, the next batch of writers (here merely *represented* by Carver, Beattie, Barthelme, as if by a decent law firm) were simply awarded that status by their publishers at the outset, their installation being confirmed by continued publicity.

The inevitable next step was to see if a writer could be championed by a publisher and turned into an early best-seller. What would happen if a publisher took a book by a "serious," "literary" writer and offered the kind of massive and expensive support that is usually reserved for Blockbuster authors? There are a number of recent examples of this kind of scheme. The rise to a certain kind of notoriety of Jay McInerney *(Bright Lights, Big City)* is a result of this kind of attention. So is the career of writer Richard Ford whose two most recent books, the novel *The Sportswriter* and the collection of stories *Rock Springs,* have been given the full contemporary publicity and promotional treatment by his editor (himself much publicized)—Gary Fisketjon. Between them, Ford and Fisketjon have succeeded in giving the writer a maximum "visibility." However, Fisketjon concedes that sales have not been, except in a strictly relative sense, extraordinary. Ford is certainly well known, a "name" now and, as well, has received the kind of prominent and prompt review attention that most American writers, even among the finest and most famous, never come to know. But the full apparatus of modem "exposure" could not quite bring out book buyers and readers in the numbers (yet) which would justify the expense and effort.

More impressive, more extraordinary, and, finally and in a deadly serious sense, far more dangerous to the declining, somewhat ambiguous integrity of American literary art, has been the story of "the Brat Pack." This is a story which also involves Fisketjon, as a principal mover and shaker, among others of the so-called Baby Editors who came into the limelight (a prominence once reserved for the likes of Maxwell Perkins and Saxe Commins) in the mid-1980s. Their latest task and challenge was at once somewhat more daunting and more cynical: to take a little group of writers—in this instance Bret Easton Ellis, Jill Eisenstadt, Tama Janowitz, and some others, all more or less in the shadow of Jay McInerney—writers of extremely limited literary talent, and somehow to sell them to the great unwashed American colonial reading public as literary celebrities and (maybe, all in due time) as at least spokespersons of their generation, if not as major literary figures and influences. What this involved was publicity, the beauty of it being that (at least in the view of the Baby Editors and their cohorts) today, as we drift into the inevitable decadence that haunts the ending of every century, it does not matter in the slightest whether the publicity be positive or negative, good or bad, the desired results will be more or less the same. The first stage proved remarkably successful. In a very short time any scholar worth his salt could have quickly put together a checklist of severely, often outrageously negative reviews in prominent places by prominent reviewers of the latest literary works of the Brat Pack. These could have then been added to an even longer list of articles about these authors as personalities, celebrities, *characters* and, as well, as social symbols of this and that, of something or other, in every kind of magazine you can think of, from the *Georgia Review* to *Vanity Fair, Gentlemen's Quarterly, People,* and the *New Yorker.* Conservative critics raged, the chic and trendy had campy good fun; but everybody mentioned the Brat Pack and usually spelled their names right. At first it was merely a whole lot of publicity, and (again) seemed to have no real effect on sales or reading habits. But, at last, by the end of 1987 the masterminds, the Baby Editors, had begun to sell some *books* on the basis of all that publicity. Whether anyone actually read or will read them remains to be seen. The important thing to note is that this late in our sad and bloody century when, it would seem, all the world would be at last more or less immune to the coarser, cruder, more vulgar and more obvious forms of hype, some cynical young people of less than (zero?) serious accomplishment could prove P. T. ("This Way to the Egress!") Barnum right as rain.

Truth is, these children of our century's old age did not invent

anything. Literary journalism was already in its place and functioning, like many other forms of contemporary journalism, more as
a matter of personalities and newsworthy events than matters of
art and life. Mailer, of course, had seen this whole thing coming,
plugged into the power of it and danced his little shocked and
shocking boogaloo in *Advertisements for Myself.* But it is hard to
believe that even *he* could have imagined a literary journalism
which would (in 1987) devote space, energy, even some thought to
such questions as the matter of Joni Evans departing from Simon
and Schuster (and, simultaneously, divorcing her boss and husband
there, Richard Snyder), going on to replace Howard Kaminsky (who
seems to have been fired over something about a party in Frank-
furt—who knows? cares?) at Random House. Then there was the
hue and cry and the counterattacks of the book reviewers when,
against overwhelming odds and well-laid plans (it seems), Larry
Heinemann won the National Book Award for his novel *Paco's Story.*
Much more space was spent on this argument than was ever (so far)
allotted to reviews of the novel. And there was so much else to write
about, to think about. There was the big J. D. Salinger lawsuit.
There was the final departure of Shawn and the arrival of Gottlieb
at the *New Yorker.* The rising and falling of certain smaller nations,
some minor wars and famines attracted less press attention than
that little episode. There were public accounts of odd little literary
quarrels. See, for instance, "Big Fight among the Little Magazines,"
the *New York Post* (June 22, 1987, p. 6), which tries to detail and
make some sense out of a battle between Robert Fogarty of *Antioch
Review,* Gordon Lish of the *Quarterly,* and Ben Sonnenberg of
Grand Street. In a roundup of important events and happenings of
1987, "Updates on '87," the *Washington Post* (December 31, 1987)
spent some time (as it and the *New York Times* had earlier spent a
good deal of time and space) considering the sad fate of a *book proposal* (!) by Joan Braden. (If you can publicize and review book pro-
posals, who needs to bother with books?) Equally important to the
Post was the case of Shere Hite, "the Sean Penn of the 1987 literary
circuit," whose latest opus, *Women and Love,* was one of the most
prominently reviewed and publicly discussed books of the year. In
fact, this may have been a moderately important story, for this was
a case which ran counter to the Brat Pack Caper. In spite of everything, it failed to live up to plans and expectations. A "Knopf insider" was quoted: "The general expectation is that publicity, good
or bad, generates sales. On this title, publicity generated sales but
not to the magnitude it should have."

The peak of literary journalism in 1987 was probably Rust Hills's
"*Esquire's* Guide to the Literary Universe" *(Esquire,* August 27, pp.

51-61), where Hills jumped aboard the bandwagon to celebrate the likes of (yes!) Gary Fisketjon, whom he declared ("The President Ordains the Bee to Be") to be "the only young editor in the business who has the power—and the inclination—to publish his contemporaries." Presumably Hills means people of Fisketjon's own age. Notice that there is no mention, not the slightest hint, of quality or excellence. Merely contemporaneity.

And that, ladies and gentlemen, is where we find ourselves as we stagger forward into the last decade of the century. What can be said of the American publishing scene in our time? That it has, in almost every way, reflected the vices and virtues of the society of which it is an odd part. That, at times and almost in spite of itself, it has allowed artists, master artists, to surface and to endure. That the great corruption, if not simply danger of the last half of the century has been the attempt on the part of the publishers to *create* (by fiat as much as fact) its own gallery of stars and master artists. That this last, while not an outright failure, for there are fine and gifted writers who have been championed by their publishers, is nevertheless not likely to improve the lot or situation of most American writers, either the discovered or undiscovered.

Nevertheless—witness this magazine, witness the incredible persistence of many small presses, the surprising success of many small regional publishers (Algonquin Books, for example)—there are other forces at work. Not the least of these is a strong new kind of regionalism in the nation, which, at the very least, goes counter to the effort to govern and control the whole country's taste from one great, dying city. And not the least force for the possible change, if not destruction of the (already) Old Order of things is technology. Even imaginable technological changes could easily constitute a revolution. But we are on the edge of almost unimaginable and surely unimagined changes which seem likely to make the whole present system of American publishing as quaintly old-fashioned as a medieval market fair. Let it come down, as the man said to Banquo.

Meantime, as if by magic alone, so many good and gifted, old and new American literary artists of all kinds carry on, often quite outside of the system. Perhaps it is appropriate to summon up magic at this point. It was no Brat or Baby Editor, but a genuine literary artist, R. V. Cassill, who has seen clearly a thing or two in a long lifetime and who said of our time: "I think we are at the end of an age, and the magicians have always appeared at the ends of ages."

First published in issue 8.3 (Fall 1988)

A Few Notes on Two of My Books

Kathy Acker

For weeks, months, now, I've been avoiding writing this: I have an almost uncontrollable desire not to talk about my writing. Why? If I had something to say about my writing outside my writing, something written which occurred outside my writing, my writing wouldn't be sufficient or adequate.

Everything is thrown into my writing.

I'll begin talking about someone else's writing. Living in England, I keep returning to American literature. That tradition. At this moment, to the books of William Burroughs. Unlike most of the writing in the contemporary novels of this country, Burroughs's writing is "immediate." "Immediate" has something to do with the sentence "I want to read something that means something to me." Most English contemporary novels, forgetting those of Ballard, bore me. At best, they entertain. But they don't talk to me. Burroughs never bores, for he and the other writers I think of as in "that tradition," "the other tradition," "the nonacceptable literary tradition," "the tradition of those books which were hated when they were written and subsequently became literary history," "the black tradition," "the tradition of political writing as opposed to propaganda" (de Sade would head this list) (here I am not talking about American literary tradition), do what Poe said a writer should do. They present the human heart naked so that our world, for a second, explodes into flames. This human heart is not only the individual heart: the American literary tradition of Thoreau, Emerson, even Miller, presents the individual and communal heart as a unity. Any appearance of the individual heart is a political occurrence.

Writers such as Burroughs, Selby, etc., have always been attacked on personal rather than on literary grounds.

"Marginal," "experimental," and "avant-garde" are often words used to describe texts in this other tradition. Not because writing such as Burroughs's or Genet's is marginal, but because our society, through the voice of its literary society, cannot bear immediacy, the truth, especially the political truth.

I've never been sure about the need for literary criticism. If a work is immediate enough, alive enough, the proper response isn't to be academic, to write about it, but to use it, to go on. By using each other, each other's texts, we keep on living, imagining, making, fucking, and we fight this society of death.

But I'm a good girl: I was told to write about my own texts so I shall do so.

In 1979 I wrote "New York City in 1979," published by Anne Turyn in her series named "Top Stories." In this short story I did two things. First, I took my present environment, the Lower East Side in New York City, and described it, its society. I hated the life which I was living at that time; I hated the society; I didn't differentiate between the two. I thought that if my friends and our society didn't find a way for adequate change, we would die and quickly. Some of us did die. I wanted radical change, however it had to come. At the same time I was aware that writing changes nothing on the larger political scale. One reason for this, of course, is that those who are most oppressed are often either illiterate or rarely read. Literature, especially novels, is written by and for the owning or the educated populace. Here is one reason why the novel is one of the most conservative art forms in our century. I wanted change, but I had no adequate tools or weapons. I was, at best, a writer.

If writing cannot and writing must change things, I thought to myself, logically of course, writing *will* change things magically. Magic operates metaphorically. So: I will take one text, New York City, the life of my friends, and change this text by placing another text on top of it.

I do know that writing or making is magic. I'm not referring to "magic realism."

As my second text, I took a story about Charles Baudelaire and Jeanne Duval. I believe, a true story. Jeanne Duval had been an incredibly beautiful black woman. Baudelaire gave her syphilis and then fell in love with her. Baudelaire said in his notebook in 1846:

Her beauty has vanished under the dreadful crust of smallpox, like foliage under the ice of winter. Still moved by her long sufferings and the fits of the disease, you gaze sadly at the ineffaceable stigmata on the beloved convalescent's body; suddenly you hear echoing in your eyes a dying tune executed by the raving bow of Paganini, and this sympathetic tune speaks to you of yourself, seems to describe your whole inner poem of lost hopes. Thenceforth the traces of smallpox will be part of your happiness.

Here was a model of change: ugliness changed through worse ugliness, even destruction, into love.

I placed the second text on top of the first text, crudely. You do what you have to do however you have to do it.

For me, the myth of Daedalus defines fiction, literature. According to Robert Graves, Daedalus was a highly skilled craftsman. His king, Minos of Cretan Cnossus, honored him until he learned that

Daedalus had helped his (Minos's) wife fuck a white bull. Then Minos made Crete Daedalus's prison.

Daedalus escaped prison by his art. He made wings for himself and his son. His son got too high, flew too high, soared into the sun, and drowned.

Art is this certain kind of making. A writer makes reality, a writer is a kind of journalist, a magic one.

Does "make" mean "create"?

When I was about fifteen and living in New York City, I had a boyfriend, P. Adams Sitney, who was making films, working at the Mekas's Film Co-Op, and editing his own film magazine. He introduced me to Jackson MacLow, Robert Kelly, and to the work of Charles Olson. At the time I felt confused, that I was understanding nothing, but something must have filtered in. Robert Kelly and his first wife, Joby, were painting Pound's dictum "MAKE IT NEW" on stones, poundstones. I'm not sure if my memories are historically valid; I never am. I remember that Robert Creeley taught that a writer, a poet, is a real writer when he (or she) finds his own voice. (Back then, "he" was important enough to include "she.")

When I was either twenty or twenty-one, I again moved away from New York City, back to San Diego where I had done my last two years of college and first two years of graduate school. I apprenticed myself to David Antin. That is, I sat on his doorstep and babysat for his kid. Blaise, the kid, and I got along great. Our favorite game was "Criminals"; a sample question: "Would you rather hold up a small bank in Kentucky or poison a rich creep who's already dying?" "MAKE IT NEW." I wanted to be a writer; I didn't want to do anything else; but I couldn't find my own voice. The act of writing for me was the most pleasurable thing in the world. Just writing. Why did I have to find my own voice and where was it? I hated my fathers.

These old feelings, questionings, and intuitions in me have done nothing but grow. I now wonder where the idea or the ideology of creativity started. Shakespeare and company certainly stole from, copied each other's writings. Before them, the Greeks didn't bother making up any new stories. I suspect that the ideology of creativity started when the bourgeoisie—when they rose up in all their splendor, as the history books put it—made a capitalistic marketplace for books. Today a writer earns money or a living by selling copyright, ownership to words. We all do it, we writers, this scam, because we need to earn money, only most don't admit it's a scam. Nobody *really* owns nothing. Dead men don't fuck.

There's another part to this argument. For a while, back in my early days of writing, I looked for a voice, a self. I placed "true" autobiography next to "false" autobiography. I learned two things. First, in fiction, there is no "true" or "false" in social-realist terms. Fiction is "true" or real when it makes. Second, if there is a self, it isn't Hegel's subject or the centralized phallic I/eye. If there is a self, it's probably the world. All is real. When I placed "true" autobiography next to "false" autobiography, everything was real. Phallic identity's another scam that probably had to do with capitalistic ownership.

Fiction is magic because everything is magic: the world is always making itself. When you make fiction, you dip into this process. But no one, writer or politician, is more powerful than the world: you can make, but you don't create. Only the incredible egotism that resulted from a belief in phallic centricism could have come up with the notion of creativity.

Of course, a woman is the muse. If she were the maker instead of the muse and opened her mouth, she would blast the notion of poetic creativity apart.

When I copy, I don't "appropriate." I just do what gives me most pleasure: write. As the Gnostics put it, when two people fuck, the whole world fucks.

In his introduction to *Imaginary Magnitude,* Stanislaw Lem talks about this "cult of the new," about modernism. We were promised, he says, that by following out the new, we could, traversing varying geographies, arrive at landscapes never before seen. We could learn what wasn't before known and, perhaps, the unknowable. In actuality, by following the "cult of the new," we have exchanged "one old, spontaneous, and therefore unconscious bondage for a new one"; we have not "cut the fetters," but have made freedom into a law.

"I myself," Lem continues, "crave a different basis for heresy and rebellion."

What basis? Right now, Lem argues, art is on the point of being totally useless, of not being, for we are living in a society that marginalizes, distrusts both art and its artists. We are also living in a society that seems bent on its own self-destruction. Though Lem is speaking about the other side of what used to be the "Iron Curtain," he could well be speaking about our world.

Unfortunately, our society's self-destruction would involve us. So the artist finds himself or herself in a peculiar position. The artist doesn't need to find out the limits of his or her medium, to "make it new"; the artist, though politically and socially powerless, marginalized, must find the ways for all of our survival.

Method has become supremely, politically important. For example, the novelist who writes about the poor Cambridge vicar who can't deal with his homosexuality is giving us no tools for survival. Whereas William Burroughs's writing methods, his uses of psychic research, are weapons in the fight for our own happiness.

When I began writing my most recently published novel, *Empire of the Senseless,* I heard myself saying to myself, repeatedly: "You can't change this society. You know this. The fucking hippies didn't change anything; maybe it's worse now even than in the McCarthy days. But despair stinks. Living every day by wanting to die. How can happiness be possible in this society?"

When I wrote my first book, *Politics,* I was living in a society that was politically and socially hypocritical. According to the media back then, politicians were men who said sweet things to babies and neither adultery nor drug abuse ever came near a middle-class white American home.

Perhaps our society is now in a "post-cynical" phase. Certainly, I thought as I started *Empire,* there's no more need to deconstruct, to take apart perceptual habits, to reveal the frauds on which our society's living. We now have to find somewhere to go, a belief, a myth. Somewhere real. In *Rebel without a Cause* the kids are desperately looking for a place so they can live.

Empire of the Senseless is my first attempt to find a myth, a place, not the myth, the place.

As it was being written this book divided itself into three sections. The first part, "Elegy for the World of the Fathers," is a description of the society which is defined by the oedipal taboo. The oedipal myth, after all, is not only one story out of many, but also just part of one myth, the Theban cycle.

To learn how the oedipal society looks, I turned to several texts, mainly to those by the Marquis de Sade and by Freud. Freud, for obvious reasons. At one point I was going to give all my characters the names of Freud's patients. (Only Dr. Shreber survived.) Anything for a bad joke. To the Marquis de Sade because he shed so much light on our Western sexual politics that his name is still synonymous with an activity more appropriately named "Reaganism." Something of that sort. As I've said, I never write anything new.

In "Alone," the second part of *Empire,* I tried to describe a society not defined by the oedipal taboo. That is, by phallic centricity and total domination on the political, economic, social, and personal levels. Some of my texts for this section were ones by Jean Genet and Pierre Guyotat, for both these writers, perhaps partly because of their sexualities, have described other than oedipal relationships. Have described different nexes between power, sexuality, and politics. Guyotat's writing was influenced by his experiences in the Algerian war. I thought, as I wrote this section, that today, as the "Great Powers," as they were formerly known, meet and meld economically, then culturally, as more and more of the known world goes Coca-Cola and McDonald's, only the Muslim world resists. A

French friend of mine who frequently travels to South Africa just told me that one town which he often visits ten years ago had twenty churches and one mosque. Today, the opposite is true. I thought, for Westerners today, for us, the other is now Muslim. In my book, when the Algerians take over Paris, I have a society not defined by the oedipal taboo.

As I wrote this second part, I learned that it is impossible to have, to live in a hypothetical, not utopian but perhaps freer, society if one does not actually inhabit such a world. One must be where one is. The body does not lie. Language, if it is not propaganda or media blab, is the body; with such language lies are not possible. If lies were possible, there would be no reason to write fiction. Specifically, I live in a world which is at least partly defined by the multinationals, the CIA, etc. Nowhere else. So the CIA kept invading the Paris in *Empire;* for this section I used various journalistic texts. As I put these texts together, I realized, as I did years ago, that the hippies had been mistaken: they had thought that they could successfully oppose American postcapitalism by a lie, by creating a utopian society. But the body is real: if one, anyone, lives in hell, one is hell. Dualisms such as good/evil are not real and only reality works.

By the end of "Alone" I found myself at the end of the second part of a dialectical argument. I was back to my original question: In a society defined by phallic centricism or by prison, how is it possible to be happy?

The last section of *Empire* begins with the text of *Huckleberry Finn,* one of the main texts about freedom in American culture. I make nothing new, create nothing: I'm a sort of mad journalist, a journalist without a paid assignment. Twain was obsessed with racism; me, with sexism.

After having traveled through innumerable texts, written texts, texts of stories which people had told or shown me, texts found in myself, *Empire* ended with the hints of a possibility or beginning: the body, the actual flesh, almost wordless, romance, the beginning of a movement from no to yes, from nihilism to myth.

If I had made up this journey, it wouldn't have interested me. Critics have often accused me, and sometimes even my writings, when they distinguish between the two, of being violent, and worse. I make up nothing: I am a reader and take notes on what I read. Whether it's good writing or bad by academic standards doesn't interest me. It never has. What is, simply is as it is. Of course I am interested in learning, in what I don't know, understanding, and if this is the "MAKE IT NEW" that Pound meant, then I subscribe to that tradition.

First published in issue 9.3 (Fall 1989)

A *Small Biography of*
The Obscene Bird of Night

José Donoso

In a 1981 newspaper interview, Gabriel García Márquez was quoted as saying that his newly published novel, *Chronicle of a Death Foretold,* was his best up to then. Bypassing the arrogance of this statement, which may or may not be correct, I should be excused for rather doubting it, not only because I know García Márquez, but because I fear authors are generally the worst judges of their own work. It is emotional conundrums that determine their opinion, plus editorial policy, plus mere stage fright, which blur the clarity of their assessments. Even more than that, let me start this chat off by stating my opinion that the novelist is always the poorest critic of his own novels.

I know that the name of Henry James will at once be brandished at me. But when I say "poorest" I use that word advisedly, stressing its connotation of "limited" rather than that of "bad." I only want to express my opinion that when a novelist speaks of his own art, he tends to show us no more than a shaving or two of his conscious intention while creating his work, at most to exhibit a couple of the wheels he was aware of setting in motion to operate his machinery, always far more complex than what he can surmise. This does not happen, of course, when the author is off guard, in his diaries, say, or his letters, like Flaubert and Virginia Woolf, who describe the pain and the drudgery and the glory of it all. But, diary and letter-writing being things of the past, one has a sinking feeling that future generations will have no firsthand material to reconstruct the life, the intention, and the work of the artist. I, an addict of diary, biography, and letters, fear that newspaper articles and interviews will never fill that void. A whole dimension of what writing is will then be lost; the picture of the artist at work, what he put in or left out, will become dim, and no one will care or even know what it is and how it feels, and how the writer goes about the task of creating a work aspiring to at least a modicum of eternity.

Yet I have to acknowledge that a novelist is hardly ever able to illuminate his novel from without it, as a student would, or a critic. When an author analyzes his own work, the result is, more often than not, that we are left with a disarray of fragments rather than with the structured universe of the metaphor. We believe a writer when he is on his own turf. But is self-criticism, is criticism, his own turf? Isn't it true that he is poaching in somebody else's? The feeling I am generally left with is flat, without projection, mostly plain preening.

The feeling of frustration which I have when reading a writer on his own writing is because, in the first place, all serious writing is an exercise in lucidity, even if we are talking of the work of Burroughs or of Raymond Roussel. Personally I prefer those novels which impress upon me the reality of the author's effort to reach the outer limits of lucidity, where he sets free the wild beast of metaphor on an uncharted path. I find in pages thus written the "whole" of the writer's self, conscious and unconscious, intelligence and imagination and sensibility and cultural references, memories and taste, past, present, and future, cast into one mold, and projected. The canvas for this "wholeness" may be tiny, as in the case of Jane Austen: but in her pages, there she is, complete with what she herself called her "elegance of mind": a mean eye for the absurd, calculating, funny, playful, and, at the end of her life, rather sad. Or it can be huge, a whole universe unto itself, such as Tolstoy's, whose projection of his "wholeness" is as boundless as Russian history and the horizon of the steppes. The thing is that both developed very distinct literary "voices": tone, diction, subject matter, vocabulary, intelligence, passion or the lack of it, style, and all the rest, cast into what Kafka himself once called "a universe which becomes an object of art," placed outside the author, unassailable by the author himself once that universe is complete.

When I say that it is desirable—not to say exciting—that the "wholeness" of the writer should be evoked in his work, I don't mean to set myself up as a champion of "literary sincerity," a quality which I feel unnecessary to good writing. I believe that quite often a literary voice is a mask or a disguise, adopted in order to make it act as go-between, a messenger from the writer to the public. A writer cannot approach his public with "naturalness." This is a latter-day affectation, popular among second-rate American writers, and stemming, perhaps, from the realist, tough-guy tradition in U.S. writing. But even their voices are essentially adopted, chosen, masks, disguises, affectations: I don't think that anyone today would be so bold as to claim that Hemingway's voice was not full of mannerisms, tough-guy pose and all. His case is extreme in one way; as Virginia Woolf's antennalike sensibility of voice would be exactly the same at the opposite extreme. In every case, the voice chosen, adopted, found, forged, contrived, manufactured, is the very essence of literature, the very flesh of it, since the quest for a distinct literary voice or the laborious manufacturing of one, lies at the center of a writer's endeavor: it is his most important creation, the most radiant at the same time as the most misty of all his metaphors. Artifice, to be sure: but Kafka, again, in his *Letters to Felice,* says: "If one is not able to lead a beautiful and perfect life, one has to create artifices." The voice adopted is the most powerful of the writer's artifices.

To get at a writer's innards, the critic should analyze his voice more than anything else in his pages. Why does Virginia Woolf use semicolons with such maddening frequency? Why are Hemingway's sentences so clipped, yet, taken together, in spite of their demand to be received as something simple, spell out a rhythm and rhyme which is sometimes so sumptuous? Why is Carlos Fuentes's prose overspiced with cultural references which often seem irrelevant, but which belong to the *tessitura* of his voice? It is his distinct literary voice that limits and gives shape and significance, at the deepest level, to a writer's work, and it sets loose the eagle of his fantasy—or the sparrow; or the hummingbird—and it is what, in short, stands in place of the author and contains him. This ring of wholeness in a literary voice, no matter what its limitations or size, is what I personally want of good writing.

There are, of course, what one could call generic voices, the voice of a period, of a culture or subculture, of a social milieu. This is true, I think, of the second-rank French novelists of the beginning of this century, Barrès and Anatole France, say. It is also true of American novelists not of the first rank, who harbor a strong prejudice against anything so "phony" as "adopting" a voice which may not seem colloquial, sincere, "natural," a rejection of language as mask or disguise, of nontraditional form or subject matter as something difficult to grasp and identify with for the reading public. This is the reason why a writer like Faulkner has receded into the classroom, a subject for studies by Ph.D. candidates rather than forming part, as in the near past, of the excitement of live culture. Harriet de Onís, light-years away from the present, rejected *Coronation,* my first novel, for the house of Knopf, on the grounds that "the reader doesn't know what side the author is on," and went on to say that "the same thing is true of Faulkner; but Faulkner is great *in spite* of this, not for this reason." What happened is that she distrusted or was not able to pick out my voice—such as it was—and understand it as a metaphor containing energy-charged particles, which under scrutiny could reveal a structure and thus a system of values.

But even the most sophisticated writers, Carlos Fuentes for instance, when he writes about his own literary voice at the level of adopted metaphor or as metaphor that the unconscious has forced upon the writer, seldom see it as an "artifice." They tend to confuse themselves with that voice, as something almost biological, socio-logical, never a device, a disguise, a willful limitation. This confu-sion of personal self with literary voice gives the impression that the frightened author wants to jump right back into his created per-sona, into the literary work which he had separated from himself, giving it a life of its own. When taking that voice apart for the ben-efit of his public, he is compelled to justify it, doesn't want it out there, as a metaphor with a life of its own and possessing its own uncontrollable energy and luminosity. Because like all metaphors, and chief among them, the literary voice is uncontrollable. When effective, it is a powerful piece of machinery which recycles nature and the experience and the imagination of an author, transforming it into something which only *that* voice and no other can structure and project, and which bears its stamp. This voice, when of superb quality, is larger and more radiant than the author's consciousness, bearing more meanings and projections than anything that author can express in a language other than that of his metaphor: when this voice reaches the outer limits of lucidity, in other words when it is successful as literature.

Once a novel is written and encased in the limits of its lucidity the author becomes totally foreign to it, at least, let me tell you this quite clearly before I proceed further, that this is my experience: the wild beast is out on the prowl to devour other creatures by moon-light; the Bengal light which illuminates the object created and at least a part of the surrounding darkness blinds him, or at least me.

Thus, an author's attempt to approach his own creation from without and take it apart with the tools of a critic is generally no more than a sample of his narcissism: "Remarks are not literature," Gertrude Stein is reported to have said, and criticism is remarks, opinion, evaluation, discernment. One must never forget to distrust an author talking about his own work. His approach to his own work from without is no more valuable—and certainly less authori-tative—than what the critics and the reading public will offer. I feel very strongly that by writing a novel one loses it and a great part of oneself, and all access both to that work and to the part of the writer that went into it becomes closed, all attempts at further pertinent insight seem banal and repetitious. Thus for the author the finished novel is an object of lambent shadows, a thing foreign, suspect, re-doubtable, strange, and finally, inert. An odd sensation to be sure which sometimes borders on repugnance, but this has been my ex-perience, for what it's worth.

I don't want to say an author should never write about his own work, taking a stance different to that of the creator. On the con-trary, one of the many pleasures of authorship is the license to say what one pleases about oneself. The result is more often than not redundant and quite beside the point. But why should I deny myself the modest pleasures of redundancy and irrelevance? A novel is, besides many other things, a story. What could conceivably be useful, or at least amusing, would be to append to that story a kind of biography of it: not *what* it is or what it is *meant* to be but *how* it all happened. Thus, a clutter of rattling trailers could become attached to the rear end of the sleek racing car that is a good novel and make it, perhaps, less forbidding. In any case, I don't doubt that the critics will take these trailers apart, place them in a different order, eliminate a few with their monkey wrenches and other suspect but I fancy necessary tools.

After this introduction, which I fear has been far too long but will at least justify what I want to say now, I'd like to tell you a bit about how *The Obscene Bird of Night* happened to me. This novel, which took me about eight years to write, is one and the same in my memory with the experience of pain and disease. This is not always the case with my novels, several of which are in my memory one with pleasure, no matter how somber their tone and subject matter. I'm not excessively clear as to what I mean by this, just as I'd be hard put to define exactly what I mean by a literary "voice," though I could give examples if we came down to the perusal of texts. Nevertheless, there they are, aren't they, these words? I've picked them up in the air while I write, all of them suggestions, approaches, rather hazy and I hope radiant metaphors which stand in place of, and mean more than, what it is my intention to convey.

As a little boy I was skinny and a bit bookish and shy, and quite frail. When I was about two years old I had some kind of sickness which made me mope a lot, the name of which, though I believe quite common, goes unrecorded in the annals of my family. I took a long time to recover: what did it was an enlightened doctor who told my parents that they should repaper my nursery with brighter wallpaper, and that my mother, while taking care of me, should try to look as pretty as possible and wear the nicest clothes.

My brothers claim that I've made all this up to start my autobiography on a dignified footing. What they don't realize is that if untrue, it is no lie, only a fantasy born in my unconscious to explain an early vocation for harmony and poetical if not literal truth. But in the clearinghouse of my memory, at the period when memory and fantasy are confused, pain and beauty seemed to go hand in hand. I also have a fantasy that it was a sickness called croup, which kept me from speaking for a while and gave me coughing fits, so you see, I may now be talking of voice, coupled with sickness and beauty and pain, because at a very early age I may have feared not to be able to find my own voice.

As I say, I was quite frail as an adolescent, nearsighted and bad at sports. In order to stay away from compulsory sports in the school I went to, I invented a pain in my stomach which, when examined, was diagnosed as the beginning of an ulcer. This disease put me outside the common run of my schoolmates since I was excused from sports and had to lie down after lunch while the others were kicking the football about. I learned the delights of being a person "different," *hors de serie* as the French say, and fantasizing that because I was sick—because there was a flaw in me, which to begin with I'd made up—I was superior. That, I guess, was my first successful piece of fiction; I had cheated the grown-ups, especially my father who was a doctor, and this made me superior to him: the theme of the reverse of power. I could never imagine at that point (I was thirteen) what huge meaning this fictional ulcer would assume later in my biography. It was also my first successful disguise and consequently the first successful "voice" which I could really call mine.

Adolescence was conflictive and difficult; so was early manhood when I began to want to write seriously. But every time I tried it, involuntary pains appeared exactly where the feigned ones had earlier been. Pain no longer seemed an ally: it was an enemy which de facto spoiled my health and separated me in some kind of real way from boys like me. Some years later a duodenal ulcer was diagnosed by X rays: fiction and disguise, which I had early chosen for myself, had become my reality and replaced what others deemed my "true" self. I had to assume the burden of pain so early invented as a subterfuge for reality: this was real. It was burrowing at my innards with a cruel beak of pain, this disguised, diseased self was my true self, a young man whose self-inflicted illness had turned him into an outcast, a derelict. It was a metaphor. It was a voice. And as I got off a bus with my first book of short stories under my arm to take to the leading Chilean literary critic, I fell in a dead faint and was taken to the hospital with my first bleeding ulcer.

About eight years after that I got married. We took a house in the country, small and cozy but quite primitive, and I decided that I was finally going to write a great novel. I had just read Cortázar, Fuentes, Carpentier, Rosario Castellanos, and I was all up in flames about them. I had just finished translating Isak Dinesen into Spanish and her wonder filled me. I told my wife with affected scorn: "I'm not one of these complicated new writers. I want to write a simple, short, straightforward fable." There was a yellow bitch roaming around the house, whining at night and scratching at doors to be let in during the hours of our intimacy, but her presence then passed unnoticed, though it was picked up a year later. But since the yellow bitch is a sort of thread running through the whole of *The Obscene Bird of Night,* I'm not too sure that it was not that skinny, scruffy, hateful beast that determined, right from the start, what my voice would be while spending all those eight years writing it. She started it all. Though I did not know it then, she was my voice.

What did surprise me was that as I sat down to write without a subject in my head, something completely unimportant which I thought forgotten forever, a tiny scrap of an anecdote of my not too distant past, sprang back into my imagination with a bound, offering itself as subject. I suddenly remembered the following: I stood with a friend at a street corner in downtown Santiago chattering away. We became so absorbed in our conversation that we neglected to cross the street with the green light. There was a car waiting for his green light right beside us while we talked and as we continued our chatter I looked into that luxurious limousine: a handsome, blond, liveried chauffeur sat at the wheel, while in the back seat I saw a wreck of a young man, beautifully turned out in an expensive-looking three-piece suit, his face a map of scars, dwarflike, hare-lipped, hunchbacked, deformed. The car after a minute went on its way with the green light and my friend and I went on to lunch, talking all the time. I did not draw my friend's attention to that strange, luxurious car. I never talked about it. And because I did not, I guess the memory sank to the bottom of my mind where I forgot it, only to float back up again for no apparent reason—or had that yellow bitch something to do with it?—when I started off my simple, short parable about a father who has a deformed son, and is so proud that he shuts him up in a house surrounded by monsters more deformed than himself. Those who have read *The Obscene Bird of Night* know just how short and how simple this fable is.

The fable grew apace. The yellow bitch scratched at the door of our bridal bedchamber and yelped by the window at night. I did not let her into my story because I did not yet know she not only belonged there, but that her cowering misery and scruffiness, her hunger and that servile look in her hateful eye, would eventually be the voice on which to string all the other motifs that were to come.

The ulcer pains began again. I was building a beautiful, roomy white house, its space full of light and the reflections of the lazy flutter of greenery. Pain struck at my bowels as soon as I sat down at my writing table: the pain was, indeed, an enemy, and to dream up the relation between my new house and my new novel, both of which were spaces created by me which were growing, I had to work against the powerful current of that pain which carried me down with it. The pain became so great that I had to quit my job as a journalist. I wrote in longhand in bed. But by quitting my job I became quite poor, unable to keep my beautiful house.

Yet, I remember that initial period of writing without a well-defined direction, of spreading myself out in the quiet of my new house without more work to do than write, as a happy period, notwithstanding the pain and the poverty. I thought back on my life. I wrote on in my fable, then called *El último Azcoitía* (The Last Azcoitía). I gave Don Jerónimo and his wife the face, the stance, the pride of a couple I was friendly with. Not only that: this couple, in my imagination, were not only perfect but *superior* to me; and I fancied that at the bottom of their hearts they despised me. It was this feeling of being despised by them that crept into the novel nowthere was no Humberto Peñaloza yet—giving the fable a new character. It was as if the initial monster seen in the car in downtown Santiago had been an inert cancer tumor and suddenly it had these metastases, the feeling of being inferior to my derelict friends. I wrote their faces into the pages I was then doing. They are by no means "portraits" in any sense of the word. Nobody is ever a "portrait" in any of my novels. Neither is a depicted physical space—a house, say, or a brothel—a replica of reality. But the way my imagination works is to pick out an emotionally charged person or space from reality, plant it in the place I need it in my imagination, and then train my imagination over as if it were a creeper, and the "real" person or space only a tutor: the tutor eventually becomes smothered by the creeper and doesn't show at all, but there, beneath the leaves, it holds the whole thing together. I'd say, pretty sure not to be wrong, that this tutor-creeper method is what I've used in most of my books. In most cases I've forgotten what or who the original tutor was. In the case of Iris Mateluna, for instance, the "tutor" was a girl I saw one evening in a back street in Santiago during no more than a minute as she passed by. My Iris Mateluna is surely very different from what that girl was, though to write about her, even to contradict her, I had to plant her image, that tutor, in my mind.

The recaptured image of Boy in his limousine produced multiple metastases: arrogance of parents who kept him so well tended, privilege, and everything that the Chilean oligarchy has. It was easy to fill out everything pertaining to Jerónimo and Inés—to my friend and his wife—with the attributes of the Chilean patriciate. I felt that things were really happening when I finally wrote the yellow bitch—a year later, perhaps? once we left our first little country house?—into the story, especially in her relation to Inés. And when we moved into our new house I found that I had to move my characters into a house of their own. I surrounded them with a house called in reality La Rinconada, the estate of an ancient spinster who kept a literary salon. I used to hear the dogs barking at night in her park outside my window. But it was not *those* dogs that barked and whined: it was really, all of them, the yellow bitch.

In this case the tutor—the real Rinconada—though widely different from the fictional one, defined a lot in the growth of my characters and atmosphere. The total lack of social justice, these serfs, these peons, were governed by this frail lady who practically owned them: in those days before the advent of the transistor radio, she refused to have electricity installed in her estate because then the peons would buy radios and they would hear about what the "outside" was like. The universe, then, defined by the "real" Rinconada was divided into two: the "outside" and the "inside," which is, again, a motif that runs through not only *The Obscene Bird of Night,* but through all of my books.

All the while I was writing and writing and writing without direction an accumulation of motifs which, notwithstanding the yellow bitch and the radiance that she cast, were left unstrung. I was horrified at how complicated it had all grown in a year or two and how encased I was by it, how impossible it became to write anything else. Just layers and layers and layers of Jerónimo, Inés, La Rinconada, and Boy. They were static. I could not go on or get out.

One night a friend and I were coming back from the beach in his car, and we ran over a drunken hobo and killed him. We took his body to the police station but they found no identification on him. No one in the surrounding countryside had ever seen him before. He was like an apparition dissolved at the very moment it flares up, nameless, penniless, almost naked such were the rags he was wearing, ageless, eternal.

I went instinctively home to my parents. There I told Nana about this death and she, so strong, began to cry. I must explain that Nana was the servant who brought us all up. She was born in my grandfather's farm, traveled as a maid to Europe with relations, and my grandmother sent her to keep an eye on my mother's probably unreliable housekeeping. She embodied the earth, the far reaches of our country and continent, the class of people whom we, from the protected middle class, would never be able to fathom or do justice to, the mystery of a race apart. Yet not quite apart. She bore a surname related to my family. Had she been born, then, or had her father been born—she made it quite clear that though she was dark her father had had blue eyes—a bastard to a gentleman of my blood? Quite possibly. It happened very frequently in Chile in those days. Nana did not know how to read or write. To this very day I cannot understand why this extremely intelligent and sensitive woman, in our home which was full of books, was never taught how to read, neither by my parents nor by ourselves who loved her. It's a feeling of guilt I have had to live with. She was the pillar of our home. Nana took close care of us, three brothers, was tender, funny, wise. Later, on many occasions, it was her counsel and her thrift and tact which kept the family going. My mother died four years ago in the same house where I was born. My father died one year ago in the same place. When he died our old house was torn down. But Nana lived on in my brother's house, funny and wise and useful until she was ninety and almost blind, occupying a corner of that kitchen with her presence and her stories while peeling a potato so as not to feel useless. For a while we had lived in another house in the old section of town, and there as a very young boy I had seen countless old women like Nana doing their little, undetermined jobs, telling their stories, engaged in their work and their strifes, or crouched over a brazier in winter, sipping maté tea, a cat or a pet hen nestling in their laps to keep them warm. Nana was all those old women, those old women were forcing themselves onto my pages with my feeling of mystery, of vulnerability, of fear, that the consciousness of social guilt provides.

She had had an offshoot: when I told her of the hobo we had run over and she began to cry, she said that she was crying because that man was surely her brother who had run away from her parents' home when he was a boy and had never been heard from again. It was an allusion to her past, to a private history and private pains we had not heard of before, connecting her with this derelict, with the nameless many whom she came from bringing with her that particular history. This motivated in me a passion—which I had also felt as a young boy when I played hooky—for roaming about the outskirts of the poorer districts of Santiago, the rubble piles and the shanties, and the abandoned projects of parks, with stunted trees no one took care of, where hoboes lived. I talked to them. I became one of them. The hobo had always been one of the images which appeared and reappeared in my psychoanalysis. It was the unarmed man, the defeated man, the man who has nothing so he cannot be afraid of anything since he can't come lower. I read a lot of Dostoyevsky when I was younger and some Gorky. But it was this feeling of a vast "outside" to which I had no access and which was embodied by Nana and the old cronies of the Casa de Ejercicios, and Nana's brothers, and the hoboes I saw and followed but never talked to, just drank them in with my eyes and my imagination, which now became the center of a vast series of visions and fantasies which I began writing about. Thousands of pages were covered with script, discarded or torn up. The man we had run over and

Nana's tears pointed to a new direction. I thought I had abandoned *El último Azcoitía* and was now writing rather desperately a completely different novel.

But people from one novel began visiting the other. The central crony in the novel of *miserabilismo* [a noun made out of the adjective "miserable"—Ed.] became the nanny in the novel of pride. From this novel, one day in a museum Don Jerónimo meets Humberto Peñaloza and makes him his secretary. The bitch began to whine in both novels. The monsters invade the novel of the convent, and so forth. It was like watercolors running into each other until I could no longer make out which was which, what stood where, what belonged in which. The years went by and with the years, an ulcer pain that I could not get rid of: it was the bitch gnawing and I used to call that pain "the yellow bitch" in my conversations with my wife.

We moved out of Chile. I left most of the papers referring to my novel behind, that is to say, to my two novels. But in Mexico the urge to write was huge, the desire to complete something, the eagerness to publish mounted. What I did was just sort of cut a limb off of the very heavy tree of *The Obscene Bird* and plant it. It was no more than a paragraph, but one of those radiant paragraphs which one sometimes achieves, containing a whole world unto itself, ten, fifteen lines which I tore off the big novel then called *El último Azcoitía,* and which I fashioned into *Hell Has No Limits* in two months of uncontrolled, mad, effervescent enthusiasm.

I owe a great deal to this little novel. In the first place, it showed me that I could begin, write, and finish a book, which was something I had begun to doubt after turning around in circles with *El último Azcoitía.* In the second, I found that I could use the elastic forms of pronouns with varying points of view and accent to what seemed to me great advantage. Third, I felt that every piece of my "big" novel was bursting with life and it was fertile. Fourth, and perhaps more importantly than anything else, I found out that disguise is voice.

I wrote at once another shortish novel and went on to teach at Iowa for two years. But they were barren years, delightful, easy, and although I felt terribly frustrated because I could not write one single word during those two years, I believe at the end I came out a winner. At the end of two years I realized that for me teaching and writing fiction did not work together—as it did for Kurt Vonnegut, who taught at the same college at the same time I did, and wrote one of his best novels there—and no matter how cozy the fastness of an American university, *I had to get out.* Which we did, and went to Spain.

There our daughter was born a few months after our arrival. And we proceeded to Mallorca, where we wanted her to spend the first years of her life in the sunny Mediterranean. Mallorca was chosen because Spain in those days was cheap to live in, and the little money which I had saved would last me about a year. I read *One Hundred Years of Solitude, Pedro Paramo, The Time of the Hero, Conversation in The Cathedral,* and very specially *The Green House,* which was a book that then filled me with wonder. It must have been while reading some of this stuff that somehow, again from way, way back, from the patios filled with old servants and braziers of my childhood, with aunts doing charity and remembering the good old days, from that distance welled up, as I opened my *Obscene Bird* papers recently arrived from Chile to start on that novel again, the image of the "imbunche," the legend of the "chonchón" which I remembered having heard but had forgotten when spending summer on my family's farms down by the Rio Maule. I remembered witchcraft. I remembered poverty, the usual derelicts. And the whole legend of the old witch-nanny and the landowner and his children and his daughter rose up within me in a matter of days onto paper, the yellow bitch following them and screaming. This legend I made up. There is no such legend in Chile that I know of. And later, I have tried to inquire, but it doesn't exist. I made it up from elements of myth which lay at my fingertips, and by creating it I welded all those disparate universes into one: the novel had acquired a voice. Still, the ulcer pain was too great to write. I spent months in bed. An operation was not advised because, it being a disease of nervous origin, it would come back soon. I wrote and wrote, layers upon layers, I had the shape and voice of the novel in my head but could not get it on paper. I told my wife I would burn everything and start another novel from scratch. She said, wise girl that she is: "Don't burn it. If you do, it will all stay inside you and you'll never get rid of it." So I didn't burn it. But we were by then out of money. So I accepted a quarter's teaching job at Fort Collins, Colorado.

A week after my arrival in Colorado, having left my wife and child back in Mallorca, I had an ulcer hemorrhage and had to have an instant operation. This episode was, perhaps, the turning point in the writing of *The Obscene Bird of Night.* Sickness and pain. A feeling of impotence, of inferiority, of incapability, above all when confronted with writing, as things had shown. Now the element of madness was added. For during and after the operation I was given painkillers, morphine, to which I am apparently allergic, and went into an incredible bout of madness—a trip, I think young people call it—hallucinating wildly, pain and terror larger than life-size, everything, every pain, every humiliation blown up into something of monstrously large proportions, paranoia, schizophrenia, politics, sex, everything became confused and took on a gigantic proportion.

I came out of it all shook up, as you say.

After about a month I was sent back home to Mallorca. Fear was still in me. I could not sleep at night because I was terrified of being trapped forever within my nightmares. I had lost thirty pounds. My hair and beard became white. My wife could not believe what she saw come down from the plane. Fear stayed with me. Fear of being followed, of being spied upon, of being vulnerable, frail, mad. We moved to Barcelona, for the island, however beautiful, became stifling.

Barcelona was then, for us Latin Americans, in its heyday. I had old ties of friendship with Mario Vargas Llosa and with Gabriel García Márquez, who were then living there, enjoying the delights of one of the great literary friendships of our time. It was the day of the "Boom," if there ever was such a thing, those years preceding 1970. Cortázar came often to Barcelona, so did Carlos Fuentes. I remember a New Year's party at García Márquez's where everyone was present. And our literary agent, Carmen Balcells, feted us continually, as did the Catalan writers, especially the Goytisolo brothers. After madness, it was party, party, party, opening nights, operas, concerts, after loneliness, friendships, being in the full swing of things. We went to Aix, to an opening night of one of Carlos Fuentes's plays with María Casares in it, and stayed at Cortázar's home in Saignon. The air was rife with political passion until, in 1970, Salvador Allende became president of Chile.

During all this time, until 1969, I wrote and wrote in my flat in Vallvidrera, up in the green hills behind Barcelona. Something very strange had happened. I had acquired a voice. My madness had given me a voice, this madness which was pain and disease, the final result of all those years of fighting it. It was all coming out, everything that during eight years had been piling up inside me: the hateful yellow bitch which had my voice and ran its crazy race through the whole novel, the deformed boy who had started everything going, the feeling of being enclosed, and the feeling of being outside things, left out; the handsome patrician couple that had hurt me so; the convent, the monsters, the derelicts, the old women, pride, poverty, injustice, everything, somehow, after this bout with madness, became sort of crystal-clear, well-cut, defined, lucid, in place, everything had an order and a voice and a meaning. In a final effort of recovery that took about eight months—a recovery of my mind, that is, for after the operation and the madness there were terrible sequels of fear and instability—writing *The Obscene Bird* was an operation of recuperating my own mind and my strength and confidence which had been under stress for so many years now. I wrote it from beginning to end, welding the pieces together and making up others as I went along. I used all the elements which had accumulated during the years, unable to find a pattern. Now, I felt as if I had been mute all these years, just like Humberto Peñaloza and shut up in that convent which is like Kafka's castle: now every experience and every feeling I had in me was shouted abroad as with a megaphone, for everyone to hear.

I could go on forever picking up from my memory the correlative in reality of every single bit in *The Obscene Bird of Night*. Everything has been recycled, it is true, but if I took the time, I could find every single tutor which held in place every single metaphor. But I feel it would be a sterile occupation, reality, after all, being no more than a tributary of fiction. For the reality which you and I share is not the name of certain streets, not the shape of certain eyes that belong to somebody with a real name, and in whose face I saw for the first time a certain smile, a certain way of looking at things, which led me to write a paragraph in my novel. What you and I share is the recycling of all this matter into something quite different from it, but which transcends and contains all of that.

I want to end by saying that it is quite possible that many steps led up to my writing *The Obscene Bird of Night:* in my biography, marrying, building a house, leaving Chile, were perhaps the most important. It was only after leaving Chile that I could "see" it, only then that I could fashion my extremely limited personal experience of my own country into what is, finally, the simple parable that I was after when I started off writing. I wish to add that, had I stayed behind, I would not have written this book, which is a possibility which, contemplated now, seems utterly incongruent. But I shared with all those Latin Americans in Barcelona, those two or three wonderful years there, an experience which is not common. There was a feeling of brotherhood. We were all, for better or for worse, doing the same thing. We all had moved away from our own countries because we found that our voices became stifled by the closeness, inaudible because of the nearness. We all thought that we could "understand" our countries, our continent, and through understanding it, understand the world, far from our countries, which would always be the emotion-charged metaphor, the splendid prism which held in our hand reflected and refracted the light our countries shed, decomposing it into what our personal limitations could transform it. We were all doing the same. There was not a single one amongst us who could or would write about anything but the country he had left behind, in the specific Spanish language of each of those countries. We were not cosmopolites. We were trying to understand, taking the long view now, from afar, after having been swamped in the mire of each of our societies. Very seldom does a country or a community, less a continent, find its own contemporary voice. And when it does it is a wonderful choir that does not last for a very long time. One such occasion was Mexican mural painting in the 1920s and 1930s: murals were the country's voice for a while, and then it was all over. Or Spanish lyrical poetry in the 1920s, when Lorca and Alberti and Cernuda and Hernández were all writing, and Pablo Neruda was the Spanish American poet in residence: lyrical poetry cast a shade onto almost all of the rest of artistic undertaking of that period.

So it is with the Latin American novel of the 1960s and 1970s. Our poetry, by comparison, is puny, and a whole continent, in its many forms and nationalities, seemed to have expressed itself, at the same time, in the same form, and made it, par excellence, the metaphor for that continent. I have said time and again that I do not subscribe to a social interpretation of literature, much less of what I have written. But, with time, I have grown not to dislike its possibility. Now, it seems to me, with age, I have acquired a degree of humility which makes me accept the possibility that, on one level, my voice is more meaningful than alone when heard in a choir.

This essay (in slightly different form) was first delivered in English as the John Gordon Stipe Lecture in Spanish at Emory University, 11 May 1981.

First published in issue 12.2 (Summer 1992)

Something to Die For

William T. Vollmann

This time the Cassandras who talk about the death of the novel may be right, because the great enemy, television, is working to bring about the death of the book. Television is ideal for people without memories. As an instrument of control it might be even more effective than the Bible or Mao's little red book. The strange and amazing thing is that television is not owned by any controllers, but only by a vague number of self-interest committees. This is why it so rarely stands for anything (although it does so when needed as a propaganda tool, as when one drops bombs in Iraq). It never seems to be explaining or conveying, only grinning like Francis Bacon's Idol of the Den.

Unlike a television program, a novel is most often the work of a single brain. This is because an individual can better afford to produce a page of typescript than two minutes of airtime. Precisely because the novel is cheaper to create, it is less respected (also, of course, because reading takes more work than "viewing"—and it would never do to work!).

Some editors (and, increasingly, agents) work to dilute the novel's uniqueness wherever possible. I have had good editors, who are in fact nothing more or less than the "ideal reader" we all write for: attentive, appreciative, skeptical, critical, and respectful of the ultimate sovereignty of the writer over his material. (Most have been this way.) I have had other editors who mucked, omitted, twisted, bowdlerized and macarooned, all with the best intentions, and compared to some other writers I have been lucky. I remember the sad galleys of one poor fellow which I was asked to read. The original manuscript itself was in places quite good. But he had meant his story to be a tragedy. The editor decided that the book would sell better as a black comedy instead. The author must have felt that he did not have any leverage; maybe he was genuinely satisfied with the "improvements," I don't know; but it sickens me now to remember how the book was spoiled and degraded.

No one is to blame for any of this. In that strange labyrinth of offices which we call "the business world," products are sold to please and sustain. If the product is not acceptable to the largest number of buyers, it will be recalled and altered. The mission of a work of literature is likewise to please and to sustain. However, precisely because of its uniqueness, its status as a metonym of the author's mind and spirit, it is not meant to be altered to please the crowd. Minds and spirits are not meant to do that. Of course, we all succumb to that tendency in various degrees: the baby becomes toilet-trained to ingratiate itself with the family, the schoolchild silently witnesses or participates in torture to gain the approval of playmates, the lover primps to gain attractiveness in the gaze of the beloved, and nationally and internationally it's all much worse. And yet the people we respect the most are those who stand aloof enough to retain some integrity while at the same time being sensitive and compassionate.

My writing as such, and my CoTangent books as objects, are attempts, however flawed they may be, to express my own thoughts and emotions, following my own aesthetic method. Because it is difficult for one person to be equally proficient in literary composition, physics, forensics, anthropology, draftsmanship, and bookbinding, my work must be inevitably weak in places. The hope is over the course of my lifetime I can continue to improve. Whenever I can, I tune out the dictates of others. If my work has value, that value will shine out. If not, then not. That is all that matters.

It is hard to say such things without sounding either boastful or defiant. I am neither. The world does not owe me a living. People are free to dislike my books on their own demerits, in which case I will go out of business. Of course people are free to do that anyway, whether I follow my own path or someone else's. Why not follow my own path, then?

A book need not be easy to read, or difficult, to be good. It need not be anything but itself. A good book is a companion, a comfort, and an inspiration to those good actions without which life is despicable. A good book is something to die for. Both readers and writers can legitimately have the privilege of living and dying for a book.

Here is a list of some of the best books I have ever read:

Tadeusz Konwicki, *A Dreambook for Our Time*
Lady Murasaki, *The Tale of Genji*
Cormac McCarthy, *All the Pretty Horses*
Lautréamont, *Maldoror*
Vasily Grossman, *Life and Fate*
Tolstoy, *War and Peace*
Yasunari Kawabata, *Snow Country*
Hemingway, *Islands in the Stream*
The *Poetic Edda*
The tales of Chekhov
The tales of Hawthorne
Njal's Saga
Sigrid Unset, *Kristin Lavransdatter*
Melville, *The Piazza Tales*
London, *Martin Eden*
Julio Cortázar, *Hopscotch*
The poems of Emily Dickinson
Faulkner, *Pylon* and *The Sound and the Fury*

Homer, the *Odyssey* and the *Iliad*

Nikos Kazantzakis, *The Odyssey: A Modern Sequel*

Heidegger, *Being and Time*

Poe, *The Narrative of A. Gordon Pym*

Pushkin, *Eugene Onegin*

Kobo Abe, *The Woman in the Dunes*

Blake, *Songs of Innocence* and *Experience*

Gyorgi Konrad, *The Loser*

Isaac B. Singer, *The Family Moskat*

Bruno Schulz, *The Street of Crocodiles*

Malraux, *Anti-Memoirs*

The poems of Lorca

The poems of Mandelstam

Ovid's *Metamorphoses*

The tales of D. H. Lawrence

T. E. Lawrence, *Seven Pillars of Wisdom*

Ivan Ilich, *Tools for Conviviality*

Mishima, the *Sea of Fertility* tetralogy

Kimon Nicolaides, *The Natural Way to Draw*

The poems of Gerard Manley Hopkins

Jane Smiley, *The Greenlanders*

Doubtless some people will want to complain about the women, blacks, reds, whites, blues, and greens I left out, but I don't really give a damn.

The beauty in these books would flourish more widely if the following social changes were made:

1. Abolish television, because it has no reverence for time.

2. Abolish the automobile, because it has no reverence for space.

3. Make citizenship contingent on literacy in every sense. Thus, politicians who do not write every word of their own speeches should be thrown out of office in disgrace. Writers who require editors to make their books "good" should be depublished.

4. Teach reverence for all beauty, including that of the word.

First published in issue 13.2 (Summer 1993)

Of Idealism and Glory

Osman Lins

What does a writer seek? A true writer, that is, one who makes the written word his reason of life. For, as with everything, and just as there are bad ministers, for example, writers have their imitators too. Those who imitate the gestures of a writer by publishing books, discussing Joyce, giving interviews, and who are not writers. These people are only looking for their name in the papers, and later for sinecures, well-paid jobs, decorations, some sort of social prestige, and the Academy, of course. These characters do not count and it does not matter what they seek: they are segregated by the same soil that produces all other kinds of impostors.

What a writer wishes to accomplish is to give to his fellow creatures, primarily those who speak his language, works he has consecrated the best of himself to. Working under restrictions, on commission, is necessary in other trades. In the writer's, commissions and restrictions mean precisely the death of the trade. Freedom is the climate in which it thrives.

Freedom? What kind? All. Beginning with internal freedom. That is, with the curbing, within himself, of ambitions extraneous to literature that might sidetrack him, make him lose his way.

This freedom, which, with greater or lesser effort, can be achieved under varying conditions, is not enough. Many other factors are necessary for the act of writing, the craft of writing, to reach its plenitude.

Let us limit ourselves, here, to the material situation of the writer. At the beginning it is impossible for him to live off his own work. Unlike the mason, or other workmen, he receives no compensation during his apprenticeship. This initial situation, which *must not perpetuate itself,* puts him, in the eyes of those around him, in an orbit to which a pompous name is applied (as generally happens to everything we wish to remain unrewarded and thus possibly destroy): idealism. The young man who, after having withdrawn into silence, timidly shows his poems, his little stories, refusing to spend his spare time on more concrete, more understandable, and immediately remunerative pursuits, is an idealist. In other words: someone naive, who does not participate in the general looting and can always be ignored with impunity. It does not take much for the young man to fall for this hoax, for this exaltation which is both malevolent and full of malice. The youth receives a crown emblazoned with his status of individual raised above the gross interests of everyone else. He does not know that they are bleeding him this way: he won't have any strength left, or he will need to expend a hundred times more energy to accomplish what he, still vaguely, plans. *Idealism,* in fact, in bourgeois dictionaries means: to live in need, dream in solitude, achieve in adversity, die unrewarded.

As I intend to be as objective as possible in this essay, I won't offer any suggestions, no matter how indispensable, as to the assistance to be offered to the future writer. I even have some doubts as to its use. Maybe it would tame the future writer's fecund wrath. A certain incompatibility is necessary. But if at the moment I had to give a piece of basic advice, or at least a warning, to the youth who wants to devote himself to literature, I would say: send those who extol your idealism to hell, they are trying to fool you. Writing is a job.

In the beginning it is impossible to live off it. Nevertheless, it is not right, nor desirable, nor useful for the writer—once he has achieved maturity—to continue underselling the product of his work (or not sell it at all). And this is what the writer is surreptitiously set up for when the label we referred to, of a fluctuating and extremely imprecise nature, is affixed to him in his youth.

This behavior, or better still, this trap, has countless causes, and I am not going to list them all. I will point out just two which are complementary and encompass all the others. The first is born of the *ignorance* of the writer's import. It is difficult to understand that the writer is a man destined not to escape the world but to plunge into its depths instead. It is difficult to understand that he is not a creature made of dreams, incapable of facing life with determination, but exactly the opposite: he laboriously learns how to see, through his practice with words. To be sure, many misguided books, which actually describe a process of escape, of avoidance, of alienation from life, are the cause of that misconception and seem to substantiate it. It happens, however, that those very books are a consequence of the opinion one has formed. They are born of authors who, without understanding well the character of their trade (it's even possible that they do not understand it is a trade) have passively accepted and complied with the general idea. They have become what we want them to be: deserters, blind, guileless people, compliant and harmless buffoons.

The second reason, and we are not striving for any paradox at all, is the consequence of the *knowledge* of the writer's import. Just as in certain milieus, without realizing the profound meaning of the act of writing, an unimportant or even negligible role is attributed

to the person who devotes himself to it; others, suspecting or guess-
ing his power, try to annihilate it by all means. This effort to annihilate has many names and takes on countless guises. It ranges from
execution and banishment to mere indifference. One of its re-
courses, by the way, and among the most subtle, can even be accep-
tance, ample remuneration, as long as the writer abdicates free and
spontaneous probing, turns into a scribe, a hired hand who works
under the orders of intellectually inferior individuals, scarcely interested in the literary worth of his text. We must note, however,
that this pressure is more typically exerted, among us, by means of
a well-constructed chain of negative reactions. If a young person
wants to be what is called a technician, that is, an individual willing
to devote his intelligence to the growth of productivity in banks and
factories, to reduce the operative costs of slaughterhouses or invigo-
rate by any means the stock market, an attentive and protective
circle immediately forms around him. How not favor such a virtu-
ous disposition? But if he intends to write—really write and not just
scribble—resistance arises. Tacit, constant, implacable. And this reveals nothing but our boundless disconcertment. Think about a
purebred dog or horse. No matter how silky the hair of this dog, how
supple the muscles of that horse, we won't advance an inch in our
understanding of the world or of what we are thanks to them. However, the writer does not receive one thousandth of the care devoted
to the orchids and animals we admire, with their patriotic yellow-
and-green ribbons, in agricultural and livestock shows. In any job
he has outside literature (because he has to have one, since it takes
so long for him to be able, at least in principle, to profit from his
writing) he will always be regarded with suspicion: one cannot expect much from him; it is difficult to make him get involved in any
other career, since he has already consecrated himself to the most
intolerable: writing. How to accept the idea that with so many other
occupations, apt to make him, if not rich, moderately well-off, and,
what is more important, of enriching other people even more, a person can devote so many hours to writing a page, endlessly replacing
one word with another?

He won't be distrusted at this secondary job alone. None of those
who, by different means, head the society he lives in will be on his
side. At heart, no matter how much they swear to the contrary, they
know they are wrong about something. This, when the others are
distracted, does not matter. Distraction is an anesthetic. But here is
a man who is not distracted: he writes. The explosion of his sentence
goes unheard. When he walks down the street it is impossible to
identify him in the crowd. The most sophisticated instruments are
unable to determine where his book in progress is. The wire service

has no information on his struggle. The truth, however, is that he is writing. If he is writing, he is not blind, contrary to what some may think. He soaks everything in, examines everything. And nothing can be done to make him change his mind. One may attempt it—and tempt him. This is almost always futile. Then only blockading is left. Maybe he will give in. Maybe he will become discouraged.

Let us be clear. No one is afraid that the writer will upset the social structure with his books. The reaction, if we may call it such, does not exactly concern itself with what the books say; rather, it concerns itself with his presence and the mere existence of those books. More troubling than anything his works might say is the fact that he exists. He was pressured to relinquish his plan of becoming a writer; they surrounded him with an attentive indifference, an indifference that manifests itself only because it is aware of his proximity; no sustenance was granted to him. Even so, quietly, his head down (like a bull charging), he keeps going and writes his novel, his stories, his poems. In the general consonance, in the general noise, there is a silence: his presence. No matter how much noise you make it is impossible to ignore this silence. Disturbing, isn't it?

The moment, overcoming all the difficulties that have arisen, the writer finally finishes a book and sends it off, naively believing that publishers, as they sometimes claim, are always on the lookout for original works; he will discover to his surprise that in order to write he has courageously put himself in a risky predicament and that publishers tend to take fewer and fewer risks. At most they offer to publish the book, but at the author's expense. This happens because even though he is dealing with a product of the intellect, the publisher, in general, has no grasp of his role in the community. Books are merchandise, they say. True. But they are not just merchandise. They are something more. And it is the degree to which they transcend their quality of simple merchandise that they demand of those who work with them a more serious attitude than that of mere merchants.

Here is the manuscript, here is the writer; at the other end a community, that of the readers; in the middle, like a bridge, an agent of communication, the publisher. The writer's mistake is imagining that the publisher, considering the position he is in, is his ally: a purveyor of culture. He is at times a purveyor of culture, even though he frequently limits himself to publishing second-rate works without any literary value whatsoever. However, he hardly ever takes into consideration the common interest. Thus the norm for him is to avoid, by many means, cultivating the living literature of his people, of his country. Besides, it is not enough to publish. A writer does not live on his book just because the book is published. The book has to be sold, has to reach the readers in order for him to derive some kind of financial security from it and so that the act of writing, reaching those to whom it is directed, may have repercussions, disseminate, find completion.

Here we come to the basic point of this argument. Literary contests, which here continue to fail to inspire the readers to buy the prize-winning books, are receiving more and more originals, not a few of which are of good quality. This, among other things, is a lesson to those who work to destroy literature in various ways, proof that a growing number of people are looking for that disconcerting silence that manifests itself in the midst of noise. On the other hand, it enrages us to think that the majority of these works will face serious difficulties before they reach the public. The fact is that, at the same time that the number of aspiring writers is growing in the country, publishers are curbing this process. Not only by withdrawing. There are those who dispense with paying royalties or pay them so irregularly that this payment becomes aleatory, something the writer cannot count on. And why should he? Why should he demand it? Hasn't a certain form of glory, albeit limited, already been bestowed upon him?

Now in the same way we repudiate those who try to foist upon us the inclination toward an idealism whose meaning is unclear even to them, we will also solemnly send anything resembling glory to the devil. Glory, for the true writer, is simply being read—mainly by his own people—as well as being able to live off his work without giving it a bad name. But being read in a sensitive way, as well as reaping a reasonable income from his honest work, continues to be difficult for the Brazilian writer.

Therefore it is necessary, it is urgent, that writers, by all means available to them, demand a change of mentality and conditions. We cannot, in any way, allow literature, already poorly served, poorly remunerated, to be solely the occupation of people well situated in the world and, perhaps because of this, lacking the intense desire to establish a vital contact with their people through their books. It is absolutely indispensable that this opportunity is available to everybody. To work without compensation is as shameful as being compensated without a reason. Amateurism is an insult to those who give themselves, body and soul, to a particular job to make a living from it.

Therefore, let writers not stop looking for the change we discussed as a basic condition for the existence, here and now, of a literature. Nor let publishers shirk their responsibilities under any pretext. Halfway between the writer and the public, halfway between the writer and the writer's complete professionalization, it is their responsibility to establish this bridge in an honorable manner. Don't let them try to change the subject of the conversation with either veiled or blatant allusions to glory and idealism. In their position the role that has befallen them cannot be eluded. If they are unable to fulfill it, let them find another job, make room for others. We need to eat too.

[1969]

Translated by Adria Frizzi and R. E. Young

First published in issue 15.3 (Fall 1995)

Bad Times

Janice Galloway

There is a place called the Centre for Contemporary Arts in Sauchiehall Street in Glasgow, a gallery space, theater and performance café sort of affair where the newest of new artistic work is not only permissible but expected. It is a welcoming place: interested, broad-minded, eclectic. Exhibitions staged there seem to assume that's what the people who come to see them are too.

A few months ago now, I did a reading at the CCA as part of a season called Bad Times: an exploration of how artists in different fields treat the subject of depression, suicide, political lean times and mean times—bad times, I suppose. I was pleased to be invited and enjoyed the reading but that is not the subject of this essay. The subject of this essay concerns the week before, when a journalist phoned me. I had one hand hauling wet stuff out of the washing machine, the other restraining a three-year-old and the phone under my jaw, but I was polite. I made time to listen. He didn't want to talk about the reading, he said. He wanted to talk about *concepts*. Fine, I said. So, he said: what did I think about all this depression and suicide business. I didn't understand the question. This nineties vogue for despair, he added helpfully. I still didn't understand the question. Well, isn't it all a bit self-indulgent? he said, lumping a lot of misery and neuroses together and calling it Art?

Now I won't pretend everything fell into place at that moment but it should have. He wasn't asking questions at all, he was suggesting dismissal: offering me a choice between reaction and complicity. I struggled on with him for a while but the subsequent article, its references to something vaguely termed "the uplifting," its demand for an art that "looks on the bright side and away from the relentless focus on the sordid" confused me for days. I had been to the exhibitions, I had thought the work wonderfully thought-provoking. His refusal to look at the work on the grounds that there are some things better not discussed or better left out of Artistic dialogue (the old "appropriacy of subject matter" chestnut) was something I was not prepared for. I was shocked. I lost sleep. Worse, I couldn't work out why. I was seeing nothing new. Attempts to silence certain subjects or voices and render them "beyond the pale"—by ridicule, ostracism, pretending they aren't there, or any other method—are hardly unfamiliar tactics; while elitist canon-making and the promotion of some ideas as "right" or "real" at the expense of others which are "forbidden" or "invalid" are everyday realities. The only reasons I could come up with for my unprepared-ness were (a) this right-wing, repressive norm intruding on the "safe" space of the CCA, and (b) (less reasonably) the fact the jour-nalist was younger than me. Neither are valid excuses. I should not, I realized after some time to think, have been shocked or even sur-prised at all.

It is, surely, uncontentious to say that the dominant context for everything and everyone for the past umpteen years, at least as far as those who govern us are concerned, is that of the "marketplace." All levels of government and media are so saturated in the lan-guage, concepts, and priorities of this "marketplace" that it is be-coming harder to avoid taking its language and priorities as givens, i.e., not open to question. The central idea, crudely, conflates MONEY, POWER, and WORTH, making this trinity the ultimate test of the "common sense" or "reality" of all else. Thereafter, market philosophy is reliably devoid of metaphor. Phrases like "good invest-ment" can usually be taken literally: invisible or abstract "return" is regarded in much the same way astronomers regard astrology—not only wrongheaded but humorously medieval. Thus balancing books, supply and demand, and hard cash are empirical proofs, i.e., "real things"; while Human Happiness, the Common Good, and Morality are rendered pale pink wooly ideas harking back to a "less competi-tive," i.e., stupid age.

From here, several other things follow. It follows, for example, that moneys spent on things that do not reap literal return is not "commonsensical." Public spending cuts become "realistic" and even improving. Education, for example, is "best served" by funding which furthers "necessary" grading exercises for employers, and elsewhere "rationalized" by cuts. Further Education, likewise, "joins the real world" when funds go on "vocational training" and cuts are applied to "Arts and recreation." Public Health is "stream-lined" and "strengthened" by cuts while Welfare cuts "help define areas of real need." By extension, social conscience becomes "trickle-down economics"; the highest morality is "good housekeep-ing"; active mutual citizenship becomes individual consumer rights, and knowing the price of everything and the value of nothing goes by the name of "sound business sense." This is generally sold to the British public by appeals to tightening-of-belts, pulling-of-selves-together, and invocations of the Dunkirk spirit. The *lumpenprole* are meant to understand why there is no jam today (and why those with jam already are to get more) if they are told some will "trickle down" to them tomorrow. And so far, at least with the Southern English population, it's seemed to work very well indeed.

Where Art fits is, simply, uneasily. There's a sort of received wisdom in all elitist hierarchies that Art, like Guinness or perhaps medicine, is "good for you"—not just because you can make it into plays that bring in tourist revenue, but in other, less definable ways. Words like *edifying* pop unbidden into otherwise "sensible" heads. Art is a refining influence, full of lofty ideas about aesthetics and the human condition. It is generally held to be "a marker of civilized society" and having some of it around makes everything look a little more . . . well . . . humane. (One of Mrs. Thatcher's greatest failings, according to the old-guard right, was that she was "a crashing Philistine," which lowered the tone uncomfortably for those who think ruling elites ought to prefer Wagner rather than Andrew Lloyd Webber with their policy-making.) Even so, we mustn't get carried away. Lofty ideas are not (polite cough) the same as practicalities, which is to say Art is all very well but not essential. Essential, that is, in the way the needs of private industry and MP's expense accounts and government PR exercises and increases in the salaries of judges and so on and so on are. It is, after all, PROFIT that makes the "real world" go around. Art must not get ideas above itself. Art is only icing: Business is the cake.

Now, if you think Art is fundamentally important to human beings—not as a notion but as a practical reality—the present anti-artistic (i.e., antihumanist) thrust of the present party-political climate has to be worrying. Art is not decoration, or something pretty by someone dead. It's not escapism or entertainment. I'm not saying there is anything wrong with any of these things but they're not Art. Art is more even than ideas. Art is the *exploration* of ideas: an attempt, I think, to make sense of the experience of being human through a process of creative skepticism. This in turn means Art is best at work when it's being prickly, querulous, and hostile to complacency of thought. It is obvious how Art itself is a problem for the new right: too many questions do not sit well with the smug face of an apparently immovable government. You don't, however, need to issue *fatwas* or offer jail sentences instead of awards to attempt to limit Art. The hierarchical, undemocratic givens of power-politics can do it a whole variety of much subtler ways, up to and including denial of access to any means of dissemination or even denial that it exists (exactly what happened to the creative work of women for centuries—and arguably still does), or by suggesting that some kinds of subject matter are "out of bounds." It can provide only an impoverished education to the bulk of its citizens, leading them to think that's all education is. It can withdraw publicity, access, and funding from certain kinds of work and propagandize as "worthwhile" the stuff that makes fewer waves or challenges only at a trivial level. Or—the one our present government seems to be pinning a good many hopes on—it can stress private sponsorship as the way forward for funding, effectively encouraging artists to self-censor for fear that any potential sponsor will deny funding if they're too "difficult" or "controversial." And while there are some private sponsors who wouldn't dream of laying down an agenda for any creative artist, we surely delude ourselves if we do not acknowledge that the "Art" most likely to "win" sponsorship will probably be at the already established, "safe bet" end of the artistic spectrum. The work of unknown composers or writers, anything deemed too experimental or unorthodox or "geared to a minority audience" or—and here we come full circle—too depressing, will be consistently starved of funds and dissemination. This is not only a recipe for encouraging work of the blandest sort, the kind that can be consumed for "relaxation" with a guarantee of no unpleasant aftertaste, but it also blunts the cutting edge of the most radical of new artistic work, the very work that opens the fresh ways of seeing on which all Art thrives. In short, what we are more likely to encourage by forcing the market model as suitable to assess the worth of creative work is an endless recycling of the same old warhorses for fear of doing anything that might fail in box-office terms (Carnegie and Albert Halls, are you listening?), work stagnant for want of radical input, work that no longer challenges or stimulates exploration of ideas, which means Art reduced to the decorative or the entertaining, which is to say NOT ART AT ALL. Maybe one can expect nothing more of a government that is so spiritually bankrupt it sees nothing ironic in hinging the notions "Art and Heritage" together as a government department, but it's awful anyway.

Once I had thought all this through, the journalist who spoke to me, his questions, their tenor and assumptions, began to look more understandable. I had simply not taken into account how much the pattern of repressive thinking had progressed in the last few years but now I was forced to look again. In Britain, after more than fifteen years of single-track policy-making, a whole new generation who cannot remember alternatives to "marketplace" meretriciousness is coming to fruition, and that, surely, has an effect on how younger people view what Art (and people) are. Disaffection (of various sorts, from a *que sera* attitude to a drug culture to a strong sense of political impotence to the notion that individual rather than collective action is the only possible form of protest) and born-again, quasi-nostalgic repressiveness are the two most prevalent manifestations I can come up with. Both are obviously evidenced in the body of new British writing and writers, though the latter, in the guise of saturated tolerance ("ENOUGH IS ENOUGH do we really need to have our noses rubbed in this kind of thing is it supposed to be modern and if so call me old-fashioned" etc.), is the one that finds most favor with our critics. I know of course there always have been and always will be attempts to control what artists do, suggestions from noncreators about what "true" creation should consist in. The present reactionary tendency, however, is more blatant and shameless than anything I can remember and the more shocking for its coming after Barthes, Foucault, Russ, Spender, et al.—i.e., great schools of thought that seemed to be beginning to democratize how we view and codify art. And it is in that, I guess, the worst of the shock resides. Mr. Major's inane BACK TO BASICS* slogan and his more recent advice to "condemn more and understand less" are, it seems, becoming our critical and artistic climate too. The apparent obverse—the kind of criticism that stresses appearance and novelty (and advances paid) rather than the ideas explored in a book—isn't: it's simply "marketplace" values in thin guise. From young women who deny their sex both in their writing and with statements about "being a writer, not a woman" for fear of sounding upsettingly "feminist" to young men who write about sex by objectifying and denying sexuality because anything else is too "politically correct"; from out-of-the-woodwork academics yearning for "the voice of restraint" to elitist critics and criticism that would condemn work for its subject matter or language being "upsetting" or "too experimental" or "last year's thing"—the absurd wish for God to be in his heaven and all simple with the world again (i.e., the way it was before we knew all this politically aware stuff) seems overwhelming. It is worrying, it is distracting, it is confidence-sapping. Most of all, it is irrelevant. I've stopped buying papers and no longer watch TV. I do still go to see exhibitions I like and watch for what the papers ignore. I try to remember that things get worse before they get better and think it's really no worse than it was in the nineteenth century. The best of our art was unlikely to be promoted, funded, or encouraged then either but it was still there. Even so, the nineteenth century had more excuses. These are uneasy times and it would be an act of the worst *mauvais foi* to fall for

---

*The current rumor in this country that the BACK TO BASICS slogan was thought up by Barbara Cartland is telling: the romantic novelist was quoted in the *Observer* as saying, "Nothing is allowed to be nice any more: everything has to be sordid"—simply a cruder version of what the journalist who called me was saying. This time it's younger rather than older fogeys who are promoting the repressive bloody nonsense.

the comforting tosh that "Art (or tolerance or inclusiveness) will out" let alone triumph. Katherine Ann Porter's splendid avowal

> I have no patience with the idea that whatever you have in you has to come out, that you can't suppress true talent. People can be destroyed; they can be bent, distorted and completely crippled. . . . In spite of all the poetry, all the philosophy to the contrary, we are not really masters of our fate . . .

says it right for me too. What we can do, however, is learn a little about our limitations. I've already learned to be much more careful about who I spend time with on the phone. We can keep in touch with each other, pick up survival techniques, keep our eyes open, be suspicious, conserve our energies to keep producing work we can confidently call Art.

First published in issue 16.1 (Spring 1996)

Impressions of a Paranoid Optimist

Mary Caponegro

The *Review of Contemporary Fiction* is a periodical I esteem most highly; it has been a profound inspiration to me for the last decade, so I couldn't refuse when asked to speak to fiction's status a decade hence, despite feeling insufficiently informed, to say the least. I offer the following highly subjective impressions as a practitioner of fiction who possesses only the meagerest knowledge of hypertext, and nonetheless strong feelings. I'm grateful to the following writers/editors for assisting me through reinforcement and clarification in conversation: David Foster Wallace, Steven Moore, David Weiss, Michael Ives, Bruce McClelland.

As to fiction's future (for which I have no crystal ball), I can only say that I have no fear for it; it looks very bright indeed, although the brightness I see is not a technologically produced illumination, such as that which emanates from this framed rectangular glow before me that saves my words as I spew them. That's not the star I'm seeking myself, or being led by, though I feel a certain guilt, an anti-quarian-rather-than-micro chip on my shoulder, because I'm yearning for a future that is anything but "istic"; reliant, rather, on a technologically unmediated imagination's endless capacity to augment, transform itself.

It is suddenly old-fashioned, isn't it?—imagination: paradoxically wholesome compared to that more trendy god, technology, who is, in my view, merely tool. Having been raised in a fairly old-fashioned way, I am, I'm afraid, a woman altogether alienated from tools: they intimidate me; I use them tentatively, ineptly, and as a defense, I suppose, I feel they should do me the courtesy of knowing their place. So I find myself stuck in the capacious consolation of an entity that saved me from stagnation in my youth and adolescence and to which I thus give utmost credibility: its name—as if you didn't know—is imagination. I must confess that whenever I think about hypertext, Internet, E-mail—please excuse my naive conflation—I have this retro impulse to crawl into some cave where I can create in darkness and peace and feel primitive, primal, especially *private,* retreat into some contrastingly sensuous *un*virtual reality that produces future as nothing glitzy at all. I want somehow to retreat into body, because that's where I find I locate imagination; the more technologically oriented things get, the more I want to find a physical locus to inhabit in fiction; I can't find an eros in anything else. And from my limited and uninformed perspective, hypertext de-eroticizes fiction. The narrative of my dreams, you see, is one which takes me through plane after plane of pleasure and desire. And when it's done—excuse my metaphorical bluntness—I damn well want to know I've come. Of course I'm talking only about me: *my* fiction, my limits, my vision, my neuroses; I'm writing out of ignorance and only because, truth be told, I was asked to, so let me continue in stating the obvious.

There is something to be said, is there not, for a sensuous reality. There is something to be said for the tactile availability of a letter, an envelope, perhaps with beautiful foreign stamps, within which is sequestered someone's elegant hand or scrawl, at least signature, a letter you can open, unfold, read half of and tuck in your pocket, hide in your drawer to savor later, or of a book you can read out loud to your partner at night, put a bookmark inside of, feel the weight of in your hand, smell. (I have a colleague who judges books by their aroma; more than cover or photo, he cared solely about how his first published hardback smelled!) Or a voice on the phone, even the voice that you keep hearing on your answering machine representing the person who perpetually eludes you, because it's at least animate, and thus antithetical to the qualities of a world gone ON-LINE. I have no affection for information per se, and consequently no desire to encourage or participate in its apotheosis. I care, and passionately, about a different line; I feel its autonomy must be defended, preserved.

But why so passionate, I must ask myself, why defensive, threatened? Given my own thoroughly un- if not antitraditional fictive proclivities, what's my problem? Am I hypocrite? Or only hypercrit? How ironic indeed that what would seem an extrapolation of all I espouse artistically is anxiety if not anathema to me. Let's settle on ambivalence: the word defining my stubborn relation, at least thus far, to hypertext. Why is it that the Garden of Forking Paths, once any of them can be summoned instantly by the push of a button—should I say the click of a mouse—ceases to engage me, ceases to be, in any case, my favorite place to stroll? To me, ambiguity is the key; I want a stability fused with instability, like Kafka's Hybrid creature and Odradek. I don't think Borges was after a literal dimension. Isn't that the paradox: that the deconstruction of linearity occurs within the constraints of linear narrative? Without that tension, that dissonance, I'm bored. Already one has a text that "never reads the same way twice" (Coover); such texts, in fact, have always been my favorite fictions, so why the need to execute, laboriously, the tantalizing implications? Why not simply bask in the overtones? I do know that the space between the screen and elsewhere is the primary site of my own creativity—in-between zones where I move a concept to the "next step." Entrapment in that framed glow precludes opportunity to lie in bed with or sit under a tree with, scribble in the margins of a printed "hard" copy, have the back-and-forth relation that makes fictive friction.

What it all comes down to, I admit, is control; OK, I'm a control freak. Fiction is manipulation, yes? I want to invite the reader in, and while I want anything but a passive guest inside my page, I want also to be mistress of my own hospitality. When the ambiguities shimmer, I'm intrigued, but once each avenue implied is played out to the hilt, the sense of play is dissipated, if not obliterated. One risks feeling that exhaustion of having seen too many rental apartments, of reading too many job applications, and how can you hold them all in mind? And if you can, then what's left to imagine?

Robert Coover, who has taught me a great deal about fiction as well as other profound matters, and who is one of the most eloquent and persuasive advocates of hypertext, says "Much of the novel's alleged power is embedded in the line, that compulsory author-directed movement from the beginning of the sentence to its period, from the top of the page to the bottom, from the first page to the last." The bottom line is that I'm in love with the line, for God's sake. Every sentence probably takes me a week to write. The tension of a finely crafted sentence—one which I attempt to fashion or one which I consume—offers me all the adventure I need—for if I never arrive at closure, to take stock of the cumulative ambiguities "between the lines," how will I know where I am? The prerequisite for residing in these "overtones," it seems to me, is surface closure. Who wants, when it comes down to it, to have all possibilities *literally* available?— any more than you'd want to realize every sexual fantasy. I want this neither when I read nor when I write, nor when I make mundane day-to-day exchanges. (Imagine how exhausting the traffic would be if every such artery were perpetually unclogged!) Some boundaries, some limitations, may be useful. Steve Moore kindly reminded me of a quote from chapter 1 of Thoreau's *Walden:* "We are in great haste to construct a magnetic telegraph from Maine to Texas; but Maine and Texas, it may be, have nothing important to communicate."

I read recently of the soon-to-come (or already available?) mode of research in which one would read an article on Beethoven and, bingo, synesthesialike, hear a sonata. Admittedly seductive, but what, I wonder, happens to the fantasy one now has no opportunity to begin constructing, of what that music *might* sound like, a speculation that would later be challenged, fulfilled or revised by the recording one would hear? In that caesura so much richness lies, it seems to me, and yet we don't think to credit it with any status but inconvenience. And furthermore, what catalysts remain for the imagination when there is no *something contained* in an envelope, or between leaves, behind a cover, the electronic medium not these latter's substitute any more than live music is supplanted by recording: no amount of technical precision serves as substitute for the sensuousness of being in the same space with an instrument, a performer. I suspect a pseudocommunication may proliferate through a technology whose sophistication perhaps exceeds *our* collective sociomaturity—yielding a promiscuity that I'd far rather imagine than participate in. I realize that the cave into which I've crawled brands me a Stone Age fictioneer, but mark my words: years hence we could be looking at a diminution—although no instrument could measure it, and hence we'd not believe it—of the power to hold something in mind *un*realized—a cosmic consequence less overt yet more dire still than carpal tunnel.

But back to the brightness: I do have a more optimistic report; it is not exclusively paranoia I bear. In fact, I can't imagine a more optimistic time for fiction, especially American fiction—when the recent publications of my mentors, friends, and idols alone keep me up to my neck in belles lettres, when I read the few excellent groundbreaking journals that inspire me, such as this one, which has kept me substantively informed ever since I was a student/aspiring writer, connecting me to an avant-garde tradition that I couldn't find much evidence of elsewhere, and which was vital to my education and evolution as a writer.

Even while the publishing industry is proving more and more limited/ing with respect to literary fiction, and great editors are in perpetually precarious positions, and best-sellers are all the marketplace approves/accepts, I think there is an alternate truth, if you will—that enough *is* getting published to keep us engaged and challenged, that language is up to something plenty provocative, and in the same old places it always was, on the page, as well as above/beyond. Meanwhile young writers I'd never heard of emerge by the dozens: new voices that move and excite me, mainstream and non- and in-between. I have the privilege of continuing to publish what I write even though it is not mainstream in the least. I have the privilege of teaching the authors I love, and of teaching young aspiring writers to write *against* the marketplace's limitations.

In my own work I am trying to undertake more elaborate projects, some collaborative, with artists/musicians etc., to push limits, boundaries, of narrative, of reality, in whatever modest ways I can muster. There are probably other worthwhile artistic goals than deconstructing mimesis, but I don't anticipate that one wearing thin for me. I know I will remain primarily a stylist. I am at this moment finishing a collection of stories whose seed was a year's stay in Italy—the last place I ever thought my fiction would take me was to my "roots," but so it did, albeit obliquely; that book was conceived nearly all-of-a-piece but executed in excruciating sequence, a trait I am, alas, unlikely to outgrow. I know that I want story to remain my medium—to continue to explore all the ways I can distort/enhance the form, particularly through comic fiction. My snail's pace is such that I move story by story; a decade probably represents significantly less volume—or should I say fewer volumes?—of published writing for me than for the other writers represented in *this* volume, and in ten years time I will simply be working on that year's story, in much the same manner, I imagine, and I would hope with a still greater depth for the intervening stories. In the end it comes down to sentences, doesn't it? I want only to fashion ever more beautiful elliptical sentences that provoke thought and give pleasure. I'm thrilled to have what audience I have; to me it seems large, and it wouldn't occur to me to measure it against a commercial writer's. I feel fortunate to have begun my career before the worst of this crisis in publishing hit. I'm overwhelmingly gratified that some readers feel stimulated, provoked enough by my work to find it compelling, consoling, intriguing, offensive (or as a friend/fan said to me, "I'd better have another cup of coffee before I try to read that stuff"). I have support, encouragement, the benefit of extraordinary mentors, a marvelous and genuinely literary agent, superb—again literary—editors, as most writers yearn for, places to publish I respect deeply, a way to make a living that allows me to have intimacy with what I love, students who inspire me, everything but enough time to write—but hey, compared to most of the populace that's hardly a complaint. There is plenty to be alarmed about for the coming decade, and deeply alarmed: political conservatism/repression on the one hand, extreme forms of political correctness on the other, and this obviously has an indirect impact on what gets read, published, taught. Education is in great jeopardy; these are things to worry about, but fiction itself will not be impoverished, I don't think; writers will continue to challenge the status quo, continue to transform the complexity of experience, to strive for that elusive, allegedly mythic beast, originality, regardless of the size of their audience in any given decade. Because I teach fiction writing, I know that there are reinforcements on the way, that those of us devoted to the expansion and dissemination of imagination, through whatever various means, are not a dying breed.

First published in issue 16.1 (Spring 1996)

Book Reviews

David Foster Wallace. *Brief Interviews with Hideous Men*. Little, Brown, 1999. 273 pp. $24.00.

In *Brief Interviews with Hideous Men* David Foster Wallace collects twenty-three pieces of fiction, most written since the publication of *Infinite Jest* in 1996. Few of these are stories in the conventional sense. Rather, the book makes into fiction many other forms: the title interviews, which provide the structure of the book; monologues; a play; pop quizzes; an outline; and harder-to-define nonnarrative snapshots of various characters and their lives. The results are both familiar, as we recognize techniques and themes from Wallace's earlier work, and surprising, as we see Wallace taking his post-big-novel work in new directions.

The various pieces here work together to explore three interconnected problems. The first is how to be human in a contemporary society that prefers to see us as things, in which we are encouraged to see others as things and to think of ourselves as things. As one of the hideous men says, "it's possible to be just a thing but . . . minute by minute if you want you can *choose* to be more if you want, you can *choose* to be a human being and have it *mean* something." The second problem is where human identity resides, someplace inside, where we know ourselves, or someplace on the outside, where others see us. This ambiguity can be paralyzing, as in the title character of "The Depressed Person," who becomes obsessed with not appearing to others as she fears she might, or despicable, as in the various hideous men, who self-consciously develop personae in order to manipulate women's reactions to them. In both cases the result is dehumanizing. The third problem is how to develop a post-postmodern literature so as to write about these problems in a meaningful way. Wallace returns here to concerns he first dealt with explicitly in his novella *Westward the Course of Empire Takes Its Way*: the self-conscious fiction of the high postmodernists has been popularized into a cheap cynicism, a celebration of surface and the denial of depth, and a tendency to label any assertion about anything as hopelessly naive; fiction needs to build on the technical and thematic innovations of postmodern literature and find a way to break through the cynicism and the superficiality of contemporary society so as to say something true about being human. "Octet," a series of pop quizzes, ends as a powerful challenge to writers and readers to remake fiction and its purposes. A fourth problem is interwoven with these three: language's ability to express the truth about the self or the world. Like *Infinite Jest* these pieces suggest contradictory attitudes toward language: on the one hand, a Jamesian desire to describe more and more obsessively, as if creating a lasso of language to ensnare the ineffable; on the other hand, a recognition of the clichéd state of language, so overfamiliar that meaning can be telegraphed ("Foxholes and atheists and so on"). This conflict is illustrated in "Adult World," where the first half of the story is narrated obsessively and the second half presented as the author's outline.

The mood of these pieces is generally grim, and the book is less frequently laugh-out-loud funny than Wallace's others. But in its form, narration, language, and ideas, *Brief Interviews with Hideous Men* is a virtuoso display that builds on the achievement of *Infinite Jest* and points the way to the future of fiction. [Robert L. McLaughlin]

Maurice Blanchot. *The Station Hill Blanchot Reader: Fiction and Literary Essays.* Station Hill, 1999. 529 pp. $29.95.

While thousands of books appear each year, few publications can be classified as genuine events: this is one of them. Station Hill has collected its previous six récits (*Vicious Circles, Thomas the Obscure, The Madness of the Day, Death Sentence, When the Time Comes, The Man Who Was Standing Apart from Me*), plus a sampling from its essay collection (*The Gaze of Orpheus*), into a single stunning, beautiful, and canonical volume.

The editorial material is quite helpful. Christopher Fynsk provides an illuminating theoretical forward, and the publisher George Quasha contributes a lucid history of publishing Blanchot in America, as well as a perspicacious argument for Blanchot's poetic or literary impact in this country, an argument too often absent from most current discussions of his work. But it is Blanchot's own writing, at once translucent and obscure, intimate and distancing, morbid and hopeful, which truly shines forth here with a brilliant, dark light.

Although I found myself missing the oddly monumental quality of those thin, exquisite earlier editions, this collection offered the opportunity to develop connections between the different sites of textual inquiry. While the volume specifically refuses to contextualize the different récits into anything resembling a totalizing whole, oeuvre or work—what Quasha calls a "thesis"—this collection does allow the texts, both fictional and theoretical, to speak to one another, to converse with one another and to ask and repeat the question of what literature is.

This is a magnificent work of writing, translating, and publishing. It should not be missed by any reader interested in contemporary literature or theory: it should not be missed by any reader interested in writing. [Jeffrey DeShell]

Stefan Themerson. *Bayamus & Cardinal Pölätüo.* Intro. Keith Waldrop. Exact Change, 1997. 242 pp. $15.95.

Stefan Themerson (1910-1988), a Polish emigrant and prominent member of the Polish avant-garde, moved to England in 1942 and established the Gaberbocchus Press with this wife Franciszka, eventually publishing such diverse voices as Alfred Jarry, Kurt Schwitters, Raymond Queneau, and

Bertrand Russell. This jarring assembly aptly describes Themerson's own motley writing. In his books we encounter philosophical parodies prosaically transcribed by a startling avant-garde sensibility. Imagine, if you can, a comic philosophical treatise composed by an utterly serious dadaist.

The two novels published in this volume provide a great introduction to Themerson's innovative style and thought. In *Bayamus* the narrator follows a man with three legs to the Theatre of Anatomy and the Theatre of Semantic Poetry. The latter is the novel's true destination, where its real concern is explored. Semantic poets insist on clear thinking and the need to free poetic words of vague and multiple associations. To do this the poet must replace each questionable word with the more precise phrasing of a dictionary definition. This method of substitution feels notably Oulipian, and, fittingly enough, Themerson's semantic rendition of "Taffy was a Welshman" has been included in Mathews and Brotchie's *Oulipo Compendium*.

Cardinal Pölätüo, while possibly even more absurd, is also more striking in its philosophical satire. The Cardinal composes a 6,940-page "Philosophy of Pölätüomism," which attempts to prove that far from undermining the Church's tenets, science is a subset and further proof of the validity of religious belief. Pölätüo is equally set on disclaiming Russell's logical positivism and on destroying that great enemy of his faith, poetry. Unfortunately, this also entails ridding the world of his eighteen-year-old, in-utero poet son, Guillaume Apollinaire.

Presented in one of Exact Change's always-elegant editions, this volume is a wonderful way to be introduced to the twisted and hilarious world of Stefan Themerson. [David Ian Paddy]

Lois-Ann Yamanaka. *Heads by Harry*. Farrar, Straus & Giroux, 1999. 320 pp. $24.00.

Following the controversial *Blu's Hanging*, Lois-Ann Yamanaka's latest book is centered around a taxidermy shop and the Japanese-American Yagyuu family who owns it. It pursues in often hilarious terms the struggles of Harry, the owner of the shop, as he tries to avoid acknowledging the failures of his daughter Toni (who is also the narrator) and the flamboyant homosexuality of his son Sheldon.

Though couched in a narrative voice closer to standard English, the dialogue of the book is primarily written in an exuberant and honest pidgin, perhaps difficult at first for readers who have not lived in Hawaii. Yamanaka is not afraid to show poverty-stricken life on the Big Island in all its glory, humor, and repulsiveness. Her characters do drugs, have all-night sex, affectionately or not so affectionately insult the hell out of each other, talk slop, hunt pigs, watch samurai movies, hang out with family, struggle through school, adopt a haole, and stuff animals. Yamanaka moves back and forth between violence and humor, showing the human lives struggling with both.

In addition to the strengths of the dialogue, Yamanaka's descriptions of taxidermy and pig-hunting are exceptionally well done, often visceral, always accurate. Though Yamanaka sometimes opts for easy solutions and at times this novel feels very similar to her other work, the comic qualities of the novel and the care and accuracy with which the dialogue is rendered make the book successful. [Brian Evenson]

Stephen Dixon. *30: Pieces of a Novel*. Henry Holt, 1998. 672 pp. $30.00.

Dixon writes apparently realistic fiction, but he renders "reality" so fully that his descriptions tend to heighten details—experiences and things (a bathroom, a wheelchair, a key)—so that these descriptions become surreal. We wonder about their factual validity. And, to complicate matters, Dixon will, now and then, offer clues that his descriptions are crafted words; he interrupts texts to cancel a word. Thus the total effect is devastating—we have to put all the pieces together, but are not sure how to create true shape.

Once we recognize that our "lives" are as perplexing and obscure as Dixon's descriptions, we begin to understand that he is forcing us to interpret our interpretations. We become unsure of the shape of a life. Does a life, indeed, have a shape—a beginning, middle, and end? Can we know how we began or how we will end? Living and reading are processes, force fields, puzzles.

The title of Dixon's novel provides a clue for interpretation. Traditionally, "30" is the sign for the end of a newspaper item, a type of closure. The novel contains twenty-nine separate sections and its thirtieth section consists of fifteen texts entitled "Ends." Therefore, there is no one ending, no sense of a final solution. The subtitle, too—*Pieces of a Novel*—deliberately fights conclusive arrangement. The pieces are, indeed, perversely arranged. One piece does not lead to another in any traditional way. There may be a "burial," but in the next piece the dead person is still alive, even younger.

The novel is, therefore, a search for origins and ends; the protagonist obsessively examines the real frames of reference. But then the frames, we find, are elusive shortcuts or incomplete bypaths. The last lines of this bold extraordinary novel reflect this labyrinth of meaning for which Dixon is legend, even "the end" here sends the reader turning back to the novel's parts. Dixon's style has so accustomed us to unexpected turns (returns, counterturns) that we can never expect "the end" to be the only possibility. [Irving Malin]

A. L. Kennedy. *Original Bliss*. Knopf, 1999. 214 pp. $21.00.

Original Bliss, a strange and unpredictable novel, explores and uncovers the various levels of abuse which Helen Brindle has been subjected to throughout her life, and moves toward a surprising salvation. As a result of a strict religious upbringing and involvement in an unsatisfactory marriage to a cold and abusive man, she is emotionally crippled. Her life changes after seeing Edward Gluck, a pop psychologist, on the Open University. She writes to him and they arrange a meeting at a conference. Gluck, addicted to hard-core pornography, is equally crippled emotionally. However, the relationship they begin moves forward, tentatively at first, and allows both of them to conquer together their parallel dysfunctions. In the end, this is a novel which becomes, surprisingly, a compelling and convincing love story.

Kennedy has written a richly understated and beautifully plotted novel which examines not only the surfaces of addiction—to violence, denial, and pornography—but also the mangled roots which allow these to grow. On one level, Kennedy explores a small world which will be familiar to the readers of Barbara Pym while, on another, her treatment of spousal abuse is reminiscent of what Roddy Doyle achieved in *The Woman Who Walked into Doors*. But she delves deeper than those two writers by locating the areas in the physical and psychological worlds from which these terrors emerge. In the end we are left with a finely rounded portrait of both the abusers and the abused with light cast on the forces that drive and manipulate human beings. *Original Bliss* is slow-moving, painful, and disturbing. It is also full of truth and executed with great verve. [Eamonn Wall]

Andrej Blatnik. *Skinswaps*. Trans. Tamara Soban. Northwestern Univ. Press, 1998. 109 pp. Paper: $14.95.

This brief collection by the Slovenian author Andrej Blatnik ranges from a one-line "Apologia" to the lengthier "Scratches on My Back" and "The Taste of Blood." Considerable narrative attention turns on the physical, tactile presence of skin and blood in situations of arousal or abuse. In the north of what was known for a while as Yugoslavia, in sometimes brutal imagery, Blatnik paints a violent landscape with some familiar, contemporary American overtones.

Blatnik renders scenes of contemporary ennui, frustration, and impotence in figures of debased horror and sometimes random violence. Can "Hodalyi" feel dread stalking him as he sweeps aside a gang of urchins' muffled threats on a muggy afternoon? Will Roman the architect ignore the "Scratches on My Back" which are Diana's hold on him—failure at his job, at friendship, at being honest with the present, here and now? A child watching a movie imagines "His Mother's Voice" and must warn of the danger lying in wait at home. To Katrina, hovering before apparent foul play, "The Taste of Blood" is her fear of two cloddish, pushy policemen divulging a more than professional interest. If scenes of outright violence usually remain subdued, all hell can literally break loose, too, on a more intimate scale.

Yet in stories like "Possibility" and "Actually," disembodied voices discourse to little apparent effect. What has changed? What if "Apologia" were taken seriously? "The Day Tito Died" may hold an ironic significance not to be lost. "Isaac" catches on to his railroad timetable too late. "Rai," closing

Skinswaps, mimics what it can of music in words. Blatnik's kaleidoscope jogs slightly. Life reels.

Home, family, language—fragile dependencies, usually taken for granted. Blatnik captures impressions of their routine evisceration, which as these distort fictional reality rarely degrade it beyond recognition. [Michael Pinker]

Christopher Sawyer-Luaçanno. *An Invisible Spectator: A Biography of Paul Bowles*. Grove, 1999. 502 pp. Paper: $15.00.

The paperback reissue of *An Invisible Spectator* is a welcome invitation to again consider Paul Bowles, one of our most enigmatic writers. An expatriate novelist, short-story writer, translator, and cultural commentator, Bowles entices his readers into fantastical worlds with simultaneously fascinating, terrifying, and compelling portraits of often ordinary people in exotic places.

Sawyer-Luaçanno traces Bowles's less-known musical career alongside fellow composers Aaron Copeland and Virgil Thompson as an exploratory platform from which many of his later fictional themes emerge. Equally influential was Bowles's relationship with wife and fellow writer Jane Bowles. Complicating their marriage was Jane's lesbianism and Bowles's own guarded sexual ambivalence. Only in a recent documentary (*Let It Come Down*) has he indicated a lifelong loathing of his own homosexuality. Sawyer-Luaçanno's presentation is devoid of lurid accounts of sexual liasions; it strives to be an objective, respectful, and somewhat distanced account of places visited, people encountered, and mental illness manifested.

A direct reflection of his subject's evasive nature regarding emotional display, the accessibility and clarity of Bowles's emotional life begins to fade following Jane's illness and death. This horrifying detachment is, however, the very stuff of which Bowles's writing is made, and is succinctly carried over in this biographer's portrait. As Bowles enters his nineties, this is an especially important representation of his life and work. Sawyer-Luaçanno accurately captures Bowles's ear as a reflection on a century poised on the edge of its last discoveries. [Anne Foltz]

Stewart Brown and John Wickham, eds. *The Oxford Book of Caribbean Short Stories*. Oxford Univ. Press, 1999. 476 pp. $18.95.

From the writings of Frank Collymore to Edwidge Danticat, from the Caribbean pioneers to the Caribbean contemporaries, from the familiar to the unfamiliar, *The Oxford Book of Caribbean Short Stories* has gathered some of the most stimulating writings from an area of the world that is thought of as being more exotic than artistically intellectual. From the plantation settlers to the revolutionaries, this collection of short stories not only details the diversity of the Caribbean writers who celebrate their Caribbea but also reveals the diversity of the islands which editor Stewart Brown describes as a "multilingual, multicultural space."

An air of isolation trickles throughout the stories creating a strong sense of how Caribbean writers have handled colonial alienation for so many years. There is a flow of strong individuality tracing the loneliness that reflects an array of people living in a tropical part of the world that is much more diverse and larger in size than most realize. The stories selected weave themes of class issues, love, racial issues, humor, and passion that take place in various Caribbean settings as well as stories of Caribbean experiences in various settings around the world.

With a thorough introduction by Brown, *The Oxford Book of Caribbean Short Stories* brings forth an insightful history of the literary movements of Caribbean literature. This is a chronological celebration of the history, the evolving lifestyles, and the people who make up the commonality of being a part of a much larger literary community of Caribbea. [Nancy D. Tolson]

Marilyn Krysl. *How to Accommodate Men*. Coffee House, 1998. 238 pp. Paper: $15.00.

Marilyn Krysl's collection of short stories, aptly titled, is a biting exploration of the relationship between men and women in societies where men, who are often obtuse, are oppressors and women are survivors. This pattern, Krysl recognizes, is not simply endemic in America but is prevalent throughout the world. Drawing on her experience of living and traveling in Asia, Krysl explores the survivability of women within a country, Sri Lanka, torn apart by civil war.

Within that reality, the payment of electric bills and the constructed notions of Western beauty are left behind; women are forced to discern a world where men employ technologies toward destruction—a destruction which is antithetical to the reproductive, maternal power of women. In the story "Iron Shard," the iron in menstrual blood flow is positioned against the iron of weaponry. The story begins with Radika's first menstruation: a cause for ceremony. However, before the ceremony can occur, soldiers take Radika's father from home. He is not heard from after being seized, though Radika's mother inquires at the local army post.

Even though the cover is too obvious (the famous mushroom cloud of an atomic explosion above a woman, dressed in a bikini, who is sheltering her eyes with her hand), the collection is satisfying since Krysl is not afraid to explore the intimate nature of societies. In "The Girls of Fortress America," Sandra learns the lesson of silence rather early. Wanting to know about her father's secret society, the Lodge, Sandra crawls up on his lap. After he asks what she wants, Sandra thinks, "Everything," while saying simply, "Nothing." Marilyn Krysl wants Fortress America to be less secure, and for that reason *How to Accommodate Men* is a successful collection. [Alan Tinkler]

Paul West. *Life with Swan*. Scribner, 1999. 300 pp. $24.00.

Paul West has done it again—written another large-hearted novel that investigates life's overlooked corners while celebrating the splendors of creation and the unpredictable. He is back in the stars, and for the first time in fiction recounts his experiences with the Viking and Voyager space expeditions. In many ways *Life with Swan* represents a delightful extension of his experiments with the roman à clef.

The narrator, a writer and professor, unexpectedly falls in love with a student, Ariada Mencken, the Swan of the title. As their relationship deepens, the professor follows Swan to Pathica where she begins graduate work, and the two quickly befriend one of the campus's most famous celebrities, astronomer Raoul Bunsen.

To those familiar with West's fiction and life, the principle characters are only thinly disguised, but the fun is with the absurd names he concocts for the minor characters—Asa Humanas, rare book librarian, Gloria Gluckstein, faculty party maven, Segundo Cieli, painter-pilot, but best of all are Bunsen's wife and son, Nineveh and Ptolemy. West revels in the deliberately eccentric and finds in each of these figures some bit of comic delightfulness.

The descriptions of the couple's life together are full of genuine moments and quirky details: their private language of love, the sound of Swan's bicycle bell as she rides up the drive, a decanter's glass stopper that throws captivating, prismatic light. As Swan says in one of the most moving passages, "You can appreciate the spectrum, or whatever that kind of thing, only if you have love of the usual kind. Without it the spectrum, the entire magnificence of the universe, is a cold block of steel, a nail file."

This is exactly what West brings to fiction—the sense of empathic inspection that results from genuine love. West loves viewing and reviewing, creating, and language, glorious language, that medium that surrounds, defines, and informs everything. West is a treasure, and *Life with Swan* is a wonderful gem of a novel. [David W. Madden]

Vladimir Makanin. *The Loss: A Novella and Two Short Stories*. Trans. Byron Lindsey. Northwestern Univ. Press, 1998. 154 pp. Paper: $14.95.

These stories by Vladimir Makanin suggest the appeal of a leading contemporary Russian writer deserving greater exposure in English. This small collection offers a range of stories connected by their different readings of *loss*. A considerable portion of the title story is devoted to a meditation on the possibilities of how this theme may be viewed in life.

In "The Loss" Makanin shows one Pekalov bossing a dwindling crew of drunks into building a tunnel under the Ural River. Why would anyone want to do this? But Pekalov does it, becoming legendary for doing it, even worthy of reverence. Yet this means losing his identity, becoming Pekalov subject and also object of speculation, Pekalov the icon, whose actual loss becomes fluid as it gains significance.

"Klucharyev" rises at Alimushkin's fall. As fate would have it, Alimushkin's loss must always mean Klucharyev's gain. For a while Klucharyev feels guilty, fretting over this peculiar fortune; he even visits Alimushkin in his decline, perhaps to offer what small comfort he may. But should Klucharyev feel responsible, if neither can avoid this cruel destiny?

"The Prisoner from the Caucausus" is rendered in a spare style, like Hemingway's war stories. Deep in the mountains, at a lull during the war in Chechnya, Sergeant Rubakhin is attracted to a prisoner whom he and rifleman Vovka are sent to exchange with some rebels. Survival requires subduing strong feelings and Rubakhin find a way to survive his crisis. After a while he, too, doesn't feel any more responsible than Klucharyev. Rubakhin is last heard marveling at the beauty of the landscape.

Makanin plays on gain and loss in three registers in these stories, each in a distinctive voice and a universal language. [Michael Pinker]

Harry Mathews. *The Way Home: Selected Longer Prose*. Atlas, 1999. 215 pp. Paper: $14.95.

At first glance, the presentations in this collection could not be simpler: "Here is an outline of my life," opens the seventy-page-long "Autobiography"; "Here is an old French regional dish for you to try," begins "Country Cooking in Central France." Each paragraph in the memoir about Georges Perec begins with the words, "I remember," and each item was initially composed without Mathews "trying to be exhaustive or particularly acute." "Singular Pleasures," sixty-one descriptions of masturbation the world over, is said to have "emerged without warning when six of its episodes sprang full-blown into being at four o'clock on a March morning in 1981." With characteristic poise, Mathews is only too happy, at one level, to let words be equal to the things they stand for. For example, the recipe in "Country Cooking," a *farce double* (fish encased in clay balls inside a lamb), is itself farcical. For stuffing, it includes a story in the form of a song that is said to be sung by the Auvergnat community during the overnight roasting break. Impossible as a recipe, the narrative is no better able to contain what it presents in any one form or frame; and neither can the matter-of-fact prose conceal a creative exuberance and a not infrequent anguish—as in the "Armenian Papers," translations without originals which "exist scarcely at all except as a desperate hypothesis."

Exuberance, anguish, and imagination-in-desperation are all attributes of the speaker in Mathews—a distinctive personality who somehow exceeds the neutral voice, blunt significations, and considerable formal and material constraints that the author chooses to work under (as the only active American in the Oulipo or, *Ouvroir de littérature potentielle*). Without the constraints, Mathews insists, and without a prose that stays close to the plainness of everyday American conversation, he could not bring his "hidden experiences," his "unadmitted self into view." As in the drawings by Trevor Winkfield attractively reproduced among the pages of the volume's title story, locating the human figure as an "identifiable object" requires activity on the part of the reader, an imaginative ability to move "by angles, along a black line inscribed on a white ground that is itself bordered by blackness." In Mathews, as in Winkler, "identity as a clear or coded sign" is only an aid to the imagination, "an occasion for rest, something to lean an elbow on while drawing fresh and not necessarily metaphorical breath." And then the process of self-creation continues through further black marks on white paper—the materiality of written language.

A fitting complement to the novels and edited compendia that in recent years have confirmed Mathews's position among English-speaking writers, these seven distinctive studies in "constrictive form" also reveal why the way home to autobiography and to recognition, over obstacles apparently of the author's own making, has taken so long. [Joseph Tabbi]

A. M. Homes. *Music for Torching.* Morrow/Weisbach Books, 1999. 358 pp. $26.00.

A. M. Homes's new novel unpacks the dysfunctional family life of Paul and Elaine Weiss, the suburban couple who first appeared in her story "Adults Alone." The action begins when Paul and Elaine deliberately burn down their house after a family barbeque—a spur of the moment attempt to erase the past so that they can put their lost lives back on track. "Like children who have been allowed to stay up late," Paul and Elaine play a variety of immature, sometimes vindictive, games (think *Who's Afraid of Virginia Woolf?*) and entertain a bizarre procession of neighbors as they struggle to find some authentic sense of themselves while trying to conform to the normalcy Elaine imagines surrounds them.

Homes succeeds in showing that no one is "normal" when we peer behind their white picket fences, and her novel is both moving and disturbing because she manages to portray the comedy and the tragedy of her characters' lives with compassion: "None are what they seem, none are what you think, none are what you'd want them to be. They are all both more and less— deeply human." The novel ends as an emergency with one of their children forces Paul and Elaine to reevaulate their perspective on their lives and to accept responsibility for their actions. My only complaint with Homes's fine novel is that the story ends rather abruptly. After watching these characters maneuver through the outrageous trivialities of their lives, I desperately wanted to see how they might cope with a real crisis. [Trey Strecker]

Hayden Carruth. *Beside the Shadblow Tree.* Copper Canyon, 1999. 148 pp. Paper: $14.00.

When James Laughlin died in 1997, newspapers around the country listed the many names of poets and writers whom he had published through New Directions. His influence on twentieth-century poetry is obvious, but his personal influence on many individuals is less well-known. Hayden

Carruth, the poet who worked with Laughlin in various capacities for over forty years, knows this influence well, and in his memoir of the man ("Jas"), Carruth recounts several key moments in their friendship. Most interesting, however, is the *way* he relates these memories; Carruth pointedly rejects checking his facts, insisting that he is not a historian and specifics such as exact dates don't matter. Still, he adds comments or justifies himself ("I'll leave what I've written as is, however, because it represents my feeling") on the bottom of the page, in effect utilizing a type of anti-footnote. Most of the time, Carruth sticks to his story, and his gruffly nostalgic tone is entertaining; but when he strays to all-encompassing remarks about the current state of poetry, he risks making his story small. (He refers several times to the "young people of today," dismissing them as "products of their time—lazy and greedy, concerned to discover the easiest way to upgrade their 'careers.' ")

By the end of the book, James Laughlin's effect on the people around him is clear, and although Carruth has moments of tangential spiraling, the love/hate issues of living in the shadow of a great man withdraw to reveal sincere admiration. In a postscript written after the death of Laughlin's third wife Gertrude, Carruth explains his loss best, and shows that his most effective words are spare and simple: "I didn't go to Gertrude's funeral. I didn't visit the grave of Jas. Everything I could have known was in my head. And all of it was insufficient." [Amy Havel]

Haruki Murakami. *South of the Border, West of the Sun*. Knopf, 1999. 213 pp. $22.00.

Hajime, the middle-aged narrator of Murakami's new novel, begins his story completely convinced of how average he is. His was, he allows, "a 100 percent average birth." The town where he grew up was "your typical middle-class suburbia. . . . Some of the houses might have been a bit larger than mine, but you could count on them all having similar entranceways, pine trees in the garden. The works." Although Murakami's stories and novels differ in how unhinged and fantastic he allows events to become, they typically begin with similar statements of calm, with two feet set squarely in contemporary normalcy. *The Wind-Up Bird Chronicle* opens with a character watching a pot of spaghetti boil. Out of this emerges more than 600 pages and all manner of odd event and metaphysical speculation. In the new novel, the events may be less odd, but his attention to the mysteries of ordinary lives that has brought Murakami seemingly contradictory comparisons to Raymond Chandler and Franz Kafka remains.

After an uneventful adolescence, Hajime marries and opens two jazz clubs in Tokyo. Everything appears 100 percent okay, but Hajime feels as if something's missing, a feeling precipitated by the appearance of Shimamoto, a woman he was friends with in grade school. The two meet periodically at one of his bars and talk. But Shimamoto remains a mystery to Hajime, more a vivid mental idea than a person. She comes into his bar, talks, and exits, leaving Hajime alone to wrestle with his feelings of opportunities lost.

Parts of Hajime's story might read like another mid-life crisis tale, particularly to American readers, but Murakami evades all of the pitfalls of the form, not allowing Hajime to conveniently escape into fantasy or to ignore his wife at home. [Paul Maliszewski]

James Purdy. *Gertrude of Stony Island Avenue*. Morrow, 1999. 182 pp. $19.95.

Though he has entered his fifth decade of publishing, James Purdy is not afraid to experiment or to take risks. In *Gertrude of Stony Island Avenue*, he takes more than a few: he creates a narrative voice decidedly different from that found in his other fiction, explores the relation of life to art, and manages to interweave a contemporary story with the myth of Persephone.

A fictional and sideways glance at the life of twentieth-century Illinois-based artist Gertrude Abercrombie, Purdy's novel is recounted by Carrie, Gertrude's mother, as she attempts to come to terms with the life of her artist/daughter, now deceased. *Gertrude* is an odd coming-of-age novel, about a mother's final move, late in life, from being a child to being an adult. As she makes that move, she discovers for the first time who her daughter is and thus symbolically brings her back from the dead.

The characters seem somewhat crazy, even to be living in another world—Purdy mentions, for instance, one falling back on the language of the Elizabethans as he speaks. The value of Purdy's art is not primarily mimetic: the value lies in his ability not to depict the world but to transform it and by so doing to cut through all that which obscures what it means to be human. The writing here is beautifully formal, Purdy refusing to opt for crudities of expression. Instead of the quick fix, Purdy allows his story to build slowly, exerting slight pressures with such evenness and exactness that one is trapped before realizing it.

Remarkably quiet at first, Purdy's *Gertrude of Stony Island Avenue* soon builds to a powerful pitch. A first-rate read, it reveals that Purdy is an artist who remains vital, impressive, and necessary. [Brian Evenson]

Jenny Offill. *Last Things*. Farrar, Straus & Giroux, 1999. 264 pp. $23.00.

Last Things is a first novel of such depth and intelligence that reading it means swallowing a time-release capsule of delight and anguish: sudden-glory bursts of understanding keep disrupting a haunting sense of a world in which a long history of wrong turns is about to prove fatal.

Grace Davitt is a smart eight-year-old with a brilliant, troubled mother and a baffled father. Also featured are Edgar—an adolescent scientific genius—and an uncle who is Mr. Science on children's TV. Grace, curious and embattled, is a compulsive observer who churns out questions about the world and gathers answers from sources of varying dubiousness. Anna

Davitt tells her daughter myths of her own invention as adroitly as she tells authentic myths and "extinction stories." Her home-schooling of Grace focuses on the "cosmic calendar" (January 1: the Big Bang . . . December 31: First humans), but Grace also gets input from the *Encyclopedia of the Unexplained*, Edgar, and Mr. Science. As a result, her brain roils with a rich brew of superstition and scientific and bogus facts.

Unknowingly, Grace follows a venerable tradition: that of seeing the world as a book readable by those who learn its language. *Last Things* brims with references to language, codes, messages encrypted in seemingly random clues. Learning to read the world means becoming adept at deciphering analogies and symbols. Alas, the solutions we find are mostly wrong, since the human mind is superb at inventing meaning where knowledge is lacking. Grace, incessantly processing myths, mysteries, facts, and claptrap, is a model of humankind trying to make sense of things by turning out ten thousand answers—about the universe, chance, love, dreams, the soul. *Last Things,* in the end, reveals the dark possibilities of this discovery process; the novel is propelled by the fear that although we are decoding the cosmic arcanum at an unprecedented rate, we may be too late to save ourselves. [Evelin Sullivan]

Tristan Egolf. *Lord of the Barnyard: Killing the Fatted Calf and Arming the Aware in the Cornbelt.* Grove, 1999. 410 pp. $24.00.

A number of reviews have praised this book as an epic of Middle American life. That's an exaggeration, but not an inappropriate one. *Barnyard* is really a contemporary tall tale, akin to the nineteenth-century dialect yarns of George Washington Harris or Augustus Baldwin Longstreet. Their frontier is gone, but Egolf finds a similarly unsettled setting in the cheap apartments, dive bars, and low-tech factories of Baker, a town in an unspecified Midwestern state. Baker tolerates the members of its lowest social stratum as long as their poverty and tackiness are invisible, and it's there that chicken farmer John Kaltenbrunner comes of age as many mythic heroes do, with the promise of high birth giving way to early orphaning and banishment. Cast out by the town's establishment, he caroms between incarceration and several almost unimaginably demeaning jobs until returning to sacrifice himself in a garbage strike that shatters public order.

Egolf tars virtually all his characters as narrow-minded or worse, but aligns himself with the people rather than the power. He occasionally troubles to delineate personalities beyond the social roles and manages to evoke sympathy for his grotesques, although they are not allowed to speak for themselves. Institutionalized thinking rather than innate human depravity is the true target, as evidenced by civic reaction to the strike. Mounting piles of garbage summon hordes of vermin, and various attempts are made to control the pests. "Had anyone stopped to consider, it might have been pointed out that whole days were being invested in scavenger hysteria, while the root of the problem—the actual pile-up itself—was growing every hour." The metaphoric equivalent of the pile-up is really our toxically pollutive economy; and although this issue is prevalent, it exists only as subtext. *Barnyard* isn't a polemic or a call to arms, just an artfully belligerent novel. [James Crossley]

Andrew Holleran. *In September the Light Changes: The Stories of Andrew Holleran*. Hyperion, 1999. 320 pp. $23.95.

In the early seventies a cohort of gay men emerged who devoted themselves to two things: the pursuit of the arts and of sex, preferring those occasions when the two merged, or as a character in this collection puts it: "I want someone who can quote Rilke, and eat my ass till his face falls off." Finding such a person has never been easy—even in the seventies, even in New York—and thus many of these gay men became disappointed and disillusioned long before AIDS whittled their number down to a handful. It has been the work of Andrew Holleran—and to a lesser extent Edmund White and Felice Picano, Holleran's friends and colleagues—to chronicle this cohort (can we even call it a sub-subculture?) of which they are survivors. As time has gone on, their fiction has taken on an increasingly epic cast because it seems less and less about individuals than about their entire culture. Although speaking of short stories as epic is oxymoronic, no other term does justice to these tales of a civilization cut to the bone. Little happens in them, and yet the little that does exposes fundamental shifts in prespective, which, of course, alter everything except, as the title story ruefully acknowledges, the human heart. These stories are Chekhovian, not merely in their psychological subtlety, lyric intensity, and haunting mixture of comedy and tragedy that make impossible distinguishing one from the other, but because, as in *The Cherry Orchard*, the tiniest incidents resonate with millennial implications as one manner of life gives way to another. Holleran reveals a sensibility so fine and an intelligence so subtle, that no matter how much attention this collection receives, it will, by definition, be overlooked. [David Bergman]

Paul Auster. *Timbuktu*. Henry Holt, 1999. 181 pp. $22.00.

After the awkward experiments in narrative voice perpetrated in *Mr. Vertigo* (1994), Auster is close to getting back on track in this novel told from the point of view of an aging dog named Mr. Bones, whose fate we follow through three masters. His original master is Willy G. Christmas, a homeless poet who models himself after Santa Claus and takes Mr. Bones wandering through America. After losing Willy in Baltimore, Mr. Bones befriends a Chinese-American boy named Henry, who teaches him that "love is not a quantifiable substance . . . and even after one love had been lost, it was by no means impossible to find another." Chased away by Henry's father, Mr. Bones wanders into Virginia, where he ingratiates himself to a generic white suburban family named the Joneses, who rename him, with appropriate banality, Sparky. The Timbuktu of the title refers to Willy's vision of the afterlife, and Mr. Bones's tale ends with him abjuring the comforts of the Joneses and attempting to rejoin his fellow economic and social outcast Willy in the far-off land of justice and equality.

The first half of *Timbuktu* is marred by Willy's annoying, extended, free-associative monologues, which don't work because their po-mo clutter and wordplay fail to enhance the novel's thematic content and because Auster can't reproduce varieties of American speech as well as writers like Don DeLillo, Ralph Ellison, or William Gaddis. But in the second half, Auster's usual spare, transparent narrative style predominates, recalling that of earlier works like *The Music of Chance* (1990) and his masterpiece *Leviathan* (1992). Although *Timbuktu* doesn't have the compelling narrative thrust of those novels, nor the sustained uncanniness of Kafka's great "Investigations of a Dog," its canine narrator offers many poignant and humane reflections on the hidden economic and psychological injuries that blight contemporary American life. [Thomas Hove]

Ralph Ellison. *Juneteenth*. Ed. John F. Callahan. Random House, 1999. 368 pp. $25.00.

Since the publication of *Invisible Man* in 1952, anticipation about Ralph Ellison's second novel has been fervent. Unfortunately, Ellison never completed the novel, but at his death in 1994 he left over two thousand pages of notes and manuscripts of the forty-year work-in-progress. According to John Callahan, Ellison's literary executor and editor of the novel, *Juneteenth* is the one narrative out of the sprawling saga Ellison envisioned "that best stands alone as a single, self-contained volume."

Readers looking for traces of *Invisible Man* in *Juneteenth* would do well to reflect on the final line of Ellison's magnificent first novel: "Who knows but that, on the lower frequencies, I speak for you?" *Juneteenth* is an extended meditation on that line, a splendid riff on the "lower frequencies" that cut through American racial divisiveness and demand acknowledgment of the complex ties that bind all Americans. It's a novel that challenges overly simplified categories of "race" to reveal, in the words of *Juneteenth*'s Alonzo Z. Hickman, "some cord of kinship stronger and deeper than blood, hate, or heartbreak."

Hickman, a horn-blowing gambler turned preacher, comes to these words reluctantly and painfully. As he sits at the deathbed of Senator Adam Sunraider, he tries to make sense of how Bliss, a child of indefinite race raised lovingly by Hickman and members of the black congregation, could reject his past, his identity, to become the racist politician now struggling for his life after being hit by an assassin's bullet. Drawing from African-American cultural forms including sermons, folk tales, the blues, and jazz, *Juneteenth* moves back and forth between past and present, its antiphonal form veering in and out of the consciousness of Hickman and Bliss/Sunraider as they grapple with the mysteries of race, identity, and nation.

Juneteenth is indeed Ellison in his prime. Callahan did an admirable job with a particularly daunting task, and whatever one's opinion of edited, posthumous novels, *Juneteenth* is essential to a better understanding of an important American writer. [Christopher C. De Santis]

Salman Rushdie. *The Ground beneath Her Feet*. Henry Holt, 1999. 575 pp. $27.50.

Rushdie's funny and rich new novel uses the history of a fictional rock band—from difficult beginnings to superstardom through the inevitable legal problems and breakup to a nineties reunion tour—to look at the stories of our time and to examine the role of art in expressing who we are and how we understand our world. Ormus Cama, musician and songwriter, and Vina Apsara, singer extraordinaire, are the driving force behind the band, and their playing out of a variation of the Orpheus-Eurydice myth, as narrated by Rai, photographer and friend to both, is the focus of the story. The thematic focus is on the clashes of competing versions of reality and art's part in articulating them. The novel is set in an alternative reality. The world Rai describes shares much with ours but in many places goes in its own direction: JFK escapes assassination in Dallas; the Nixon presidency and Watergate exist only in a political novel; Stephen Dedalus is the great novelist of the twentieth century. Ormus's genius and eventually his obsession result from his being able to see into another, competing world (clearly, our world), which he foresees invading and shaking apart his world.

Knowledge of these worlds, any world, is mediated through art. Rai tells his story via a plethora of artistic references and allusions: from myth, Western and non; music, classical and pop; literature, highbrow and low. (N.B. Pynchon fans: Rushdie even supplies an ending for the notoriously inconclusive *The Crying of Lot 49*.) But the sheer pleasure one takes in the wealth of knowledge displayed here is countered by an undercutting of art's ability to make new worlds possible. Ormus's revelations become routinized as they are explicated and critiqued by reviewers and commercialized as the band's fame grows. Moreover, the novel's anticipated apocalyptic moment is deferred as the mundane asserts itself and takes over.

The Ground beneath Her Feet is a brilliant novel, delighting us with the many worlds it contains and the stories they're told through, challenging us to think about how stories can help to make and unmake worlds. [Robert L. McLaughlin]

John Yau, ed. *Fetish: An Anthology*. Four Walls Eight Windows, 1998. 318 pp. Paper: $15.95.

In his introduction, John Yau explains his hopes for this compilation of short pieces, that he wanted to "satisfy [his] desire for an anthology that would neither replicate previous anthologies nor settle for an already defined category." With that in mind, Yau solicited some favorite writers to contribute and therefore, some of the writing is appearing for the first time. The range of authors and topics is vast—Cris Mazza's "first" bra to Charles Bukowski's mannequin, Wang Ping's crush to Ben Marcus's resuscitated wife—but they are conveniently separated here by fetish code: I-You, I-It, and Us-Them. Each section has at least one story that stands out in originality and presents surprising relationships among the characters and their need-things or the unspoken desires that exist between them: Jonathan Lethem's "The Spray," Michael Brodsky's "The Son, He Must Not Know," and Shelley Jackson's "Jominy" particularly make the anthology worthwhile. The lesser-best are the cringeworthy recognizables: the fun-with-excrement fable, torture devices as plot necessities, minor porno scenes that do not deviate from their expected results, etc. Surprisingly, Gordon Lish shows up to chat about John Yau's feet and ask why no one except for Gordon Lish is "looking truth square in the eye." I'd have to argue with his judgment; every writer here is definitely looking truth "square in the eye." The believability of that truth's reflection is what sometimes falters. [Amy Havel]

Julian Barnes. *England, England*. Knopf, 1999. 288 pp. $23.00.

In this satire set in the twenty-first century, a business magnate creates the ultimate tourist destination by constructing a replica of England on the Isle of Wight, outdoing the original to the point where even the Royal Family is persuaded to relocate. For all the half-affectionate laughter at "Old England's" expense, however, *England, England* is a novel of downright Swiftian darkness and ferocity. A modern-day counterpart to the island of Lilliput, the slickly run theme park that Barnes imagines in the English Channel is a stinging caricature of contemporary England's spiritually void heritage industry.

The crux of Barnes's narrative is the elusive search for something "real" to replace the vapid offerings of the leisure market. Of course, "the real" is nowhere to be found. The best we can have is "seriousness," the book's protagonist reflects, because "If life is a triviality, then despair is the only option." The "entirely local and the nearly eternal" are where we should look for answers, she concludes.

Whether we read it as a lament for Old England, or a jeremiad against deracination by worldwide market forces, *England, England* chills with the bleakness of its cultural panorama. [Philip Landon]

Harold Brodkey. *Sea Battles on Dry Land*. Henry Holt, 1999. 450 pp. $30.00.

This valuable collection contains essays Brodkey wrote between the early 1980s until his death in 1996. In four sections—"Celebrity and Politics," "Wit and Whimsy," "Love and Sex," and "Language and Literature"—the essays demonstrate his preoccupation with masquerade, sexuality, memory, and consciousness. They vary in quality, of course, but every one is provocatively tense.

Here I can mention only the most fascinating essays—or sentences from them—to offer a brief suggestion for future exploration. "My Time in the Garden," from the second section, is a beautifully written description of sensual delight. Brodkey describes a hidden garden: "They were not an Eden but offered a sense of profusion and of shade with a sense of difference from any other Italian landscape and, then, because of the staggering, interlocking complexities of branches and tree trunks, they had an almost fairy-tale quality of grotesque crowdedness of vegetable incident, of biological life." The long, seductive rhythm of the sentence reflects the garden, interlocking complexities of yielding one's self to some terrifying beauty (or beautiful terror).

Although each essay offers Brodkey at his best, the fourth section on "Language and Literature" is, without doubt, the most intriguing part of the book. Brodkey's essay on Jane Austen versus Henry James is brilliant. He re-creates a Jane Austen who understood sexual intrigue, social ambivalence. And he is quick—too much so—to alert us to James's "sexlessness": "James's is an invented female voice, extremely intelligent, entirely self-involved in a disguised way. Austen manages to be everyone." Not only is this collection a tribute to the wide range of Brodkey's work, from film reviews to celebrity profiles to memoir, it is also proof of a master writer. [Irving Malin]

Ian MacMillan. *Village of a Million Spirits: A Novel of the Treblinka Uprising.* Steerforth, 1999. 257 pp. $24.00.

In his most recent novel, *Village of a Million Spirits*, Ian MacMillan makes clear the work's purpose through one of its own characters. Upon realizing that his friend has died at the hands of the Nazi guards, Janusz Siedlecki comes to understand why he must survive: "All these people have been made to vanish from the earth, the reality of their existence wiped away, but for one thing: the presence of one person to see and remember. And in fact he was ordering Janusz to see Treblinka according to the long view. I order you to survive. I order you to see and remember, and then to survive." MacMillan not only recognizes the importance of remembrance, but the greater importance of retelling. Through what starts as a myriad of voices each telling its own story of life in the concentration camp, MacMillan comes to weave together the individual voices to tell a single story: the uprising at Treblinka. In doing so, MacMillan does indeed offer the long view; the stories told are those not only of the victims, but of the victimizers; not only of the living, but of the dead.

His story both fact and fiction, MacMillan does not fall victim to hiding the reader from the truth of this moment in history. In an expertly woven and highly moving narrative, the author struggles to bring to light the incomprehensible horrors that occurred behind the fences of Treblinka: the victims' struggle to survive, the torture and joy that victimizers found in carrying out their duties, the gruesome reality of the gas chambers, and the inspiring story of one people's decision to re-obtain their humanity through revolt. It is through MacMillan's adept style and desire for remembrance that he has been able to provide readers with such an unforgettable and invaluable work concerning such a dark moment in history. [Michael J. Martin]

———————

Juan Goytisolo. *The Marx Family Saga*. Trans. Peter Bush. City Lights Books, 1999. 186 pp. Paper: $10.95.

Fans of Goytisolo and avid readers of the postmodern will both find *The Marx Family Saga* an insightful journey into the ideological chaos of "the new world order." Beginning with a boatload of Albanian refugees who arrive at an Italian resort in search of the paradise called "Dallas," the novel intersperses a wry sense of humor with a biting attack on transnational capitalism. With the craft of a skilled movie director, Goytisolo pulls back from the confrontation between hungry refugees and indignant vacationers to reveal the Marx family in a barren flat, channel-surfing before dinner. Karl enters and watches the television screen as scores of refugees are detained while waving photocopies of dollar bills and reciting "God Bless America" in heavy accents. Living in a historical limbo, Karl Marx witnesses "the dismantling of the systems supposedly based on his thought."

For those concerned with the fate of politics after poststructuralism, *The Marx Family Saga* provides a brutally vivid characterization of the intricacies of social commitment in a world which consumes more television than literature. In narrative gestures typical of his earlier work, Goytisolo posits a number of surreal hypotheses: How would Karl Marx explain his work if he were alive today? Would he answer the media interest in "scandals"? How does one write about Marx today?

Goytisolo is one the finest masters of the postmodern. Rarely using punctuation, his narrative has a remarkable sense of rhythm and a strong element of self-reflection. The dilemma of writing in today's market functions as a concern equal to the reaction of a fictitious Marx to the collapse of communism. When the author must face a Faulkner-ish editor (who chastises him for complex style) and his consultant, Dr. Lewin-Strauss, a feminist sexologist (who criticizes Marx's treatment of the family servant), the reader is thrust into an odd world of hyper-intertextuality and bizarre twists of history. [Sophia A. McClennen]

———————

Steve Erickson. *The Sea Came in at Midnight*. Avon, 1999. 259 pp. $23.00.

Steve Erickson's latest millennial tale navigates a psychic landscape of spiritual exhaustion and existential confusion that will be familiar to readers of his earlier work. Kristin, the novel's young protagonist, narrowly escapes a cult suicide as 1,999 women and children walk off a California cliff at the stroke of the new millennium. As the novel opens, Kristin remembers how she came to the edge of the cliff before fleeing to Tokyo and becoming a "memory girl" at the Hotel Ryu, where she shares her story with a customer who has died. Desperate and homeless, Kristin had answered the strange personal ad of a man known as the Occupant, who had needed someone to console him after his true love—not coincidentially, the dead Japanese man's estranged daughter—mysteriously disappeared. An apocalypologist, the Occupant keeps a calendar mapping "the routes and capitals of chaos" and searching for a scheme to order the inexpicable horrors of modern life. This obsession grows out of his effort to understand a personal apocalyptic event from his childhood—a shooting involving his parents during the May 1968 student revolts in Paris.

For Erickson's characters, apocalypse is intensely personal. These traumatic events must be remembered as a part of the "ever-fluid, ever-transforming map" of identity. As the characters struggle to find meaning in their lives, readers trace the looping plotlines that link the characters and their stories in this tangled web of time, where the present exists in an uneasy balance between our dreams of the future and our memories of the past. The cyclical nature of these "apocalytic tide[s]" signals the beginning of new millennia and allows Erickson to leave open the possibility of redemption, either real or imagined. [Trey Strecker]

Will Self. *Tough, Tough Toys for Tough, Tough Boys*. Grove, 1999. 244 pp. $23.00.

Will Self has never seemed to lack fictional premises, and the new collection of stories is no disappointment. In one, a man discovers a huge vein of crack cocaine underneath his London apartment and begins the slow, industrious work of mining it. In another, a man terrified, even angered, by the presence of insects in his home comes to achieve a macabre kind of détente with the bugs. In a monetarily unified Europe, a baby in England bosses around his bewildered parents in fluent business German, while in Munich a deputy director for Deutsche Bank is reduced to baby talk. A man who believes himself surrounded by people named Dave, some of whom have only recently and suspiciously changed their names to Dave, is asked, quite calmly, to change his to Dave too.

But while the premises of Self's stories get the most attention, his fiction and its satiric qualities are severely diminished by any recitation of the daffy premises alone. Any of the above are ideas only and may seem indistinguishable from an episode of *The Twilight Zone*. By themselves they are all contrivance and mechanical juxtaposition. Satires, however, are more than a series of inventive premises; in Self's case, the premise is only as good as the language that expresses it, and Self's language continually surprises with its gradual unfolding and delights with each unexpected exaggeration and detail.

While many of Self's earlier fictions have been set in London, here his references to London suburbs and the surrounding countryside have become more dense, his observations of livelihoods and daily habits more germane and particular to the satire. Self shows himself to be a fine observer of the people, commerce, and geography of individual neighborhoods, attuned to the manner in which cities fall and rise and fall again only in the space of a few blocks on the same street. [Paul Maliszewski]

Sena Jeter Naslund. *The Disobedience of Water*. David R. Godine, 1999. 212 pp. $21.95.

Of the eight stories in this book, several have appeared in literary periodicals, and two are taken from earlier books. Naslund's characters continually face the opacity of surfaces, at risk because of what they can neither grasp nor affect. At the same time, the reader is astounded by stunning turns of revelation and lovely passages. What at first might seem self-consciously literary slips back into the normality of the unexpected occurrences of life, coincidental or not. Naslund lets us into the consciousness of her characters, many of whom are highly literate, well educated, or artistic, though her range here takes us to children, as in "I Am Born," in which a young girl's very personal nickname is taken and given to a new baby, or in "Burning Boy," in which racial codes and sexuality elude young Skeet.

"The Death of Julius Geissler" introduces us to a virtuoso violinist, European in origin, playing in the U.S. with a new, young accompanist. Geissler's recollections of his sister, her relationship with Geissler's manager Alex, and his playing of Tartini's "The Devil's Trill" allow us to recognize the beauty and self-absorption of the artist and to witness both the world he has made in concert halls and his attraction to the common, playing in parks while Alex frets over Geissler's health, safety, and the Stradivarius. The writing, depicting the music and the feeling it engenders, carries readers deeply into the scene and its effects, jarred occasionally by Alex's material concerns and other external forces that threaten the delicate beauty we witness. Like Tartini, in this story and elsewhere, Naslund combines strong technical and poetic qualities. We should thank Godine for publishing this author; my only regret was the absence of the lovely "Five Lessons from a Master Class" (*Ice Skating*); this author writes wonderfully about music and character, and that sense of nuance resonates throughout this collection. [Richard J. Murphy]

Alois Hotschnig. *Leonardo's Hands*. Trans. and foreword by Peter Filkins. Univ. of Nebraska Press, 1999. 146 pp. $12.00.

Rarely can the language in a work of fiction reflect its story successfully; often the best one may hope for is a gossamer connection to certain isolated indicatives. However, Alois Hotschnig's harrowing tale of desperation and addiction achieves this with a style both intimate and powerful. The unique language lines each passage with teeth, sharply tearing through the facades built up by its characters. Tracing the bizarre aftermath of a fatal car accident through a myriad of affected voices, the novel unfolds with an underlying vibration of defeat, of utter disintegration. The characters' growing detachment from the world around them is reflected perfectly in the hopeless tone of the novel which syphons passion from every word, leaving a bare language which foreshadows the characters' imminent fate. While this detachment, inefficacy, and guilt-laden fear surround them, the novel's theme of hopelessness cannot be usurped by the attempted loving connection of its two main characters. The grasp for understanding and love becomes nothing more than "a killing hand that caresses."

Benefited in no small part by the wonderful translation of Peter Filkins, *Leonardo's Hands* is a simply told, complexly provocative work that exploits the madness and secrecy of the human psyche. Alois Hotschnig takes the reader on a disturbing yet exhilarating journey through the synapses of two flawed souls and reveals the hidden fears and inconsistencies of the human condition. [Brian Budzynski]

Frederick Busch. *The Night Inspector*. Harmony Books, 1999. 278 pp. $23.00.

This remarkable historical novel has one of the most interesting narrators in recent American fiction, a former sniper for the Union during the Civil War named William Bartholomew. His story plays out in 1867, in Manhattan's nightmarish Five Points neighborhood, where he befriends a customs inspector—one Herman Melville, whose fiction he at one time read and admired. Melville enthusiasts should be satisfied by Busch's portrayal of him and its sensitivity toward recent developments in Melville scholarship and biography. But Busch judiciously keeps Bartholomew at center stage, his story reflecting and extending the economic preoccupations and moral ambiguities of Melville's fiction. Half of his face having been shot off in the war, Bartholomew wears a mask that recalls the "pasteboard mask" of visible reality through which Melville's Ahab wants so badly to strike. To Ahab, one thing that mask stands for is the inhuman logic behind both the Christian problem of evil and the global capitalist system. But instead of hunting for a white whale, Bartholomew attempts to find redemption within that increasingly impersonal system by planning to rescue a shipload of children from slavery. This attempt serves as a tragically ironic endeavor for a sometimes ruthless social Darwinist who is dismayed that the only victor in the Civil War was money.

Into this plot he drags the unwitting Melville, whom, in the overdetermined manner of Melville's Confidence Man, he treats as both a friend and a pawn. Much more compelling than this rescue plot, however, are Bartholomew's gruesome Civil War flashbacks and his vivid evocations of the language and substance of everyday life on the mean multicultural streets of Melville's "insular city of the Manhattoes." This is historical fiction at its best: nineteenth-century in style and subject matter, late-twentieth in form and attitude. [Thomas Hove]

Howard Sounces. *Charles Bukowski: Locked in the Arms of a Crazy Life.* Grove, 1998. 310 pp. $26.00.

While an author can't dig up dirt on a self-professed dirty old man, Howard Sounces's biography of Charles Bukowski, like the old man himself, has an objectivity that makes squalidness fascinating. *Locked in the Arms of a Crazy Life* does justice to a life that was miserable for fifty years, then had a second act of rising contentedness.

The blunt self-image Bukowski created doesn't leave much room for biographical analysis. What Sounces adds is the depiction of the whole career, the sense that "this bum is going to make it." We see the teen with debilitating acne, the suicidal wanderer, the enslaved post office clerk, the race-form scouring ladies man, and the semi-reluctant celebrity. All familiar Bukowski characters, but here they grow one from the other. That continuity is absent from the author's own work.

Like cigarettes, Bukowski hooks most of his victims at a young age, and often gets dismissed as a bad habit. He is the father of transgressive fiction, the gross-out trend in which incestuous circus freaks provide first-person narrative. But who can out-freak a man whose first wife lacked a neck? And who got a rejection slip from *Hustler* magazine for being too harsh? Although Bukowski's work appears shameless, the baldest attempts to shock are never poseurish. His stamina in the face of (often self-imposed) grotesquery is spectacular, though best not admired.

A revelation: Bukowski was probably not an alcoholic. Abstinence came in easy stretches throughout his life. He was a respectable father, too. Still, on the occasion of making crude, day-long passes at a woman by defaming her recently dead husband, he was capable of all the savagery his image suggested. Deeply anti-intellectual, he was never anti-aesthetic: he knew about art and he knew what he liked. [Ben Donnelly]

Tomek Tryzna. *Miss Nobody*. Trans. Joanna Trzeciak. Doubleday, 1999. 296 pp. $23.00. (Also published as *Girl Nobody* by Fourth Estate, 1999, same translator.)

When Marysia, a fifteen-year-old Polish girl, moves from the rural flatlands to an industrial city, she hopes big changes will result, but most specifically she just wants to avoid ending up like her troubled parents. Life with her new friends proves adventurous and offers a whole new set of emotional, sexual, and psychological experiences. Marysia's vivid imagination supplements these experiences in ways to make sense out of them; over and over, when she is overwhelmed by her own feelings, she finds a way out by creating a new fantastic scenerio. Her eccentric friends, Kasia and Eva, play her as a pawn in their own game of deceit, and so the naivete which was so useful in creating a fantasy reality unfortunately ends up hurting her. All of the action (real or imagined) is interpreted through Marysia's absolutely adolescent point of view, and Joanna Trzeciak's excellent translation keeps the originality and specificity of Marysia's voice intact.

The transitions between Marysia's two realities are usually seamless and dreamy, only rarely causing moments of confusion. With such artful description and maintenance of voice, it is hard to believe that *Miss Nobody* is Tryzna's first novel; he portrays the sometimes brutal environment of adolescence perfectly and with much skill. Also, Tryzna's statement on Poland's development away from Communism is subtle but evident; while these characters chronicle a story about the end of individual innocence, they also epitomize the necessity of growing up fast in the unpredictably changing Polish culture. [Amy Havel]

Rikki Ducornet. *The Fan-Maker's Inquisition: A Novel of the Marquis de Sade.* Henry Holt, 1999. 212 pp. $22.00.

"A fan is like the thighs of a woman," begins Rikki Ducornet's new novel, "It opens . . . with a flick of a wrist. It produces its own weather. . . ." From this prime image, *The Fan-Maker's Inquisition* grows into an allegory of imagination's effect on the world. In place of the embuggering/throat slashing scenes in Sade's own work, the novel first follows the citizens' trial of Gabrielle, a confidante of Sade and maker of erotic fans. Sade's letters to her are brought in as evidence of her perversity, as is their co-authored novel about officially sanctioned atrocities by the Spanish in Mexico. The book then switches to Sade, imprisoned within earshot of the guillotine as he reads Gabrielle's letters and imagines meals, gardens, books—and the erotic scenes she painted on fans.

With bows to the historical Sade, Ducornet creates exquisite lists—a Sade book of hours, calendar of days—and the novel becomes a poetic rendering of this author's philosophy of the abject, a tradition extended by Georges Bataille and so prominent in contemporary body art (see Cindy Sherman's vomit photos). Here, knowledge of the world comes from the body as well as the mind, and is most eloquent about reigns of terror. Sade's literary valorization of the vile exposes that which is hidden by platitudes and other "enlightened" justifications for the literal atrocities committed routinely in the name of God and country (though, of course, the self-interest of rich aesthetes escapes critique in this aristocrat's telling). Perversity is thus revealed as a matter of inversion, a matter of perspective—a creation of the aggressive eye—the perfect complement to Ducornet's approach to art through the sublime language and meticulous attention to form that is characteristic of her prose. [Steve Tomasula]

Denis Donoghue. *The Practice of Reading.* Yale Univ. Press, 1998. 298 pp. $30.00.

"Are we quite sure," asks Denis Donoghue early in this newest collection of his work, "that we have devised methods of reading responsive to our own new needs and to the literature we have still to read?" The fifteen essays gathered here attempt an answer, the first eight by raising questions about how we read, the final seven by offering implicitly exemplary commentary on individual texts (from *Othello* and *Gulliver's Travels* to Cormac McCarthy's *Blood Meridian*).

Donoghue remains enamored of those critics who first shaped his critical thinking (Eliot, the Leavises, Empson, Kenneth Burke), and throughout *The Practice of Reading* he makes a persuasive case for the value of a formalist aesthetics. What is unfortunate about the ideological approaches to literature in vogue today is that their "common motive," Donoghue insists, "is the mortification of the subject" via "the deployment of themes, arguments, and morally charged conclusions." Consequently, critics see their job as the exposing of manipulative messages read out of texts that tend in the process to become more or less generic.

Donoghue, following Kenneth Burke and others, would see art rather as symbolic action, as performance, the point of which is to provide texts worthy of emphatic contemplation. That contemplation ought properly to result not in acts of interpretation but of careful description, acts of close "attention to objects that ask only to be perceived," literature being, first and foremost, a generous incitement to "imagine being different."

Donoghue might have done more to transform these fifteen lectures and journal articles into a book with a sustained argument. Regardless, *The Practice of Reading* more often than not proves provocative, urbanely argued, helpfully corrective of current truisms, and demonstrative of the fact that formalism needn't be either a dull drive down a dead-end street in a conservative neighborhood or a trip away from the world beyond the word. [Brooke Horvath]

Arthur Salzman. *Understanding Nicholson Baker*. Univ. of South Carolina Press, 1999. 209 pp. No price given.

Nicholson Baker, one of our most puzzling writers, seems to do without plot or character. He devotes his energy to the mysteries of language and consciousness. He will, for example, spend pages analyzing the functional beauty of objects, spending so much time on them that they are transformed into ritualistic havens of meaning. Saltzman writes: "Baker defamiliarizes the landscape by being so in-depth about his inventories; by providing such relentlessly exploded views." Perhaps, as I once suggested in a review of his essay collection, *The Size of Thoughts,* he is a "religious" writer, hoping, like Henry James, to see the obscure radiance of words as worlds (or vice versa).

A clue to Baker's concern with "enlarging" small thoughts about the material which surround us—books, shoelaces, toys—is the fact that the hero of "The Mezzanine" carries a copy of the *Meditations* of Marcus Aurelius. From the battered copy, the hero reads: "Observe in short how transient and trivial is all mortal life; yesterday a drop of semen, tomorrow a handful of spice and ashes." Saltzman, in his analysis of the story, sees

Baker's skills at work and explains that it "is nothing if not a campaign against the maladies of transcience and triviality."

Although I may have incompletely analyzed Saltzman's book—the first one to examine Baker's strangeness and beauty—I must say that it is wonderful criticism. It offers close investigation—not arcane theory—and poetic readings. The last sentence serves as an excellent example: "By demanding an erotics of attentiveness, [Baker] does as much as any contemporary writer to keep things on the record." Thus Baker and Saltzman mirror each other; the reflection is dazzling. [Irving Malin]

Books Received

Agee, Jonis. *Taking the Wall*. Coffee House, 1999. Paper: $14.95. (F)
———. *The Weight of Dreams*. Viking, 1999. $24.95. (F)
Ageyev, M. *Novel with Cocaine*. Trans. Michael Henry Heim. Northwestern Univ. Press, 1998. Paper: $11.95. (F)
Alsop, Derek, and Chris Walsh. *The Practice of Reading: Interpreting the Novel*. St. Martin's, 1999. $65.00. (NF)
Ashbery, John. *Girls on the Run*. Farrar, Straus & Giroux, 1999. $20.00. (P)
Baker, Gary L. *Understanding Uwe Johnson*. Univ. of South Carolina Press, 1999. $29.95. (NF)
Banville, John. *Mefisto*. David R. Godine, 1999. Paper: $13.95. (F)
———. *The Newton Letter*. David R. Godine, 1999. Paper: $10.95. (F)
Barker, Adele Marie, ed. *Consuming Russia: Popular Culture, Sex and Society Since Gorbachev*. Duke Univ. Press, 1999. Paper: $19.95. (NF)
Bayard, Louis. *Fool's Errand*. Alyson, 1999. Paper: $12.95. (F)
Beidler, Peter, and Gay Barton. *A Reader's Guide to the Novels of Louise Erdrich*. Univ. of Missouri Press, 1999. Paper: $19.95. (NF)
Bely, Andrei. *Kotik Letaev*. Trans. and intro. by Gerald J. Janecek. Northwestern Univ. Press, 1999. Paper: $17.95. (F)
Bénichou, Paul. *The Consecration of the Writer, 1750-1830*. Trans. Mark K. Jensen. Preface by Tzveten Todorov. Univ. of Nebraska Press, 1999. Paper: $25.00. (NF)
Benjamin, Walter. *Selected Writings: Volume 2, 1927-1934*. Ed. Michael W. Jennings, Howard Eiland, and Gray Smith. Trans. Rodney Livingstone et al. Belknap Press/Harvard Univ. Press, 1999. $37.50. (NF)
Bergson, Henri. *Laughter: An Essay on the Meaning of the Comic*. Trans. Cloudesley Brereton and Fred Rothwell. Green Integer, 1999. Paper: $11.95. (NF)
Bernanos, Georges. *The Imposter*. Univ. of Nebraska Press, 1999. Paper: $20.00. (F)
Bernstein, Charles. *My Way: Speeches and Poems*. Univ. of Chicago Press, 1999. Paper: $18.00. (NF)
Bjørneboe, Jens. *Moment of Freedom*. Dufour, 1999. Paper: $15.95. (F)
Blanchot, Maurice. *Awaiting Oblivion*. Trans. John Gregg. Univ. of Nebraska Press, 1999. Paper: $15.00. (F)
Bosshard, Marianne. *Chantal Chawaf*. Rodopi, 1999. Paper: $25.00.

(NF)

Boulé, Jean-Pierre. *Hervé Guibert: Voices of the Self*. Liverpool Univ. Press, 1999. £36.00. (NF)

Brautigan, Richard. *The Edna Webster Collection of Undiscovered Writings*. Intro. Keith Abbott. Houghton Mifflin, 1999. $14.00. (F)

Brodsky, Michael. *We Can Report Them*. Four Walls Eight Windows, 1999. $16.95. (F)

Brody, Dylan. *The Warm Hello*. Silk Label, 1999. Paper: $7.99. (F)

Broyard, Bliss. *My Father, Dancing*. Knopf, 1999. $22.00. (F)

Bruccoli, Matthew J. *The Only Thing That Counts: The Ernest Hemingway-Maxwell Perkins Correspondence*. Univ. of South Carolina Press, 1999. Paper: $21.95. (NF)

Burgin, Richard. *Ghost Quartet*. Triquarterly Books/Northwestern Univ. Press, 1999. $25.95. (F)

Burnam, Clint. *Airborne Photo*. Anvil Press, 1999. Paper: $10.95. (F)

Byatt, A. S. *Elementals*. Random House, 1999. $21.95. (F)

Calaferte, Louis. *C'est la Guerre*. Trans. Austryn Wainhouse. Marlboro Press/Northwestern Univ. Press, 1999. Paper: $14.95. (F)

Caputo, Philip. *The Voyage*. Knopf, 1999. $26.00 (F)

Cisco, Michael. *The Divinity Student*. Buzzcity Press, 1999. Paper: $14.99. (F)

Clark, Brian Charles. *Splitting*. Wordcraft of Oregon, 1999. Paper: $9.00. (F)

Clavell, James. *King Rat*. Delta, 1999. Paper: $11.95 (F)

Cloonan, William. *The Writing of War: French and German Fiction and World War II*. Univ. Press of Florida, 1999. $39.95. (NF)

Condé, Maryse. *Land of Many Colors* and *Nanna-Ya*. Univ. of Nebraska Press, 1999. $12.00. (F)

Cooney, Ellen. *The Old Ballerina*. Coffee House, 1999. $23.95. (F)

Craze, Galaxy. *By the Shore*. Grove, 1999. $24.00. (F)

David, Robert Murray. *Mischief in the Sun: The Making and Unmaking of "The Loved One."* Whitston, 1999. $18.50. (NF)

Davis, Amanda. *Circling the Drain*. Morrow/Weisbach, 1999. $23.00. (F)

DeLillo, Don. *Valparaiso*. Scribner, 1999. $18.00. (D)

Devlin, Kimberly J., and Marilyn Reizbaum. *Ulysses: En-Gendered Perspectives*. Univ. of South Carolina Press, 1999. $55.00. (NF)

Di Blasi, Debra. *Prayers of an Accidental Nature*. Coffee House, 1999. Paper: $13.95. (F)

Dickey, James. *The James Dickey Reader*. Ed. Henry Hart. Touchstone/Simon & Schuster, 1999. Paper: $16.00. (F)

———. *To the White Sea*. Delta, 1999. Paper: $11.95. (F)

Disch, Thomas M. *The Sub: A Study in Witchcraft*. Knopf, 1999. $24.00. (F)

Dixon, Stephen. *Sleep*. Coffee House, 1999. $15.95. (F)

Dorfman, Ariel. *The Nanny and the Iceberg*. Farrar, Straus & Giroux, 1999. $25.00. (F)

Dunmore, Helen. *Your Blue-Eyed Boy*. Back Bay, 1999. Paper: $13.00. (F)

Dyer, Geoff. *Paris Trance*. Farrar, Straus & Giroux, 1999. $23.00. (F)

Emshwiller, Carol. *Leaping Man Hill*. Mercury House, 1999. Paper: $14.95. (F)

Engel, Howard. *Murder in Montparnasse*. Overlook, 1999. $23.95. (F)

Fante, Don. *Chump Change*. Sun Dog Press, 1998. Paper: $14.00. (F)

Fast, Howard. *Redemption*. Harcourt Brace & Co., 1999. $24.00. (F)

Fiffer, Sharon Sloan, and Steve Fiffer, eds. *Body*. Bard/Avon, 1999. $23.00. (F, NF)

Flanzbaum, Hilene, ed. *The Americanization of the Holocaust*. Johns Hopkins Univ. Press, 1999. Paper: $16.95. (NF)

Fontenay, Charles L. *Target: Grant, 1862*. Silk Label, 1999. Paper: $9.99. (F)

Foster, Ken. *The Kind I'm Likely to Get*. Quill/Morrow, 1999. Paper: $12.00. (F)

Freed, Lynn. *Home Ground*. Story Line Press, 1999. Paper: $14.00. (F)

Fry, Stephen. *Making History*. Soho Press, 1999. Paper: $13.00. (F)

Furman, Jan. *Toni Morrison's Fiction*. Univ. of South Carolina Press, 1999. $12.95. (NF)

Gardiner, John Rolfe. *Somewhere in France*. Knopf, 1999. $24.00. (F)

Garréta, Anne F. *La Décomposition*. Bernard Grasset, 1999. No price given. (F)

Gass, William H. *Reading Rilke*. Knopf, 1999. $26.00. (NF)

Gates, David. *The Wonders of the Invisible World*. Knopf, 1999. $22.00. (F)

Gay, Peter. *Mozart*. Viking (Penguin Lives), 1999. $19.95. (NF)

Germain, Sylvie. *Night of Amber*. Trans. Christine Donougher. David R. Godine, 1999. $23.95. (F)

Giannone, Richard. *Flannery O'Connor and the Mystery of Love*. Fordham Univ. Press, 1999. $33.00. (NF)

Graywolf Silver Anthology. Edited by the staff of Graywolf Press. Graywolf, 1999. Paper: $16.00. (F)

Green, David. *Atchley*. Barrytown Ltd., Station Hill, 1999. Paper: $12.95. (F)

Guy, Barbara J. *Khaki Killer*. Vantage, 1999. Paper: $10.95. (F)

Hammett, Dashiell. *Nightmare Town*. Knopf, 1999. $25.00. (F)

Harnisch, Antje, Anne Marie Stokes, and Friedemann Weidauer, eds. *Fringe Voices: An Anthology of Minority Writing in the Federal Republic of Germany*. Berg, 1998. Paper: $19.50. (F, NF)

Harpman, Jacqueline. *Orlanda*. Trans. Ros Schwartz. Seven Stories

Harris, Mark. *The Self-Made Brain Surgeon and Other Stories.* Intro. Jon Surgal. Univ. of Nebraska Press, 1999. Paper: $17.95. (F)

Hellenga, Robert. *The Fall of a Sparrow.* Scribner, 1999. Paper: $14.00. (F)

Herzogenrath, Bernd. *An Act of Desire: Reading Paul Auster.* Rodopi, 1999. $44.00. (NF)

Heym, Stefan. *The Wandering Jew.* Trans. by the author. Northwestern Univ. Press, 1999. Paper: $16.95. (F)

High, John. *The Desire Notebooks.* Spuyten Duyvil, 1999. Paper: $14.95. (F)

Hill, Kathleen. *Still Waters in Niger.* Triquarterly Books/Northwestern Univ. Press, 1999. $24.95. (F)

Hoffmann, Yoel. *The Christ of Fish.* Trans. Eddie Levenston. New Directions, 1999. $21.95. (F)

———. *Katschen & The Book of Joseph.* Trans. Eddie Levenston, David Kriss, and Alan Treister. New Directions, 1999. Paper: $11.95 (F)

Holman, Sheri. *The Dress Lodger.* Grove, 2000. $24.00. (F)

Huston, Nancy. *The Mark of an Angel.* Steerforth, 1999. $21.00. (F)

Jarry, Alfred. *The Supermale.* Exact Change, 1999. Paper: $13.95. (F)

Jones, James. *From Here to Eternity.* Delta, 1999. Paper: $13.95. (F)

———. *The Thin Red Line.* Delta, 1999. Paper: $13.95. (F)

———. *Whistle.* Delta, 1999. Paper: $13.95. (F)

Joyce, James. *On Ibsen.* Ed. and intro. Dennis Phillips. Green Integer, 1999. Paper: $8.95. (NF)

Kamau, Agymah. *Pictures of a Dying Man.* Coffee House, 1999. $23.95. (F)

Kerouac, Jack. *Atop an Underwood: Early Stories and Other Writings.* Ed. Paul Marion. Viking, 1999. $24.95. (F)

———. *Selected Letters: 1957-1969.* Ed. Ann Charters. Viking, 1999. $34.95. (NF)

Klein, Olaf Georg. *Aftertime.* Trans. Margot Bettauer Dembo. Hydra Books/Northwestern Univ. Press, 1999. $24.95 (F)

Kolocotroni, Vassiliki, Jane Goldman, and Olga Taxidou eds. *Modernism: An Anthology of Sources and Documents.* Univ. of Chicago Press, 1999. $75.00. Paper: $30.00. (NF)

Kureishi, Hanif. *Intimacy.* Scribner, 1999. $16.00. (F)

Lafarge, Paul. *The Artist of the Missing.* Illustrated by Stephen Alcorn. Farrar, Straus & Giroux, 1999. Paper: $13.00. (F)

Lisicky, Paul. *Lawnboy.* Turtle Point Press, 1999. Paper: $13.95. (F)

Lively, Penelope. *Spiderweb.* HarperCollins, 1999. $22.00. (F)

Locklin, Gerald. *Go West, Young Toad.* Water Row Press, 1999. Paper: $14.95. (F)

Lucas, John. *The Radical Twenties: Aspects of Writing, Politics, and*

Culture. Rutgers Univ. Press, 1999. $50.00. Paper: $20.00. (NF)

Lyotard, Jean-François. *Signed, Malraux*. Univ. of Minnesota Press, 1999. $29.95. (NF)

Maud, Ralph, and Sharon Thesen, eds. *Charles Olson and Frances Boldereff: A Modern Corrsepondence*. Wesleyan Univ. Press, 1999. Paper: $24.95. (NF)

Maurel, Sylvie. *Jean Rhys*. St. Martin's, 1999. $35.00. (NF)

Maurensig, Paolo. *Canone Inverso*. Holt, 1999. $21.00. (F)

Memmott, David. *Shadow Bones*. Woodcraft, 1999. No price given. (F)

Minghelli, Marina. *Medusa: The Fourth Kingdom*. City Lights, 1999. Paper: $10.95. (F)

Misha. *Red Spider White Web*. Wordcraft of Oregon, 1999. Paper: $12.00. (F)

Mones, Nicole. *Lost in Translation*. Delta, 1999. Paper: $12.95. (F)

Morris, Christopher D., ed. *Conversations with E. L. Doctorow*. Univ. Press of Mississippi, 1999. Paper: $18.00. (NF)

Motte, Warren. *Small Worlds: Minimalism in Contemporary French Literature*. Univ. of Nebraska Press, 1999. $45.00. (NF)

Mueller, Daniel. *How Animals Mate*. Overlook, 1999. $23.95. (F)

Nabokov, Vladimir. *Speak, Memory*. Knopf, 1999. $17.00. (NF)

Nakadate, Neil. *Understanding Jane Smiley*. Univ. of South Carolina Press, 1999. $29.95. (NF)

Nakagami, Kenji. *The Cape and Other Stories from the Japanese Ghetto*. Stone Bridge Press, 1999. Paper: $12.95. (F)

Nicholson, Geoff. *Flesh Guitar*. Overlook, 1999. $23.95. (F)

North, Charles. *New and Selected Poems*. Sun & Moon, 1999. Paper: $12.95. (P)

Nye, Robert. *The Late Mr. Shakespeare*. Arcade, 1999. $25.95. (F)

O'Connor, Frank. *My Father's Son*. Syracuse Univ. Press, 1999. Paper: $17.95. (NF)

Pagani, Dalia. *Mercy Road*. Delta, 1999. Paper: $11.95. (F)

Perec, Georges. *53 Days*. Ed. Harry Mathews and Jacques Roubaud. Trans. David Bellos. David R. Godine, 1999. $23.95 (F)

Pérez, Loida Maritza. *Geographies of Home*. Viking, 1999. $23.95. (F)

Poirier, Richard. *Trying It out in America: Literary and Other Performances*. Farrar, Straus & Giroux, 1999. $25.00. (NF)

Porter, Dorothy. *Akhenaten*. Serpent's Tail, 1999. Paper: $13.99. (F)

Postman, Neil. *Building a Bridge to the 18th Century*. Knopf, 1999. $24.00 (NF)

Redd, Louise. *Hangover Soup*. Little, Brown, 1999. $23.00. (F)

Reed, Kit. *Seven for the Apocalypse*. Wesleyan Univ. Press, 1999. Paper: $16.95. (F)

Riehl, Joseph E. *That Dangerous Future: Charles Lamb and the Critics*. Camden House, 1999. $55.00. (NF)

Ríos, Julian. *Loves That Bind*. Trans. Edith Grossman. Vintage, 1999. Paper: $12.00. (F)

Robinson, Bruce. *The Peculiar Memories of Thomas Penman*. Overlook, 1999. $24.95. (F)

Said, Kurban. *Ali and Nino*. Overlook, 1999. $24.95. (F)

Saramago, José. *The Tale of the Unknown Island*. Trans. Margaret Jull Costa. Illustrated by Peter Sís. Harcourt Brace, 1999. $16.00 (F)

Schmidt, Arno. *Radio Dialogs I*. Trans. and intro. by John E. Woods. Green Integer, 1999. Paper: $12.95. (NF)

Sebald, W. G. *The Rings of Saturn*. Trans. Michael Hulse. New Directions, 1999. Paper: $14.00. (F)

Selimovic, Mesa. *The Fortress*. Trans. E. D. Goy and Jasna Levinger. Northwestern Univ. Press, 1999. Paper: $19.95. (F)

Skei, Hans H. *Reading Faulkner's Best Short Stories*. Univ. of South Carolina Press, 1999. $39.95. (NF)

Stephens, M. G. *Where the Sky Ends*. Hazelden, 1999. $20.00 (NF)

Straus, Botho. *Living, Glimmering, Lying*. Trans. Roslyn Theobald. Northwestern Univ. Books, 1999. $26.95. (F)

Swift, Edward. *My Grandfather's Finger*. Univ. of Georgia Press, 1999. $24.95. (NF)

Tammi, Pekka. *Russian Subtexts in Nabokov's Fiction*. Tampere Univ. Press, 1999. Paper: $24.00. (NF)

Tennant, Emma. *Strangers: A Family Romance*. New Directions, 1999. $22.95. (NF)

Thomas, Lyn. *Annie Ernaux*. Berg Publishers/NYU Press, 1999. $65.00. (NF)

T'ien-wen, Chu. *Notes of a Desolate Man*. Trans. Howard Goldblatt and Sylvia LiChun Lin. Columbia Univ. Press, 1999. $19.95. (F)

Townsend, Sue. *Ghost Children*. Soho Press, 1999. Paper: $12.00. (F)

Treadwell, Elizabeth. *Populace*. Avec Books, 1999. Paper: $10.00. (P)

Tusquets, Esther. *Never to Return*. Trans. Barbara F. Ichiishi. Univ. of Nebraska Press, 1999. Paper: $15.00. (F)

Ugresic, Dubravka. *The Museum of Unconditional Surrender*. New Directions, 1999. $24.95. (F)

Virgin Fiction 2. Morrow/Weisbach, 1999. Paper: $14.00. (F)

Waldrop, Rosmarie. *Reluctant Gravities*. New Directions, 1999. Paper: $12.00. (P)

Wanso, Pak. *My Very Last Possession and Other Stories*. Trans. Kyung-ja Chun. M. E. Sharpe, 1999. $45.00. (F)

Warner, Alan. *The Sopranos*. Farrar, Straus & Giroux, 1999. $24.00. (F)

Weaver, William Fense. *A Tent in This World*. McPherson & Co., 1999. $20.00. (F)

Wilcox, James. *Polite Sex*. Back Bay, 1999. Paper: $13.00. (F)

Wills, Gary. *Saint Augustine*. Viking (Penguin Lives), 1999. $19.95.

(NF)

Wong, Sau-ling Cynthia. *Maxine Hong Kingston's "The Woman Warrior."* Oxford Univ. Press, 1999. $45.00. (NF)

Yarbrough, Steve. *The Oxygen Man*. MacMurray & Beck, 1999. $20.00. (F)

Zekowski, Arlene. *Against the Disappearance of Literature*. Whitston, 1999. $23.50. (NF)

Zinnes, Harriet. *The Radiant Absurdity of Desire*. Avisson, 1998. Paper: $13.50. (F)

Contributors

KATHY ACKER (1948-1997) is the author of several novels, including *Great Expectations, Blood and Guts in High School, Don Quixote, Empire of the Senseless,* and *My Mother: Demonology.*

MARY CAPONEGRO is the author of *The Star Café* and *Five Doubts.* She teaches at Syracuse University.

CAMILO JOSÉ CELA, born in Spain, has published over fifty books of fiction, criticism, and travel writing. His novels include *Family of Pascual Duarte, Hive, San Camilo,* and *1936.* He was awarded the Nobel Prize for Literature in 1989.

JULIO CORTÁZAR (1914-1984) lived in Argentina and France. He is the author of *Hopscotch, 62: A Model Kit,* and *Blow-Up and Other Stories.*

JOSÉ DONOSO (1924-1996), born in Santiago, Chile, is the author of *Coronation, The Obscene Bird of Night, This Sunday, Sacred Families, Charleston and Other Stories, A House in the Country, Curfew,* and *Taratuta.*

JANICE GALLOWAY is the author of one book of short stories, Blood, and two novels: *The Trick Is to Keep Breathing* and *Foreign Parts.* She lives in Glasgow.

GEORGE GARRETT has published many books of fiction, poetry, and criticism. Among his novels are *Which Ones Are the Enemy?, Do, Lord, Remember Me, Poison Pen,* and the Elizabethan Trilogy: *Death of the Fox, The Succession,* and *Entered from the Sun.*

JUAN GOYTISOLO was born in Barcelona. He is the author of over a dozen novels, including *Children of Chaos, Masks of Identity, Count Julien, Juan the Landless,* and *Quarantine: A Novel.*

B. S. JOHNSON (1933-1973) is the author of *Albert Angelo, Trawl, The Unfortunates, House Mother Normal, Christie Malry's Own Double-Entry,* and *See the Old Lady Decently.*

OSMAN LINS (1924-1978), born in Brazil, is the author of *Avalovara* and *The Queen of the Prisons of Greece.*

HARRY MATHEWS is the author of numerous novels and collections of short fiction, among them *The Conversions, Tlooth, The Sinking of the Odradek Stadium, Cigarettes,* and *Singular Pleasures.*

CLAUDE OLLIER has published more than fifteen books of fiction, drama, and criticism. His novels include *The Mise-en-Scène* and *Disconnection.*

ROBERT PINGET (1919-1997), novelist and playwright, was born in Switzerland and lived in France. His novels include *The Inquisitory, Someone, Fable,* and *The Apocrypha.*

CLAUDE SIMON is the author of *The Wind, The Grass, The Flanders Road, The Palace, The Georgics,* and *The Invitation,* among other works of fiction. He was awarded the Nobel Prize for Literature in 1985.

GILBERT SORRENTINO is the author of several novels, including *The Sky Changes, Steelwork, Imaginative Qualities of Actual Things, Aberration of Starlight, Mulligan Stew,* and the trilogy *Pack of Lies.*

LUISA VALENZUELA was born in Argentina. She is the author of *Strange Things Happen Here, Other Weapons, The Lizard's Tail,* and *He Who Searches.*

WILLIAM T. VOLLMANN is the author of numerous books of fiction and nonfiction, including *The Ice-Shirt, Fathers and Crows, The Rifles, Butterfly Stories,* and most recently, *The Atlas.* When not traveling, he lives in Sacramento, California.

Annual Index

References are to issue number and pages, respectively

Books Reviewed

Reviewers' names follow in parentheses. Regular reviewers are abbreviated: BE=Brian Evenson; DWF=David William Foster; AH=Amy Havel; TH=Thomas Hove; IM=Irving Malin; RM=Robert L. McLaughlin; MP=Michael Pinker

Amburn, Ellis. *Subterranean Kerouac: The Hidden Life of Jack Kerouac,* 1: 208 (Tim Hunt)

Anderson, Perry. *The Origins of Postmodernity,* 2: 145-6 (TH)

Auster, Paul. *Timbuktu,* 3: 171-2 (TH)

Barnes, Julian. *England, England,* 3: 174 (Philip Landon)

Bataille, Georges. *The Bataille Reader,* 1: 183-4 (James Sallis)

Beard, Richard. *Damascus,* 1: 187 (Matthew Roberson)

Beattie, Ann. *Park City: New & Selected Stories,* 1: 194 (BE)

Berberova, Nina. *The Ladies from St. Petersburg: Three Novellas,* 2: 146-7 (MP)

Blanchot, Maurice. *The Station Hill Blanchot Reader: Fiction and Literary Essays,* 3: 159 (Jeffrey DeShell)

Blatnik, Andrej. *Skinswaps,* 3: 162-3 (MP)

Borges, Jorge Luis. *Collected Fictions,* 1: 175 (IM)

Borinsky, Alicia. *Dreams of the Abandoned Seducer,* 1: 198-9 (Alan Tinkler)

Bove, Emmanuel. *A Winter's Journal,* 1: 186-7 (BE)

Bowker, Gordon. *Through a Dark Labyrinth: A Biography of Lawrence Durrell,* 1: 182-3 (Julius Rowan Raper)

Braschi, Giannina. *Yo Yo Boing!* 1: 202-3 (DWF)

Brodkey, Harold. *Sea Battles on Dry Land,* 3: 174-5 (IM)

Brooke-Rose, Christine. *Next,* 2: 127-8 (Brian McHale)

Brown, Rebecca. *The Dogs: A Modern Bestiary,* 2: 139. (Joanne Gass)

Brown, Stewart and John Wickham, eds. *The Oxford Book of Caribbean Short Stories,* 3: 163-4 (Nancy D. Tolson)

Burgin, Richard, ed. *Jorge Luis Borges: Conversations,* 2: 140-1 (DWF)

Busch, Frederick. *The Night Inspector,* 3: 179 (TH)

Bush, Peter, ed. *The Voice of the Turtle: An Anthology of Cuban Stories,* 1: 192 (DWF)

Butts, Mary. *Ashe of Rings and Other Writings,* 1: 185-6 (Allen Hibbard)

Calvino, Italo. *The Path to the Spiders' Nests,* 1: 190 (David Ian Paddy)

Canetti, Elias. *Notes from Hampstead: The Writer's Notes: 1954-1971,* 1: 181-2 (Allen Hibbard)

Caponegro, Mary. *Five Doubts,* 1: 187-8 (RM)

Carruth, Hayden. *Beside the Shadblow Tree,* 3: 167-8 (AH)

Cixous, Hélène. *FirstDays of the Year,* 2: 135-6 (Nicole Cooley)

———. *Stigmata: Escaping Texts,* 2: 135-6 (Nicole Cooley)

Cohen, Marcel. *Mirrors,* 1: 193-4 (Jeffrey DeShell)

Coover, Robert. *Ghost Town,* 1: 174 (RM)

Croft, Barbara. *Necessary Fictions,* 2: 128. (Nicole Lamy)

Davenport, Guy. *Objects on a Table,* 2: 126. (Alexander Theroux)

Day, Aidan. *Angela Carter: The Rational Glass,* 1: 205 (Joanne

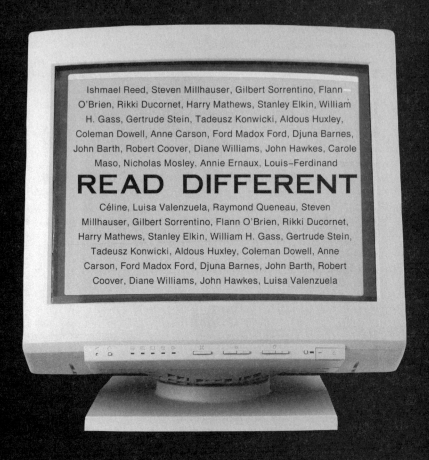

BILLY AND GIRL

a novel by Deborah Levy

$13.95, paperback (1-56478-202-6)

"Comic, absurd, and always tinged with tragedy, *Billy and Girl* reads at times like a cross between Anthony Burgess's *A Clockwork Orange* and Beth Nugent's *City of Boys*."—*Voice Literary Supplement*

"Movies and comics aiming to be somewhat like *Billy and Girl* are produced all the time these days, but the vast majority aren't very good. Levy, though, is the genuine article; if you're into surrealistic, nightmarish stuff, go no further."
—Harvey Pekar, *Austin Chronicle*

"If, by some sick twist of fate, Dickens were still alive and kicking, he'd write like this: dirty old man's writing, splashed with rage."
—Dayana Stetco, *Metro Times* (Detroit)

"The apparent senselessness of the kids' actions exhibit a poetic and hilarious reply to the shit they've been dealt. . . . Levy writes swift and original prose that does not patronize its characters, nor does it dwell too long on cultural criticisms."
—Rachel Kessler, *The Stranger* (Seattle)

www.dalkeyarchive.com

DALKEY ARCHIVE PRESS

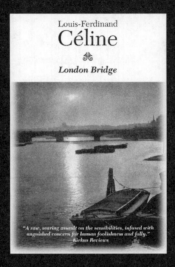

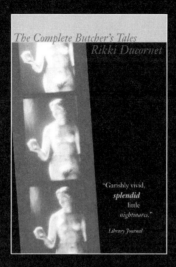

CRYSTAL VISION
a novel by Gilbert Sorrentino

-$13.50, paperback (1-56478-159-3)

"There is in *Crystal Vision* enough beauty, truth, and humor to fill up several novels. . . . It is a remarkable achievement."—*Saturday Review*

"*Crystal Vision* is a remarkable work of transparence, both artfully faceted in its construction and vital—full of speaking fossils—in the life it remembers . . . . Stories abound, wonderful anecdotes about the futile horse-playing and heroic girl-chasing, family eccentricities and accidents, the daily activities of the under-employed and self-educated."—Thomas LeClair, *Washington Post*

"A marvelous mix of slapstick and the sublime."—*San Francisco Chronicle*

"Sorrentino has established himself as a major novelist, a cross between Studs Terkel and John Barth, whose work deserves our attention."—*Virginia Quarterly Review*

www.dalkeyarchive.com

DALKEY ARCHIVE PRESS

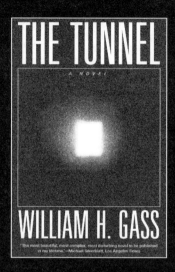

ANNIHILATION
a novel by Piotr Szewc

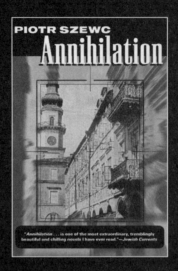

$10.95, paperback (1-56478-205-0)

"Szewc knows that life is made up not of years but of instants. So he collects them and welcomes them between two blinks, between two sighs, between two regrets. He knows, and so do we, that the city in his story . . . no longer exists."
—Elie Wiesel, *Newsday*

"One of the most extraordinary, tremblingly beautiful and chilling novels I have ever read."—*Jewish Currents*

"A considerable literary achievement. . . . A deeply moving novel."
—Stratis Haviaras, *Harvard Review*

"Beautifully translated. . . . Exquisite and compelling."—*Forward*

"A single day is minutely and lovingly resurrected, all of its lost opportunities and inconsequential details savored."—*Library Journal*

www.dalkeyarchive.com

DALKEY ARCHIVE PRESS

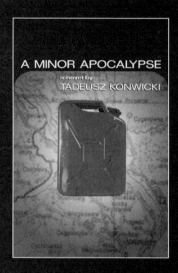

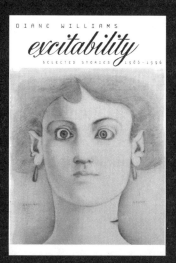

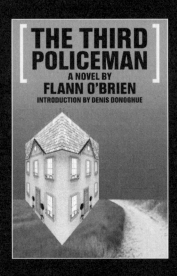

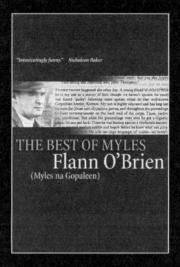

THE REVIEW OF
CONTEMPORARY FICTION

SUBSCRIBE

Individual Subscription Order Form

To subscribe to the *Review,* please fill out this order
form and mail it to us along with your credit card
information, check, or money order.
(For library subscriptions, please call 309-438-7555)

___ One Year (3 issues) $17.00 USD
___ Foreign postage $3.50 USD

Name:

Address:

City:

State:

Zip/Postal Code:

Country:

E-mail:

Payment Type:

☐Visa   ☐ Mastercard   ☐ Check   ☐ Money Order

Visa/Mastercard Number:

Expiration Date:

Checks should be made out to the Review of Contemporary
Fiction and in US dollars.

Mailing Address:

The Review of Contemporary Fiction, Illinois State University
Campus Box 4241, Normal, IL 61790-4241

If you have any questions please e-mail us at
contact@dalkeyarchive.com or call (309) 438-7555.

ANTIOCH
the REVIEW

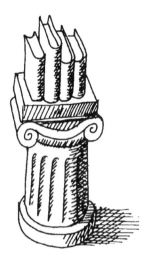

"The Best Words in the Best Order"

"The *Antioch Review* publishes the best writing in America. It is edited with good taste, outstanding judgment, and great care. Its poems, essays, stories, and reviews are always compelling."
Mark Strand

"Here is a literary magazine that does not trade in the cheap commerce of the expectable but which— always thoroughly, sometimes gloriously— honors the principle underlying the tradition of the American literary magazine—namely, freely to serve the mind and heart of a free reader."
Gordon Lish

"The best of America's independent literary reviews. The standard bearer of a tradition that must be maintained."
Stephen Jay Gould

The Carolina Quarterly

A Publisher of Fine Writing since 1948.

The work of Conrad Aiken, Russell Banks, Wendell Berry, Doris Betts, Rosellen Brown, Anthony Burgess, Raymond Carver, Evan Connell, Annie Dillard, Richard Eberhart, Lawrence Ferlinghetti, George Garrett, Paul Green, Barry Hannah, Michael S. Harper, Denise Levertov, Archibald MacLeish, Robert Morgan, Guy Owen, Reynolds Price, Kenneth Rexroth, Lee Smith, William Stafford, Max Steele, Thomas Wolfe, Ed Yoder, and many other fine writers has appeared on the pages of *The Carolina Quarterly* through the years.

Yearly subscription rates are $10 for individuals and $12 for institutions.

Greenlaw Hall CB#3520/University of North Carolina/Chapel Hill NC 27599

Leslie Fiedler
and American Culture
Edited by STEVEN G. KELLMAN
and IRVING MALIN

Leslie Fiedler and American culture have made a tumultuous marriage throughout much of the twentieth century. Fiedler's prolific career, as scholar, critic, novelist, memoirist, translator, and professor, has been a series of provocations.

While men of his age still wore hats, Fiedler was baldly both stretching and relaxing the diction of literary discourse. He was challenging the canon when the proper reaction was still reverence. He was practicing cultural studies and gender studies without a license, reading American Indian literature and science fiction when to do so was raffish. From the wilds of Missoula and Buffalo, he challenged the assumptions that dominated cultural conversation. Polyglot and polymath, Fiedler confounded categorical minds by writing about Edgar Rice Burroughs, Margaret Mitchell, and Olaf Stapledon with the same intensity he devoted to Dante, Donne, and Shakespeare. Described by Gore Vidal as "America's liveliest full-time professor and seducer of the *Zeitgeist*," Fiedler has always been ahead of his time, but he also defined and clocked it. An ageless child of the century, he ripened into one of its venerable ancients.

Leslie Fiedler and American Culture marks the start of its subject's ninth decade. The first such collection devoted entirely to Fiedler, it gathers together spirited responses to his work by scholars, critics, and poets. Also included is a reprint of Fiedler's most influential essay, "Come Back to the Raft Ag'in, Huck Honey!"

ISBN 0-87413-689-X $36.50

t h i r d

coast

A journal of poetry and fiction

"*Third Coast's* poetry and fiction is always unexpected and engaging. There's writing in here with teeth, heart, and strength."
—**Gian Lombardo**

"I love *Third Coast*—one of the best journals."
—**Alice B. Fogel**

"The *Third Coast* lineup—from rookies to seasoned veterans—is always grand, and always excitingly various. But beyond that (for mere 'names' are easy enough to compile) issue after issue is filled with the crack of home runs batted out to the reader."
—**Albert Goldbarth**

Subscriptions

Advisory Editors

Stuart Dybek
Arnie Johnston
Nancy Eimers
William Olsen
Jaimy Gordon
Herbert Scott

Past Contributors

Edward Hirsch
Heather Mc Hugh
W.S. Merwin
Reginald Shepherd
Chase Twichell
Nancy Van Winckel

Send subscription orders to:
Michele McLaughlin, Business Manager
Third Coast, Department of English
Western Michigan University, Kalamazoo, MI 49008-5092
http://www.wmich.edu/thirdcoast
(616) 387-2675

Rates are as follows:

Single Copy: $6
Back Issue: $5
One Year Subscription/Two Issues: $11
Two Year Subscription/Four Issues: $20
Three Year Subscription/Six Issues: $29

Please include your address and telephone number with your check or money order, made payable to *Third Coast*.

NOON

EDITED BY DIANE WILLIAMS

NEW

PLEASE SEND FICTION

1369 MADISON AVENUE   PMB 298   NEW YORK   NEW YORK   10128-0711